The Letters *in the* Books

Take care of each other!
Stephanie Verni

STEPHANIE

VERNI

The Letters in the Books is a work of fiction. Names, characters, and places are the product of the author's imagination. All people and places are used fictitiously. Resemblances to actual persons, living or dead, events, locales, or establishments are coincidental.

Cover design: Stephanie Verni

ISBN 978-0-692-90054-3

MIMOSA
PUBLISHING

For empaths everywhere, whether you know you are one or not.

For my family, who inspires me to continue on this journey every single day.

I love you all.

Books by Stephanie Verni

Beneath the Mimosa Tree
Baseball Girl
Inn Significant
Little Milestones
The Postcard
Anna in Tuscany - A Novelette
From Humbug to Humble
The Letters in the Books

The Letters
in the
Books

STEPHANIE

VERNI

Prologue

Thursday, December 7
Midnight Madness

Light snow begins to fall on the evening of Midnight Madness in Annapolis. The city sparkles in its holiday greens and sparkly lights, as people attend the annual holiday event in the city. Carolers sing in front of decorated shops, and a small holiday parade makes its way up Main Street. Shoppers scurry from one destination to another, and friends and families enjoy each other's company in the many restaurants, packed with holiday cheer.

However, in one particular restaurant at the bottom of the street, four people dine alone.

Eva Levoni taps her foot to the acoustic guitar player's music and curls her fingers around a dry martini. She slowly brings it to her lips. She feels the warmth of the gin slide down her throat, and she moves a long strand of hair from her eyes and reaches for the small mirror in her purse. She reapplies the raspberry plum lipstick to her lips, careful to stay within the lines. Emily, her tenant, will be moving out soon, and she's feeling anxious about the upcoming interviews she's scheduled with people interested in renting the cottage on her property. Eva leans on the rent payment to help pay her bills. Eva takes another sip and tries not to think of Kyle. She's still angry. He's been gone for nearly six months, but the mental release of him is still in progress. Letting go of him has been one of the hardest things she's had to do. She gave away everything that belonged to him except his books.

Lily Webster checks her watch and takes a sip of wine. Her blonde, mid-length bob is on point, having left the salon an hour ago. She's early, but she wonders what time her supposed blind date will show up. Lily checks her phone. Maria, Lily's friend and colleague, had badgered her to go on a date with a guy named Paul, a friend of Maria's husband. Lily wasn't in the mood for dating and had become adept at living on her own and managing her boutique. She peeks at her watch again. Still, no sign of Mister Wonderful. She sips her drink. Her phone pings. There's a message from Paul: *Sorry. Won't be able to make it tonight. Stuck in D.C. Let's try again next week. My apologies.* The server catches her eye, and she points to her empty glass, motioning for him to bring her another, as she breathes out a long sigh of disgust.

Reid Jones positions himself on the stool in the corner of the dark bar. His guitar is perched next to him. He's catching the commentators dissecting Washington's offensive line on ESPN on the televisions around the perimeter of the place. His parents are selling the home he grew up in, and it's depressed him; he was hoping he would have enough cash to buy it from them himself. At thirty-three, he's still trying to figure himself out and correct the mistakes he's made along the way. The only thing that makes him feel content is when he's playing his guitar. He takes a swig of his drink and catches a glimpse of his reflection in the Guinness mirror that hangs across the bar. He doesn't like what he sees. He looks at his watch, picks up his guitar, and begins to play *Free Falling*. Yes, I am, he thinks.

Dimitri Vassos raises his glass of Johnnie Walker Black to his lips, his damp scarf with flecks of snow on it still around his neck. He berates himself for the millionth time for marrying his ungrateful ex-wife, who left him for a very wealthy man. At the age of thirty-nine, he's become a pathetic, divorced accountant who's been miserable in his career for nearly twenty years. Dimitri knows that he could never have made that woman happy, but it doesn't minimize the hurt. She's the most materialistic person he's ever met. How could he have loved someone so shallow? He rubs his brow. Perhaps some things are just not meant to be.

At the top of the street, Meg Ellis adjusts the wreath on the front door of the bookstore she owns and feels the swirl of the December air. She laughs, acknowledging that the forecasters may be correct this time about the snow. The store's becoming more crowded, and Meg makes her way back to the counter. She reaches into her bag for the ten letters she placed inside it earlier. Accustomed to doing this every day, she removes the letters and places them in their special basket underneath the counter hidden from view but ready to be placed inside books for those who need them most. She looks around the bookstore and takes a deep breath.

Eva, Lily, Reid, and Dimitri—they are four melancholy people before they walk into the bookstore that night.

That is, until they meet Meg, and everything begins to change.

Before the Letters

Earlier that Year

Eva

Memorial Day Weekend

Eva's dog drops the frisbee in front of her for the one hundredth time, but all Eva wants to do is read her book and stretch out on her lounger in the sun. However, Brownie is so adorable, Eva sets the book down and throws the frisbee yet again. The yard is perfect for a dog Brownie's size. Eva absolutely loves living in Eastport, just over the bridge from Historic Annapolis. She walks everywhere—to the pubs in Eastport and Annapolis, to the small ramp where she keeps her kayak, and to the shops in town. She walks to work most days or rides her bike. She bought a new teal beach cruiser last year and had Kyle install the basket for her. Of course, she has a car. But for small runs to the grocery store, the bike basket works just fine.

If she never had to get into a car, she'd be thankful. The confinement of traveling in a car bothers her; the idea of being strapped into a seat, tethered to it, possibly perishing inside it in a burst of flames frightens her. She drifts momentarily to the memories of headlights in her eyes, shattering glass, and the haunting sound of metal crunching. She was seventeen when it happened, yet it feels like yesterday. So, she only gets behind the wheel when she absolutely has to, for some reason or another. Kyle drives when they're together, so she gets away with avoiding it pretty well.

Brownie sniffs around the loungers and then plunks down

next to her in the little bit of shade from the cherry tree. The sun is hot already at noon, and Eva picks up her new novel, places her large Audrey Hepburn-like shades on her face, and loops her long, dark hair into a knot on the top of her head.

When the wind blows, Eva can smell the lilac tree that has just bloomed along the white picket fence. The fragrance reminds her of her early childhood, of days spent outside, barefoot with her sister, Amelia, running through the grass on their large farm on the Eastern Shore, their mother and father drinking lemonade on the front porch. She wishes Amelia were here to smell the lilac tree. They would giggle and Eva would say Tom Bowden's name out loud, which would immediately make Amelia turn all shades of red. Eva smiles thinking about Amelia's huge crush on Tom. It still breaks her heart that Amelia endured the loss of a person she loved deeply.

Eva places the sunglasses on her face and reclines, swinging her legs up and onto the chair where she stretches out, content and happy. It's a Saturday, and all is well with the world. She's worked hard this week, and the weekends are her chance to get caught up on the stack of books she keeps on her nightstand. She's excited for a few mysteries, a contemporary romance, a World War II bestseller, and a fantasy book that's been highly recommended. She's always been someone who loves to read, to escape into books that take her away from the stresses of life. She also prides herself on the aesthetics of the bookshelves in her living room, carefully selecting and arranging them by color and size. She takes great pleasure in books that take her away, allow her to feel what characters feel, and inform her about history, love, and war. She knows her troubles are minimal compared to those heroines she reads about in her books. Overall, Eva's philosophy on life mirrors the saying she has on a sign that hangs above her small library inside her home: READ, REST, REPEAT.

Kyle left the night before to drive home to Kentucky to be with his parents, who are aging. He typically visits twice a year for extended periods of time, and he decided to use some vacation days to go for two weeks. Eva had volunteered to go with him, but he said she'd just be bored. Kyle and his father have plans to declutter their house in order to prepare it for the market. Kyle's mom is a bit of a pack rat, and they know it's going to be difficult. So, in a sense, Eva supposes she is better off not being there as they gang up on Kyle's mother—a person she adores. Kyle's mother has always been kind to her, even though they've never married, something both of Kyle's parents had very much hoped might happen for the two of them.

Eva and Kyle have never chosen to marry. They simply decided that a piece of paper wasn't critical to ensure their commitment to each other, and they've happily lived together all these years, rarely arguing, rarely at odds. It's always been easy, just as she imagined a good relationship would be.

The cottage on Eva's property is vacant this weekend. It's fully furnished and has a bedroom, bathroom, kitchen and living area that Eva decorated herself. Her tenant, Emily, has traveled home to Virginia for the weekend to be with her family. Emily's lighthearted approach to life has complemented Eva's intensity, especially with her work. But the weekends are time for Eva to unwind, and she doesn't mind a little bit of quiet.

Brownie pants and plants herself in the small bit of shade next to Eva's chair. Eva moves the dog's water bowl to the shade so Brownie can access it easily. Car doors open and close in the distance, and Eva hears the sounds of people laughing and walking through town. Music drifts from another backyard, and Eva smells the aroma of a grill. It's Memorial Day weekend, and the city is always crowded on holidays. She's excited to meet her friend, Ellen, for dinner tonight.

They reserved a table on Maryland Avenue to make sure they have a spot.

Eva leans back and folds the book over her stomach, taking a minute's rest before she dives into the novel. The sun warms her body, and she can feel the heat despite the breeze.

She doesn't remember dozing off but wakes to feel the sprinkling of rain on her body. She folds up the book, calls Brownie, and they dash inside while the short rain shower passes.

Eva loves not being tethered to a schedule on the weekends. There's such liberation in it.

*

The rain shower now over, Eva walks over the Eastport Bridge toward the city of Annapolis. It's a short walk, and one she enjoys. There are people everywhere, and traffic is backed up a little around the circle in town. A few street musicians are performing near the Market, and boats parade in and out of Ego Alley, the waterway that ends at the Harbor at City Dock. Eva wonders what Kyle is up to at the moment; it always feels strange when he's not here, but she's glad Ellen could meet for dinner tonight. She adjusts her red sundress dress and walks up Prince George Street and approaches Maryland Avenue.

Ellen is talking on her cellphone when she sees Eva and begins to blow her air kisses.

"So good to see you," Ellen says, ending her call. "You look amazing! That red dress—oh my!"

"Thanks, so do you," Eva says back, meaning it.

Ellen's always had the looks. Her brown hair is cut into a sharp bob with perfect highlights, and the Botox she admits to getting leaves her skin looking youthful and radiant. At thirty-seven, Eva has promised herself to age gracefully, although she's certain half her salary is spent on an inordinate amount of skin creams and eye creams as preventative measures.

Eva's brown hair receives the occasional highlight from her stylist and has only seen a few gray hairs. She's thankful for that. She seems to be taking after her dad more so than her mom, who went snow white sometime in her early forties and has colored it ever since.

"So, how are things?" Ellen asks.

"Good. How about with you?" Eva puts her arm around Ellen's shoulder and gives her a squeeze as they enter the restaurant and are seated.

"Same. Still trying to figure out how in the world I have two kids in high school." Ellen is a few years older than Eva, and her daughter, Sophie, a dancer, provides most of the sunshine in Ellen's world. Ellen's son, Adam, plays football, and Ellen claims he's the one giving her the wrinkles.

"So, where's Kyle this weekend?" Ellen asks, placing the napkin across her lap.

"Taking care of his parents. He went back to Kentucky for a couple of weeks to help declutter. I think his parents are ready for a smaller home in a retirement community, although his mother is putting up a fight. What did Bette Davis say? 'Growing old ain't for sissies.' I couldn't agree more."

"I hear you, sister," Ellen says. "So, no talk of marriage yet with Kyle?" Ellen sips her water and dabs her face with the napkin.

"No," Eva says. "We don't address it at all. It's not even the elephant in the room. It's just not discussed."

"Well, you two are happy, and that's what matters most. Just be happy being with him."

"I am happy with him," Eva says, meaning it. She misses him terribly when he's not around.

*

When dinner is over, Eva gives Ellen air kisses goodnight and begins the walk home in the moonlight. Ellen offers to drive her home, but Eva looks forward to the walk. She counts it as her exercise for the day.

Main Street is lit up and people are carousing in the streets. The line for the ice cream parlor is out the door and down the block a bit. The sidewalks are full, and the warm breeze blows. The stars are out in numbers, hanging over the harbor. A mime who is performing by the Market hands Eva an imaginary flower, and she takes it from him with a curtsy. She walks past the hotel and back over the Eastport Bridge, Spa Creek glowing from the reflection of the moon and the boats on the water.

As she puts the key in the door and hears Brownie scurry toward it, the house phone is ringing. She opens the back door to let Brownie outside to relieve herself, as Eva runs inside and sees Kyle's number on the Caller ID.

"Well, hello, there! I'm so glad you called. I'm just getting in from dinner with Ellen. It's a gorgeous night here. How is everything going? How was today? Fill me in on everything," Eva says, breathless from running to the phone.

"Eva, we need to talk," Kyle says.

In that split second, in hearing the tone of Kyle's voice—a voice she knows so well, a voice that she has learned to interpret over the years with all of its nuances—suddenly sounds quite distant and aloof.

Along with the deliberate way in which he begins to say the difficult words, Eva realizes that what he has to say is not at all about his visit with his parents, but rather about something altogether different. She slumps to the floor in the kitchen as Kyle begins to talk and unveils, in a matter-of-fact way during the short conversation, that things have changed for him and that he no longer has feelings for her—the kind of feelings that he should have for her if they are to spend the rest of their lives together. It doesn't take long for Eva to understand the magnitude of the hurtful words Kyle is saying to her. Over the span of a fifteen-minute conversation, she realizes that it's quite likely she may never see Kyle again.

Lily

Fourth of July Weekend

"How can you possibly move on if you're still staking out his house?" Maria asks.

"Maybe I don't want to move on. Maybe I'm still wishing I had a fire-breathing dragon as a pet. Maybe I want his privates to fall off. Maybe I want him to pay a little more attention to his high school senior now and then instead of his twenty-something fiancée with big boobs," Lily says, vigorously stuffing the packing back into the boxes that have arrived only hours before the July 4th shoppers begin to walk through the door. It's early on a Saturday morning, and the duo is preparing for a busy day at the boutique.

"He turned into an asshole, Lily. What can I say? You know you're better off without him. Have you decided whether or not you'll attend the wedding?"

"Cora wants me to," Lily says. "She wants me to play nice and for us all to get along. I think she really just wants me to be there for her because it's going to be so awkward."

"That's fair."

"Fair to whom?" Lily asks and rolls her eyes.

Maria changes the subject. "Where's Cora today?"

"She's going out on her friend's boat. I'm crossing my fingers that there isn't too much alcohol involved. You know teenagers."

"Well, she's a good kid. You've raised a good kid. She's far better than I was at seventeen, and my parents were together, though I sometimes wonder why. And Cora actually loves her mama," Maria says, as she blows Lily a kiss from across the room.

"I know, I know. I still worry, that's all. I wonder what my life would have been like had I not married at twenty-one. I can't imagine not having Cora in my life. I honestly don't know what I'd do without her, although she did leave me with these hips."

"You have good hips," Maria says. "Curvy and sexy."

"Curvy is just another term for 'eats too many cupcakes.'"

"Well, we all like cupcakes, so it's understandable."

"But why can't my curves be in my boobs instead of my hips?"

"Your ex-husband didn't leave you because of your boobs."

"You mean my lack of boobs." Lily points to them and poses for Maria.

Maria chuckles. Lily can be funny at times.

"You just need a date. Should we put you on a dating site?"

"Good God, no."

"Just trying to help," Maria says. "I'm here for you."

"I know, Maria," Lily says. "You and Cora have kept me sane the last two years. I'm just thankful the store is doing well. I couldn't handle the added pressure of a failing shop."

Lily turns on her favorite 1940s playlist and raises the volume of the speakers she recently had installed. She swears she was born in the wrong era. She's always loved the fashion of the 1940s, and her love of clothing and style inspired her to open the boutique. There's one hour until the doors open, and the two women are diligently getting things in order. It's a hot day in Annapolis, the humidity a bit stifling even at this early hour, but the sun is out, there's no rain in the forecast, and Lily's boutique typically does great business over the

Fourth of July weekend.

Lily wipes the beads of perspiration off of her forehead and turns the thermostat down to get the air conditioning cranking in the shop. In her opinion, there's nothing worse than walking into a store that feels as oppressive as the outside air. She sets up a large, glass dispenser of lemonade for her patrons as refreshment near the entrance. After owning this store for over ten years, she never grows tired of the work she puts in and the people she meets daily.

When they are finished with set up, computer log-in, organizing the music for the store for the day, and rearranging the front sale table, Lily props the door open, flips the sign to say "open," and puts a few selected items on the rack out front. She looks across the road and sees the shoppers begin to take to the streets. She notices a man walking her way and squints in the morning sun to see who it is.

Brad.

She'd know that gait and swagger anywhere. She remembers seeing him walk down the halls in high school to see her; she recalls his strut after throwing that touchdown pass from half field; she feels a pang when she thinks of him stepping down from the altar to take her arm on their wedding day.

"Hi Lily," he says, as he approaches her. They are alone on the quiet street at the moment. No one is heading in their direction, and she notices he looks a little leaner than the last time she saw him. And tanner.

"Hi Brad," she says, feeling a bead of perspiration on her forehead.

"I thought I might catch you this morning before you're swamped."

"You could have called, you know. My phone does work."

"I didn't want to call. I wanted to talk to you in person, without anyone around."

"Do you mean without HER around?" Lily asks. She knows she sounds bitchy, but she doesn't care.

"Yes, without Melanie around."

"You can say her name, but I won't," Lily says, bitterly.

"Look. I know this isn't easy for you. I never imagined it would be. But Cora wants you to come to the wedding. She wants you to be there. Now, I can understand if you can't..."

The thousands of dollars she's thrown at therapy makes it easy for Lily to say what she wants to say, so she interrupts him midstream. "Can you? Can you imagine what it will feel like for me to be there? To watch you marry someone else? Unlike you, when I said 'for better or for worse,' I meant it. I meant it, Brad. And now you're going to say it to someone else and you expect me to come and witness that?"

He's quiet for a second, a sense of defeat in his eyes. "Yes. For Cora's sake, I'm hoping you will."

They'd had their fights and rages. Saying how she feels one more time won't change anything. Lily realizes this and folds her arms and looks at him. It pisses her off that at thirty-nine, he still looks like he did at twenty-five. It pisses her off that the woman he is dating is only a couple of years older than Lily was when she married him. It pisses her off that he lacks the ability to put himself in her shoes. It eats away at her that he hasn't suffered the way she has. Life isn't fair sometimes. It just isn't.

"I have done a lot for my daughter. She knows I'd do almost anything for her. But I'm not sure attending your wedding to Barbie is allowed to be on that list."

"I'd come to your wedding if you invited me," he says.

"Would you? Really? That's because I didn't break your

heart." She folds her arms and stares at him.

"No matter the hurt, if it were your wedding, I'd come. I'm sorry, Lil. I've said it a hundred times. I'm sorry I hurt you. I'm sorry for all the crap I've done that's made you miserable, both while we were married and after. Sometimes I wonder what happened. But I don't understand why we can't be friends."

"Let me correct you. You're sorry you didn't want to be married to me anymore. Marriage in general seems to suit you just fine," Lily says. Her stare grows more intense, and she can feel the daggers shooting from her eyeballs. If murder were not against the law, she may have attempted to rip his heart out right from underneath those fit pecs of his.

Brad is still waiting, unaffected by her nasty comment, his lips slightly apart, as he longs for her to say they can be friends, but Lily knows inherently this is not possible. It will never be possible. She still loves him—has loved him since high school—and the thought of watching him begin a life with someone else is far too much pain for one fragile soul to manage. She would scream at him right now if it weren't for the young, happy couple strolling hand-in-hand toward her boutique. So instead, she takes a deep breath and exhales, something her therapist taught her to use regularly when the anger she feels hits her in the middle of the night, or at any time of the day, for that matter.

"I need you to go now. I've got a store to attend to," she says.

"Please think about it, Lil. For our daughter's sake."

In her imagination, she is lunging toward him, about to scratch his eyes out, like a character from a cartoon. In reality, she rolls her eyes and turns her back to him, leaving him alone on the brick sidewalk, as she marches through the air-conditioned store to go about her day.

"Was that Brad?" Maria asks.

"If you know what's good for you, Maria, you won't ask me one thing about that ridiculous person I used to be married to," Lily says, and Maria obeys. She is her friend, but also her employee, and Maria has learned how to strike that balance daily.

Maria also knows all too well what Lily Webster is like when her heart is shattered into a million pieces and there is little that anyone can do to help put it back together again.

Reid

Reid's mother has gone to great lengths to bake his father's favorite birthday cake: a three-tiered coconut cake that looks like something that comes from a high-end bakery rather than from a home kitchen. It's picture-perfect, and it's perched atop the white ceramic stand on display in the center of the kitchen table. Reid kicks off his work boots and leaves them next to the door. Hot, tired, and sweaty from laboring on an elaborate deck for one of his clients, he could have gone home to change, but his father had asked him earlier to throw a few things in the back of his pickup truck and take them to the dump for him in the morning. He figured if he has to haul more crap, he didn't need to bother with a shower. His parents are used to his grimy appearance. He uses the bathroom to wash up and wipe the sweat and dirt off his face, hands, and arms.

His parents are standing around the kitchen island when Reid approaches, ready to cart the food out to the patio.

"You look tired," his mother says. "Do you want an iced tea or a beer?"

"Beer works, Mom," Reid replies.

He takes the beer from his mother's hand and plants a kiss on the top of her head. She is a head shorter than he is, and she pinches his behind, something she's done to him since he was a child. He follows his dad out the screen door to the grill, where he is fiddling with the filet mignon. It's his father's favorite meal that his mother makes—surf and turf. The shrimp is prepared just the way his father likes it, with lots of Old Bay seasoning and a side of dipping sauce.

"Still drinking, I see," Reid's father says. Reid looks at him squarely. "Any news about that job with Robert?" his father asks.

"Not yet. I'm not sure what the story is with that."

"Well, you're working and making money, and that's all that matters right now."

"I guess," Reid says.

He hates talking about jobs and work with his dad. Every single time they land on this topic, he goes home feeling like the biggest loser. At night, when he can't sleep, the lingering sting of his father's disappointment regarding his career choices keeps him awake. If only he'd done what he should have from the beginning. If only he hadn't pissed away the scholarship money and embarrassed them all. So many "if onlys."

His mother joins them with two sides of corn-on-the-cob and her pasta salad, and they sit at the table to eat. Reid's sister and her husband, who live an hour away, couldn't make it because one of her two children is sick, so it's just the three of them tonight, which explains the abundance of food.

Reid is grateful for a home-cooked meal. He cooks at home, but it's just not the same making a meal for himself in his shabby little apartment. And Lexi used to cook when they were together at her place, but it's long over now. Almost two years over.

"Should we tell him now?" his father asks his mother.

"I suppose so," she says. "Now is as good a time as ever."

Reid feels a pit settle in his stomach. Is someone sick? It's always the first thing that crosses his mind. His parents aren't getting any younger; his mother was thirty-five when she had his sister, Emme. And she was nearly forty-four when he came along—a big surprise to them, as he's been told.

"What is it?" he blurts out.

"Mom and I have decided to sell the house," his father says. "It's too much for us now, and we think we may want to split our time between Annapolis and Florida, still to be determined. We're ready to do the real retirement thing, and perhaps own a condo in each location."

Reid stops chewing and looks at them both. He feels the place slipping away. He's always imagined buying this house from them in Murray Hill. He's dreamed of owning the house for years, ever since he heard the first rumblings of moving, but he didn't expect it to be so soon. The architecture and the grand porch on the outside of this home is his favorite of all. Inside, the beautiful wood floors, the high arches of the woodwork and columns, and painted blue ceiling are full of worn-in charm. This house has always felt like home to him, even though it's been a decade since he's actually lived here. Coincidentally, it's also been a full decade that he's consistently disappointed his father.

"We know you've always mentioned that you'd like to buy the house from us, but we need the money to buy two condos, so it's got to go. And we know you don't have the cash to buy it now."

"You're right, I don't. I wish I did, but I don't." He can feel the pangs of regret wanting to swallow him whole.

"We understand, Reid. Honestly, we do. We just wanted to let you know that it's going to go on the market in late September or early October," his mother says.

Reid shakes his head and swallows hard. He does his best to choke back his emotions, something he's been doing regularly for years. He totally understands where they're coming from, but it still hurts to hear it. This is his childhood home. And he's never fallen out of love with it. His old fort is still in the backyard; his markings from where he would throw the baseball against the brick chimney are still on the side of the house; the kayaks they bought during his senior year of high school are still mounted on the rack along the side fence. Call him sentimental, but he had imagined raising his own family here, in time.

He can sense his parents' eyes on him. He knows they probably feel awful about having to share this news.

"I wish I'd never let you down," Reid mumbles. "I wish I'd stayed the course and done the right things."

His father clears his throat. "It's no matter now, Reid. It's all water under the bridge. We make our own beds, and we have to lie in them. There's no harm done to me, or to your mother. It's you we are worried about, and now you've proven to us that you're happy doing what you're doing."

"I don't know if I'd actually call it being happy, Dad." Reid can't seem to look them in the eyes, and instead focuses on playing with the food on his plate.

"You seem happy," his mother says. "Are you not?"

"Not exactly happy. I spend most nights wondering what the heck I've done with my life. Wondering why I made stupid choices and decided I was too smart to listen to anyone else's advice. So I guess I'm not really happy." Reid continues to mess with the food on his plate as his parents look at each other. He feels badly about dumping his feelings on his parents during this conversation, especially since it's his father's birthday, but he's feeling sour. Really sour. The day hasn't gone as he expected, and he's worried that he could really put a damper on this celebration. Everything is slipping through his dirty, calloused fingers little by little, one piece at time. Some days, he can't even stand the smell of himself. His arms hurt from working on properties that are not his own, and his back aches every single night he crawls into bed. And doing the manual work and managing his partnership with Don—all the paperwork, estimates, miscalculations, and hiring part-time workers—is getting to him.

His father rubs his chin. "So, what will it take to make you happy?" his dad asks him. The question seems genuine enough, but still Reid knows this isn't a conversation worth having this evening. The house will be sold, and he'll have to move on from all the ideals he's been imagining over the last few years, even if he's no closer to achieving them today than he was five years ago.

"Let's not talk about any of this now," Reid says. "It's not the day for it. Let's toast to your health and your birthday, Dad. Cheers to another great year ahead."

His parents raise their glasses, and Reid gives them a smile. It used to be a million-dollar smile, as his mother used to say when he was a teenager and the girls never stopped calling the house. But now, it's just an empty smile—a regretful, lonely, and sad smile that he wears—the expression of a man who can't seem to do anything right or gain any control over the trajectory of his life.

Dimitri

Saturday, August 25

Dimitri stubs out his cigarette in the old yellow ashtray he found in the basement as he sits outside on his stone patio. He's started smoking again, although before now, he hadn't touched a cigarette in over ten years. He was never an everyday smoker, but the stress of losing money playing cards with his buddies or throwing down money on the horses at Laurel Park reignited his desire to inhale and exhale his Marlboro Lights. He couldn't believe how much a pack costs in today's world where smoking is entirely frowned upon and you're a leper if it's your bad habit. I really need to quit again, he thinks, as he smells the tobacco on his fingertips.

Despite all the bullshit he's been through this year, Dimitri has embraced the turmoil that his life has been wrapped in for the last several months. He's not stupid, but he's having trouble controlling the anger and grief that engulfs him on a regular basis. He has bad habits. Recognizing them is half the battle; he knows that he has an addictive personality, and it's been known to get him into trouble. At times, he goes spiraling downward, like the time he lost over a thousand dollars in one night at the Blackjack table two years ago. He was so close to winning, so close to bringing home the winnings to his wife, so close to finally having something to show for all his nights at the track or at the slots. But she didn't care. She wanted more. Way more.

With a thousand dollars less in his pockets that cold, windy night in January, he walked through the door to the home they had shared for eight years and his wife's closet had been emptied. Her dresser drawers were bare. There, on the bed, was an envelope with her handwriting on it.

She didn't even have the guts to say what was written on the pages to his face. She wrote her words in a damn letter that she left for him to find.

And the thing was, she knew he hated letters. They were a bad omen for him. He would have hoped she'd have been more considerate than to leave a letter telling him it's over, that their relationship meant nothing to her anymore, and that she decided to move on with her life.

When Dimitri's mother died of breast cancer when he was thirteen, his father gave him the letter his mom wrote before her death. She had directed his father not to give it to him until after the funeral. Nothing in the world can break your heart like reading a letter from someone you love more than anyone in this world and knowing you can never tell her how much she meant to you, no matter how painful it was to comprehend. At thirteen, Dimitri's heart was broken, and there's still a place deep inside him that aches the same way it did all those years ago thinking of the loss of her.

Dimitri read his mother's letter five times and then stuffed it into a shoe box where he kept the few things he's saved over the years, along with a couple of swim team medals, several ticket stubs from his favorite concerts, pictures of his old house on Cedar Street, photographs of his summers on the Eastern Shore, and an old pocket watch from his grandfather. He can still picture his mother's face, although the image of her has become fuzzy over the years. But he can still recall her dark eyes, long black, wavy hair, and olive skin. He looks more like his mother than his father and inherited all of her exotic features. She grew up in Greece until she was fifteen when her family immigrated to New York, and she met his father when they were in high school in Brooklyn. The family relocated to Maryland when Dimitri was five years old.

Thinking of his mother now, he realizes he hasn't opened that box in many years.

As for the letter from his ex-wife, he threw that one into the fire-pit on their back patio and watched it burn. He watched it disintegrate. It was a pleasure to witness her words dissolve into ashes.

The truth was, his wife, while not a gambler, loved money more than he did—more than anything, in fact. Money bought her things, and she liked to collect material things. She was impressed with wealth, having never had it as a youngster nor to the extent she wished to have it as an adult when she was saddled to Dimitri. True, he was able to provide for her well, but not to the extent that having a millionaire fiancé could buy her. Her new guy had a lot of money. After a quick Google search, Dimitri found out the guy had made a fortune as a commercial real estate developer. The harsh reality was Dimitri couldn't earn that kind of money, no matter how hard he worked his ass off and tried to make her happy—despite trying his best to care for her after the first miscarriage. And the second.

Dimitri walks to the refrigerator to get a beer. He pops it open and looks in his recycle bin. This is his fifth beer. The compulsion to drink is real—and drinking alone has become a more desperate measure to dull the pain.

The pain of a divorce, maybe, but somewhere in his brain, Dimitri knows it's much more than that. His father, a good man, was too busy providing for the family to be a hands-on father. He had to work crazy hours to hold down the fort and raise four kids on his own, so the kids raised each other. Dimitri's three siblings live all over the country now, and he is the only one who stayed in Annapolis. His father lives about six miles from him, and they see each other once a month for breakfast at the diner on Main Street. Dimitri realizes he should spend more time with his father.

Dimitri has also come to realize that he allowed his wife to come between him and his father. She had disliked his father's manner, his Greek working-man heritage, his quiet disposition, and because of this, she sensed that he disapproved of her. Too tired to fight her constant hammering at his father's lack of a personality, Dimitri decided that his father and his wife didn't need to spend a lot of time together. It wasn't worth the angst of listening to her incessantly complain about his father's humble way of living and simplistic outlook on life.

A bluebird flies overhead and lands on the patch of landscaping near the patio after the long, hot summer. He watches the bird peck around and find something it needs. Its feathers ruffle, and the bird is off and away, flying over the picket fence in the backyard.

Instantly, he is reminded of the bluebird that landed on his mother's coffin on the day of her funeral. Bluebirds had been her favorite. Could that bird have been a sign, a spirit, or perhaps a messenger? The memory of it all—the pain of losing his mother—lingers, and Dimitri thinks about picking up the phone to call his father.

He opens the pack of Marlboro Lights, strikes a match, lights a fresh cigarette, and inhales once again.

Meg
Saturday, Labor Day Weekend

Meg Ellis folds the letter for the millionth time and tucks it into her drawer where she's kept it these last ten years. It's part of her morning regimen. She wakes up, uses the bathroom, begins her morning stretches on the floor of her bedroom, and then, just before she brews her morning cup of coffee, she always reads the letter.

For as long as she is able, reading the letter will be an instrumental part of her morning routine.

The sun streams through her large, picture windows that overlook the creek and are adjacent to her bed, and she closes her eyes and says a quick prayer. Years ago, when her faith was tested and she couldn't help change a situation, despite her innate ability to be positive and find spiritual grounding, she found herself moving into a dark period of time, questioning why things happen the way they do. Initially, she found no answers.

She turns on the coffee pot in the bright kitchen, which is painted a yellow to mimic a perpetual state of sunshine. In the throes of turning herself around, she pledged that if she ever had a place of her own, she would put vibrant colors on the walls, not the dull greys and muted tans used as backdrops of modern furnishings she sees in today's magazines. Yellow, she knew, meant happiness, but after researching the psychological meanings of colors, she found it represents so much more: optimism, positivity, vigor, intellect, and remembrance.

And she dearly wants to remember.

She boils an egg and puts a piece of wheat bread into the toaster oven. Her light brown, wavy hair falls to her mid back when she removes the hair tie; it feels heavy today in the heat of the warm morning. Meg left the windows open all night. Yesterday was one of those rare days when you could actually smell the creek, and it reminded her of the summers spent here, of being helpful.

She opens the sliding glass doors of her condominium that lead to her covered outdoor porch that faces Spa Creek to let the fresh air inside. She wipes off the outside pine table where she had placed fresh flowers on the table she purchased at the market on her way home yesterday. After preparing her meal, she relaxes and opens up the newspaper on this warm, but cloudless September day. She keeps tabs on what's happening in her city—her new home. She believes this just may be the place in which she stays for a while. There are places she's been and seen, but Annapolis feels most like home.

After Meg finishes eating, she puts her coffee into her travel mug, and walks down to the dock across from her condo. She climbs aboard her still unnamed boat that her aunt and uncle gifted her, an 18-foot Bayliner, perfect for cruising the river. She feels the sunshine on her face. Across the way, folks prep their sailboat, and she hears their voices echo across the creek. She watches them for a few moments and wishes she had more people to share her love of boating with, knowing she needs to make a better effort to make friends. One step at a time, she reminds herself.

Since opening up her store over a year ago, she is content and is often in disbelief that she made it happen, saving every penny, as she watched her dream come to fruition. She now thankfully owns a store. She gratefully owns a condo and a small boat. The hours of retail require a seven-day commitment, but the labor of love is so intense for her, that she never minds. In fact, today she is interviewing someone for the job of assistant manager, and she's hoping she will be a big help and allow her to have some days off now and then.

When she initially decided to take the plunge, she visited Annapolis twice and stayed at the Maryland Inn across the street from what is now her bookstore. She remembers her agent turning the key to the musty place, its charming framed door with the window in it, and stepping inside, immediately imagining what the store's potential could be. After the quick tour with the commercial real estate agent, it only took a few seconds for her to know the location was right for her, as she got a deep feeling inside that said, "This is it." She appreciated the affirmation.

The store's size was its other selling point. It wasn't too small, nor was it too big. It was two stories, with a basement for storage. It felt comfortable, manageable. Where she had previously been docile and tepid, after the letter, she allowed her passions to awaken and she developed a plan. She found herself. Her faith returned. And in a small way, she was finding others. It was all part of her new approach to life that had been brewing ever since she received the letter years ago.

She rests her hands on her knees as she lets her thoughts drift and concentrates on each breath she takes. She says Brodie's name mentally three times with each of three breaths she takes. Remembering. She thinks about her feet, her toes, and imagines the energy from the earth empowering her feet to her core to the top of her head. She has found that this exercise each morning grounds her, protects her, and shields her from anything toxic that may come her way. Meg revels in this sensation, and when she has been contemplative for several minutes, the warmth of the sun enveloping her, she comes away both peaceful and stronger. She ends each session with a quiet "thank you, God," and takes one last breath, looking across to the water.

She glances at her watch and acknowledges that she has about an hour before she has to leave for work. Her part-time associate, Ray, opened the store this morning and has been with her since she started, but Meg had understood his time with her was only temporary. He's leaving his position next month to begin his own adventure—teaching English to students in Kyoto, Japan. A recent college graduate, he and his best friend have decided to explore this opportunity for the next year. A woman named Clarke Morgan answered the "help wanted" ad. According to her application, she lives locally and loves bookstores.

Back inside her condo, she opens the drawer to the old armoire on the porch and pulls out samples of the stationery she ordered for the store. While she sells books, she also has a small section of stationery, note cards, gifts for readers, and bookmarks in the store, as well as a handful of journals. This particular stationery looks like worn, old paper with little muted roses on the right-hand corner. She thinks it's beautiful.

Meg pulls out her favorite black felt pen, straightens the piece of stationery on the table, and begins to write the last five of ten letters she's committed to writing each day.

Each handwritten letter of every word flows from memory—or from the heart. Just like the letter she keeps in her own drawer, Meg's letters draw on words that offer hope. She watches her hands create the cursive letters that build the words that make up the sentences, stringing together the various messages of the letters. She enjoys writing every single one.

That is the promise she made to herself when she committed

to owning the bookstore: to sell books, but also to invest in and connect with people. This is her quiet way of doing just that.

Eva

Saturday, September 22

By the end of the summer, Eva's bad mood is in full swing, especially having seen posts by her various "friends" on Facebook that Kyle will be marrying his high school sweetheart. In a matter of months, he has gone from being by Eva's side every minute of the day, to becoming swiftly engaged to Christa, his former high-school girlfriend and a twice-divorced mother of five.

Eva and Kyle had spent ten years together. They'd traveled together. They'd taken cooking classes and sailing classes together. They'd trained Brownie together. Kyle had sworn up and down that he didn't want to marry. That he wasn't the marrying kind, and Eva, a professional woman who was raised to be independent, agreed to the terms of this relationship. She was confident in their mutual love for each other.

Frigging liar, she thinks to herself. You think you know someone, and then, like a magician's disappearing act, in a puff of smoke, he's gone.

At first, Eva was numb, but the temper tantrum that ensued the night after Kyle's phone call was a moment to remember. In an absolute fit of rage, she tore everything out of his closet, leaving heaps of clothes in piles all over the floor. She screamed. She cried. Brownie cocked her head and barked a couple of times when she was in manic mode. She threw his bottle of cologne across the room and cracked her mirror.

And then, when she calmed herself down with a shot of whiskey—or two—she got to work.

Eva wasn't one to sit around and brood over things. The purge was therapeutic. With all the lights on in the house, she went through room by room and began to dump. She piled up all of his work clothes and went online to schedule the Salvation Army to come pick up his things. Feverishly working to clear any memory of him, Eva spent all night getting her house back to the way it was before he was in her life.

It was three-thirty in the morning when she heard the rapping on her back door. Nervously, Eva wound her way down the stairs to see Emily standing outside the back French doors, looking bewildered. Eva opened the door.

"What's wrong?" Emily asked.

"Why are you up at this hour?" Eva asked back.

"Working on a paper for my summer class. I couldn't sleep and noticed all your lights were on."

Eva motioned for her to come in and she sat on the floor, as did Brownie, the dog's sleep clearly disturbed by the commotion, and she placed her tired head on Eva's lap. Emily followed suit, and the three sat as Eva's raw emotions and fresh tears, in concert with the pain of her storytelling, kept them all side by side talking until dawn, when Emily put the kettle on for tea and they ate breakfast as the sun began to rise.

Now, months later, Eva regrets that she has not made much progress on her mental road to recovery from a broken heart—and a brutal, figurative slap in the face. She is pulling weeds from her front beds early in the morning and watering her flowers and plants when

Emily appears on her bike, her basket full to the brim with brown bags and coffee and croissants from the market up the street. On the back of the bike, she has fastened a large bouquet of flowers.

"Hi, Em," Eva says.

"You're up early," Emily says, positioning the bike on the sidewalk and putting the kickstand down. She reaches for the flowers. "These are for you," she says, handing them to Eva.

"Thank you, but you have got to stop doing this," Eva says, as she admires yet another bouquet from Emily. The flowers are wrapped up in brown paper with a label from a mobile flower truck that makes rounds in the area.

"I know, I know. I just like going to the truck and building my own bouquet. Are you still taking that boat ride today?"

"Yes, I am. I appreciate the flowers, Emily."

"No problem. I also have to chat with you about something else."

"Sure, what's up?" Eva asks, wondering what is coming.

"I wanted to give you plenty of notice. It looks like I got into the Ph.D. program I applied for, so I'll be leaving for New York after this semester ends in early December. I'll be moving in with a friend who has a three-bedroom apartment there. One of her roommates is getting married and moving out, so I can take her room. I'm sad to leave, and I'll miss you lots."

"Aw, Emily, I am so happy for you, but I'm sad for me. I sure will miss you. You've been such a great tenant and friend to me these past few months, and I can't thank you enough for that."

"We'll keep in touch, right?" Emily asks.

"Of course. I won't even bother to advertise the place until November, so don't feel rushed. Take your time. I'll figure it out. Sadly, I always knew you wouldn't stay forever, but it's been wonderful having you," Eva says, meaning it. It is the least of her worries right now. Work has been crazy, and she's been seeing a therapist, although the hours she's been putting in at work haven't allowed for a lot of free time.

Emily is ten years younger than Eva, and even though Emily has taken good care of Eva since Kyle left, Eva has felt equally protective of Emily, garnering a sense of what motherhood must feel like to her friends who were lucky enough to have children. Kyle claimed he never wanted any. Eva was on the fence about it, but now that she thinks about it, was she just saying that because Kyle was opposed to having a family? And now he's inheriting Christa's five children—all girls. Good luck with that, Eva thinks bitterly.

When she finishes watering the flowers, she changes, applies makeup, and grabs her dark sunglasses for the ride. She has to get to the boat before ten o'clock to make the trip across the Chesapeake Bay to visit her sister in St. Michaels. The boat trip allows her to have three hours in St. Michaels, just enough time to have lunch and visit a couple of shops. Taking the boat frees her from driving and from a fear she must overcome at some point—but she's survived and managed this way since high school, so who knows if she'll ever beat it. But traveling by boat, well, that's just pure pleasure. She's always loved the water.

The weather is gorgeous and she's thinking this excursion will be therapeutic for her. Plus, she hasn't seen her sister in a while.

More than likely, she and Amelia will probably do a post-mortem during lunch and discuss Kyle and their split, even though Eva would prefer to do anything but talk about Kyle. And, more than likely, Eva bets that sometime during the lunch, Tom Bowden's name will be brought up just like it always is when they venture down the road of nostalgia and try to dissect the meaning of life. The loss of

Tom and the events of the accident have forever bonded Eva with her older sister, and she's thankful to have her in her life. The true miracle is that both of them survived the accident, at least physically they did. Navigating the after-effects of Tom's death continues even today, all these years later, as the two of them still feel the sadness that never seems to wane whenever his name is said aloud.

A life gone way too soon.

Through the work she's done in the therapy sessions with her counselor, Eva has had to talk about losing Kyle. Talk of loss led her to talking about Tom and her sister in therapy, as well, forcing Eva to face feelings she has suppressed. Perhaps it's because the love that Amelia had for Tom was unlike anything she had ever seen before, and as a little sister, Eva was quite impressionable and held their relationship in high regard.

What else are big sisters for? In Amelia and Tom's case, Eva saw true love.

Even now, Amelia's husband, George, is a doting husband and father. He adores her. He would never leave her to be with his high school girlfriend.

Thinking about all of this makes Eva question everything she's done for the last ten years with Kyle. Was any of it true? Was it all a charade?

Eva winces a little. Therapy definitely has its pluses, but it also makes you see things as they are, and not as you imagine them to be.

Lily
Saturday, October 10

Lily arrives at the venue and swallows hard before she walks into the atrium room where both the ceremony and the reception will be taking place. It took all the strength she had to muster up the courage to attend this function. She is wearing a strapless, red dress with rhinestone heels from her own boutique, and her blonde hair, has grown longer and past her shoulders. Her stylist straightened her hair and pulled it off to the side with a sequined clip. A neighbor, who is a cosmetologist, came over earlier and applied her makeup. She feels as if she looks decent, the best she can do for an occasion such as this.

Her hands tremble as she walks in, and she sees Cora across the room in her bridesmaid's dress. Swallowing hard, she attempts to catch her breath. The anxiety is finding its way to every part of her body, and her knees feel especially wobbly. There are only two bridesmaids—Cora, and Melanie's best friend. Lily swallows hard but musters up a smile and a little wave to Cora. People Brad and she knew and socialized with come up to her to say hello, and Lily makes small talk while grabbing a glass of wine to help calm her nerves. She had told Cora that she would attend the wedding for one hour—that's all she could do. One hour. She's been watching the clock since she walked into the room.

"Ah, Lily," Charmaine Andrews says to her, as she loops her arm through hers. "You are a brave one for coming today." She kisses Lily on the cheek.

A former neighbor, Lily has known Charmaine for as long as she can remember, and she's one of a few mutual friends who truly understood the devastation Lily felt when her marriage ended. There were countless nights she cried on Charmaine's shoulder, and she was also one of the only friends who checked on her periodically and stopped by her house with homemade treats just to let Lily know she was thinking of her. They would sit side-by-side on Lily's couch, as Charmaine listened and provided support. Fifteen years older than Lily, Charmaine has a wickedly dark and snarky sense of humor—one that Lily finds amusing, especially when she wants to lambaste Brad—and extraordinarily big hair. Charmaine is one of those rare people who doesn't give a flip about what you think of her.

"One can only hope the bride trips or has a sneezing fit as she walks down the aisle. A little drama never hurt any wedding," Charmaine whispers into Lily's ear.

Lily snickers. She is also thankful Charmaine's here to lean on at the moment, as her own daughter is of no comfort because of her duties as a member of the bridal party. Charmaine has an uncanny talent for making Lily laugh and forget her troubles. At the very least, Charmaine has helped Lily feel less humiliated throughout the entire divorce debacle. As for her other friends who smile at Lily and wish her well? It's all for show. Divorce always makes everything uncomfortable.

As the guests begin to move into place, Lily sees Brad enter the room. As she guessed, he looks handsome and dapper and ten years younger than his actual age, his chiseled features and bronzed skin looking amazing in the tuxedo he has chosen to wear for the occasion. Lily remembers the way he looked on their wedding day all those years ago and is forced to admit that he looks even better now. He has grown into his age and good looks and has matured in a way that suits him. For a moment, she is dazzled by his charming presence, just as she had been all those years ago. Brad is smiling as he chats with his best man, his brother Chase, a person Lily has not talked to in over a year since the divorce. Lily senses that Brad's nervous. He touches the edges of his wavy, thick hair and messes it up a bit, something he has always done to calm his anxiety.

Charmaine has gone to the bar to replenish their glasses of wine, and Lily stands, holding herself in perfect posture, sucking in her tummy, eyeing Brad's every move. If only she hadn't loved him so much. If only she hadn't fallen deeply for him in high school. He is the only man she's ever loved, ever passionately kissed. She may never recover from the heartbreak of their failed relationship. Briefly, she curses having gone to the same high school, having cheered for his team, and having been smitten with him from the first moment she had a conversation with him. Perhaps it would have been better if she'd never met him at all—how different her life might have been. But then, she wouldn't have Cora.

As she returns her gaze to Cora, she realizes that Cora has been watching Lily watching Brad. Cora feigns a smile to Lily. Lily knows her daughter desperately wished that her parents would get back together. When that didn't happen, Cora asked her parents to put aside their bitterness, and to be cordial for her sake, and for the sake of their future relationships with each other. Who can blame a child for wanting the fairy-tale ending for her parents? Brad was too far gone. There was no chance for a reconciliation. Lily tenses, remembering how badly Cora wanted them to fix their problems. Cora waves and blows Lily a little kiss, which Lily mimics catching, and blows a kiss back. Calm on the outside, but feeling panic on the inside, Lily looks around the room and comprehends this reality.

Brad is marrying someone else.

The room is lit with candles and the harpist in the corner of the room plays soft music as people begin to move into place. Brad catches Lily's eye from across the room and looks at her. The two hold a gaze that feels endless. The corners of his mouth turn up, and he stares intently at her. Lily, unable to take her eyes off of him, offers a half-smile back, nods, and swallows hard. She blinks back tears, doing everything in her power to keep them from falling.

Cora, still watching her parents, sees the exchange take place. Lily attempts another smile across the room and notices Cora rocking back and forth, her big bouquet of flowers held down low in front of her. At seventeen, and as an only child, Cora has ridden a roller coaster of emotions over the last two years over the demise of her parents' relationship and her father's new relationship with Melanie. Perhaps neither Brad nor Lily took the time to understand the lingering effects of dissolving a relationship and creating a new one, although they certainly both heard her desperate pleas to work things out.

Then, without warning, Cora begins to run from the room, tossing her bouquet at the floor of the make-shift altar that that consists of a flower trellis. Lily and Brad both watch in shock, and Brad's mouth drops open. Lily is frozen.

The mood of the room turns to one of concern. The harpist looks up from her instrument, searching for the wedding coordinator's guidance, and continues to pluck the strings so the room does not become dead quiet. The guests begin to whisper, and Brad darts from his position at the trellis and runs out the door after his daughter. The bride has yet to appear for the ceremony. Lily, seemingly stunned and shaken by this sudden turn of events, hears Charmaine nudge her and say, "Go after her." Lily feels her heart begin to race and scurries toward the doors that open to State Circle, where Cora has bolted from the impending ceremony and venue altogether.

Reid

Halloween, October 31

Reid's costume doesn't fit quite right, and he has come to despise Halloween. If it weren't for his buddies Dan and Greg, he wouldn't even be leaving his apartment. He would lock himself in and watch another stupid Freddy Krueger movie. And yet he is on the verge of participating in another shitty night out, he thinks. Plus, he's starting to feel too old for the Fells Point crowd. It's mostly college-aged kids, and he's well past that now.

He's wearing the zombie costume Lexi had made for him two Halloweens ago. They had gone to a party for couples that Lexi's friend was throwing, and she had spent the time making matching costumes. He remembers every moment of that night—the way the two of them were laughing at their ridiculous costumes, getting lost on the drive to the party, the countless photos they took for social media, and the way he felt like his life was finally getting back on track. They laughed, they played games, they drank. When the party was over, Lexi drove home, because she knew of his propensity to drink far too much. She pulled into his apartment complex. She wouldn't get out of the car and come inside.

"Come on in, Lexi," Reid said. "Stay."

"Reid, I'm glad we've had fun tonight, because I wanted to have fun with you one last time."

"What?" Reid was stunned by her words, and he tried to make sense of what she was saying.

"I wasn't sure how to say what I need to say, but I'm just going to be honest and say that this relationship is not making me happy, Reid. I have to move on. My feelings have changed and I—"

He cut her off by holding up his drunken hand. What was happening? He had a diamond ring that he'd saved money for sitting in his bedside table drawer in his apartment. It wasn't the biggest ring, but he'd been able to buy it second hand from an antiques store. He had been waiting until Thanksgiving to give it to her.

"I'm sorry, Lexi. What am I missing?"

"I just can't anymore."

"You can't what?"

She pushed the zombie costume off of her shoulder as a piece of it was hitting her right eye while she tried to talk to him, turning her body slightly as she sat behind the steering wheel to face him, to look him in the eyes.

"I can't do forever with you. I'm sorry."

"Where did this come from?" he asked.

"It's been brewing for a while."

"Clearly," he said. He watches her play with the stitching on the costume.

"I'm sorry, Reid. I really am. You drink too much, you can't seem to get your act together, and I don't think this is something I want to live with."

Inside, he could feel his heart shattering, bit by bit, pieces of his heart breaking off and scattering inside him. His head felt heavy.

"I'll quit," he says. "I'll quit drinking."

She stared at him.

"I'll get a better job."

"You never do," she said.

He said nothing, and then she whispered the last few words. "I'm sorry, Reid. I really am."

He wondered if she really was sorry. Her voice sounded flat, devoid of emotion, and there were no tears. After being together for slightly over two years, in a matter-of-fact way, as if she were ending a relationship with a repairman or beautician, as she'd been known to do frequently, she ended their relationship.

Reid reached for the car door handle, opened it, and then slammed it shut behind him. He staggered toward his apartment in a state of disbelief, another bad decision made in the long list of bad ones he'd made for years. Before he got to the door of his apartment, he turned and watched her car drive away. Once inside his place, he cracked open a beer and sat in silence on the sofa in the dark.

*

Remembering that night, Reid looks into the mirror and hates this pathetic costume, resents that he's being bullied by his drinking buddies to go to Baltimore, and despises the fact that he's in this small apartment sprinkled with random furniture he's picked up here and there or that were given to him by friends. The place feels nothing like a home. Spending the night with Freddy Krueger is way more appealing than mingling and parading the cobblestone streets impersonating a zombie when he already feels dead inside. He takes off the costume and walks outside to the complex's dumpster and tosses the zombie garb into the bin. Then, he grabs his phone and sends the text to Dan and Greg telling them he can't make it.

Reid's also feeling down because it looks like his parents have a buyer for their home. His mother had called earlier to let him know, and he has the sinking feeling that soon they will be in Florida half the time and here, in some sort of rental or condo, and his connection to his boyhood home is done. He will never set foot inside that home on Christmas or attend one of their backyard parties ever again.

An era is ending, and Reid scratches his head and ponders how odd it is that you can fall in love with a place almost as much as you can fall in love with people. He would never tell anyone that he's a bit of a romantic, or that he had clear visions of someday owning that house and making it a nest for his own family. There isn't any place he loves more than that old place, with its huge, wraparound porch, its quirky staircase, the wood moldings, the claw-foot tub, and the private backyard with mismatched gardens and quirky ornaments.

He calls his parents and asks if he can come over. His mother is surprised, and tells him it's no problem at all.

As Reid decides to walk the mile and a half to their home to get some exercise, he finds himself breathing in the cool, October air. People are out and about in Annapolis, some in costume, some not, and as he turns down the street toward Murray Hill, he remembers what it felt like to be a kid without responsibility. Without regrets.

His mother greets him at the door, and he kisses her on the cheek.

"I'll spare you the trouble tonight," he says, reaching for the candy bowl she has next to the door, just like always.

"Are you sure? I thought you might be out for the night."

"Not this year, Mom. I'd rather spend this Halloween here."

She smiles at him. He can tell she has an understanding of his sense of hopelessness.

"You know, Reid, no one holds the cards to your future better than you do," she says softly, and she rubs his arm.

He nods. He wants to cry, break down. But he doesn't. He

hides those emotions.

Instead, he takes the candy bowl and walks out the front door to the porch, pulls up the rocking chair and sits in it, ready to hand out candy to little trick-or-treaters who smile and giggle and are full of hope.

Dimitri

Friday, November 2

When the boss calls Dimitri into the office for their regularly scheduled Friday four o'clock meeting, he thinks nothing of it. Work has been exhausting. He goes in, gets his job done, and works hard for the company. He regularly brings work home with him, and despite not loving the accounting field, he's good at his job. Accounting was never his first love; it was never something he wanted to do, yet he knew he needed a secure job to live as he wanted to live. He thought it would have been enough for his wife to live in a nice home in the city, but clearly she wanted more. So Dimitri is left with a house in Annapolis that's too big for him and a job that pays the bills.

Grant tells Dimitri to sit down, and as Dimitri begins to open his folder of notes, Grant tells him those notes aren't needed for this meeting.

"Dimitri, the company has decided to downsize, and unfortunately, I regret to tell you that your position is being eliminated," he says.

Baffled, Dimitri scratches his head, adjusts his ponytail. "Is this a joke?" he asks.

"Unfortunately, no. I did my best to try to save your position, but management has other plans. It is not a reflection of your work ethic or anything you have done, it's just a decision by management.

I'm so sorry."

Dimitri feels as if there is a boulder sitting on his chest. He's unable to move. Completely flabbergasted, he can't look Grant in the face, the sense of humiliation trickling through his being, the words echoing in his head: *your job has been eliminated*. He doesn't know how he will tell his father this one. His father, who sacrificed so much and wanted to see his son yield success, will be worried for him. And the last thing he wants to do is worry his father any more than he already has.

"You'll be given a twelve-week severance package. Unfortunately, this is your last day, and you have a half an hour to clean out your desk and turn in your keys before security will walk you out," Grant says, his voice shaky. Dimitri actually feels bad for Grant, that he has to be the bearer of this type of news to someone.

"I've spent fifteen years at this firm. This is some send off," Dimitri mumbles. He stands, feeling a little weak at the knees, and tosses the folder of information that he spent hours working on at home onto Grant's desk. He reaches into his briefcase and pulls out two additional folders of information and hands them over as well.

"We'll also need your laptop," Grant says.

Dimitri shakes his head and exits the room. Thirty minutes later, he is escorted out of the building, not sure as to where he will go.

*

Dimitri turns the car toward downtown Annapolis. He decides to walk through the historic area, meandering in and out of the side streets and ends up on the docks. He breathes in the air and watches the few sailboats that are leisurely gliding on the water. The water has always calmed him, and this particular spot where he has planted himself, is his. He never shared it with his ex-wife. Never told her this is where he goes to clear his head. A fast-moving motorboat powers by, leaving ripples in the water and rocking the sailboats, as they bob in the wake the boat leaves behind. A momentary thought of buying a boat and sailing far away enters his mind, but it is fleeting. He's too much of a realist for any sort of life-changing spontaneous action.

His life has taken a surprising turn for the worse. He thinks about playing the slots at the casino but decides against it. He may be stupid with his money at times, but he knows he only has twelve weeks to figure this disaster out, and the severance won't last too long. He could sell the house. It all reminds him of her, anyway, with all the feminine touches, the abundance of pink accents throughout the main level, the white kitchen, and the Easter-egg colorful throw rugs. He should have gotten rid of it all, but he didn't. He scratches his head and wonders why.

After realizing that no matter how long he sits here, things won't get better, he gets up and walks toward his favorite tavern on Main Street. There's a guy setting up his microphone and amplifier, getting ready to play guitar. The place is full for a Friday night, and Dimitri squeezes into a spot at the bar. He orders a gin and tonic—he's not in the mood for a beer—and turns to watch the guy sing and play. He's pretty good, Dimitri thinks, envious that the musician probably loves what he does.

After a few drinks, Dimitri leaves the bar, and heads back to his spot, wrapping his coat tightly around him. This time, he sits on the bench, and tries to calm his anxieties. The temperature has dropped, and Dimitri stays only for an hour this time, before walking back home and into the empty house with the bright pink rug.

*

Sitting in front of the television, Dimitri's still reeling and questioning everything. Why do people attach so much self-worth to their jobs? Then, in the same breath, he wonders why he was let go and who else was let go? How much downsizing is happening? And is it real? He'd like to know the answers to these questions, but realizes he'll probably never get any.

He also surmises that he most likely won't be able to sleep, his anxieties riding high. Therefore, he tosses his overcoat on the chair, loosens his tie, makes himself another mixed drink, and finds himself at his piano.

That's one positive outcome of his divorce. He can play the piano whenever he wants and at whatever volume he wants, no matter the hour. It's nearing midnight. His fingers stretch across the keys—no sheet music needed—and he begins to play some of his old favorites that he learned in his twenties. It's amazing how the songs stay in his head and come out through his fingertips. A Billy Joel song. An Elton John song. A couple of contemporary tunes from John Mayer. His music teacher told him he has a nice voice, but he's never quite believed it, yet when he's by himself, he'll sing softly as his fingers glide across the keys. Dimitri can also play by ear, something he believes he inherited from his mother.

When he's done playing those songs, he fiddles with a few he's written himself. He's been creating his own music since he was in his late teens. He knows they aren't great, but they are catchy, if not a little sappy, but he plays them anyway. John Mayer's music can be sappy, too. He'd written the songs long before he met his ex. In fact, one of the songs is called Marianne, about a girl he fell in love with during his junior year of college. The two were inseparable for several months, until she opted to date one of his friends, a football player. Since he's not on Facebook, or any social media, for that matter, he has no idea what happened to Marianne, and often wonders how her life turned out. Better than his, he would imagine.

The house echoes with Dimitri's music—the C-chord, then the G-chord—a song comes into his head, one that his mom would play when he was younger. Dimitri fiddles with the keys, but he can't remember all the words or exactly how the song goes. So much time has passed. He feels that old familiar ache in his heart when he thinks of his sweet mother, her kind eyes, and the way she would tousle his hair. When Dimitri's eyes begin to blur from a blend of the memories and tiredness, he takes one last sip of his drink, walks upstairs, strips off his suit until he's in his boxers and t-shirt, and crawls under the covers, falling into a deep and tipsy sleep.

Meg
Thanksgiving Morning

Meg wakes up to a bright Thanksgiving morning. The sun is out, and she pulls the curtains open so she can see the glistening water outside her window. Across the way, she can see the trees still holding the last of their autumn colors. She breathes in and begins her morning routine, which includes stretching and reading the letter.

After she eats her breakfast and drinks her morning coffee, she showers and dresses. She will not wear black today. Orange was Brodie's favorite color, so she takes the orange sweater dress from the hanger and pulls it over her head, slips into her tall boots, and wraps a big, black checked scarf around her torso and neck. It's a beautiful day, one that does not require a coat for a Thanksgiving Day in Maryland. After a quick call to her parents in Virginia to wish them well this holiday, she grabs her keys and heads out the door. If she didn't have to open the store so early the next morning for Black Friday shoppers, she might have considered driving the five hours to their house, but it didn't seem worth the hassle. Her parents are hosting several of their neighbors this year for dinner. Although she'll miss being home, Meg knows a large crowd will keep them entertained.

Meg knows where she needs to be this morning, and it's with Brodie.

As she starts the car and begins her drive, she takes notice of how quiet the roads are. She reflects on her life to this point and genuinely feels thankful for all that she has, for all that she has been given. She'll be thirty-six in a few weeks, and the feelings of gratitude fill up her heart for what she has been able to do over the last year.

She thinks of her Uncle Ben and her Aunt Nancy, who have been like another set of parents to her. She remembers Brodie, his eyes, his wavy hair, and his crooked smile—especially when something funny was said and they'd share a laughing fit. She remembers how the stories she read to him were the bright spots in his days, how he liked to sit outdoors in the shade wearing those silly blue sunglasses she bought him, and how much he loved them and insisted on wearing them, even when he was indoors. She remembers how she and Brodie would spend the entire summer together, and that she was supposed to be the source that lifted him up. If only he knew it had been the other way around.

She stops off at the little florist shop around the corner, which was scheduled to be open until noon on Thanksgiving, and she selects a bouquet of orange and white mums. Brodie will like that—Orioles colors. He'll like the colors of the flowers. He loved his orange Orioles t-shirt, and when Meg closes her eyes, she can picture him wearing it. He would park himself in front of the baseball games on TV, and in the early years, he wanted her to tally the scores on the small chalkboard that Aunt Nancy kept next to the television. They called it their own "out-of-town scoreboard" just like the Major League ballparks display. They even made it to a few games in Baltimore, and the ballclub arranged for him to meet his favorite player before the start of the game. Brodie's face lit up, and Meg will never forget how happy he looked, especially when his favorite ballplayer signed his glove.

She drives in through the large, wrought iron gates, the flow-

ers beside her in the passenger seat, and loops around the circle to
the spot where she normally parks. The reds and oranges and yellows
and muted greens on the trees serve as a beautiful autumn backdrop.
There are other people strolling the grounds, as well, doing the same
as she is doing: visiting a loved one.

She removes the keys from the ignition and picks up the bouquet. Once parked, Meg knows exactly how many paces it takes to get
to his spot: one hundred and fourteen, exactly. She watches her feet
take each step, and when she counts the one-hundredth and four-
teenth step, she has reached Brodie. It's been several years since his
death, and she must rely upon the memory of him to recall his face, as
she kneels beside the tombstone.

Every time she reads the headstone, a tear falls. It's as if seeing
his name and the dates on the headstone makes it all the more real,
even though she knows it is real. She had promised Uncle Ben and
Aunt Nancy that she would visit often now that they no longer live
in Maryland and have retired to coastal South Carolina. They could
never give up their life of boating, but they wanted to retire to a cli-
mate that had a little longer boating season, and Hilton Head offers
them that.

The birds are chirping in nearby trees, and Meg thinks that
it must be peaceful for Brodie to hear the birds and see the fading
weeping willow blow gently in the breeze.

She places the flowers next to the headstone and sits in peace
with Brodie for several minutes. Then, she reaches inside her purse
and removes Brodie's favorite book of poems with his favorite by
Henry Wadsworth Longfellow. She begins to read, softly, but aloud
so that he can hear. She is able to get through it okay, but as the poem
continues, she fights to hold it together as she reaches the last two
stanzas:

And forever and forever,
  As long as the river flows,
As long as the heart has passions,
  As long as life has woes;

The moon and its broken reflection
  And its shadows shall appear,
As the symbol of love in heaven,
And its wavering image here.

She closes the poem and sits in the grass in silence. He always did love that one the most.

*

When she returns home at noon, feeling emotionally drained, she resorts to warming up the turkey soup she made yesterday and channeling her energy elsewhere. There's no need to fuss with a big turkey when it's just her. Besides, she's going to take her boat for a little spin today. She prepared snacks to take on the boat for Clarke and her husband, who said they would come down in the early after-noon for a quick boat ride in the river before they go to their friends' home for Thanksgiving dinner.

The phone rings and startles her out of a trance.

"Hey kiddo," the voice on the other end of the line says. "How are you?"

"Great, Uncle Ben. Happy Thanksgiving!"

"Oh, same to you, sweetie. Aunt Nancy sends her love."

"Thank you. Send it right back to her for me."

Meg can hear Uncle Ben relay the message to Aunt Nancy,

shouting it across the room, and then he asks her if she's having tur-key for turkey day.

"Close...I had some turkey soup I made yesterday. Does that count?"

"I think we can count it," he says with a laugh. "Did you visit our boy today?"

"Of course, I did. I put some Orioles orange flowers on the grave today, and the gardens in the fall looked amazing. Truly beauti-ful. It's a well-manicured place."

"Good. Glad to hear it. We have sent our love to him from afar. We're also planning to visit the cemetery over Christmas and spend some time with you. Are we still on for that?"

"Of course!" Meg says. "I wouldn't have it any other way."

"Great! We won't bother you with accommodations—we'll stay with Aunt Nancy's sister."

"You don't have to," Meg says. "This place is technically yours."

"No, my dear," Uncle Ben says. "Technically, it is yours. How's the boat?"

"Taking it out later, as a matter of fact. It's beautiful here, and the water is calm. My friend and her husband are going to come for a spin."

"That's terrific, honey," Uncle Ben says.

Meg feels for Uncle Ben and Aunt Nancy. It breaks her heart that they lost their only child. Even though she feels like crying, she fights it because she knows Uncle Ben has had enough tears over the last few of years.

"Well," Meg says, as she has said for two years, "I can't thank you enough, once again, on this beautiful Thanksgiving Day for all the things you have given to me. I'm happy and the store is doing very well."

"Music to my ears," Uncle Ben says. "We love you, Meg."

"You, too, Uncle Ben."

"Alright, we'll see you in less than four weeks! Can't wait."

"Me, either," Meg says. "Really looking forward to it."

Rereading the letter, she is reminded of something she has learned along the way. Connections bind us together, and taking initiative to do for others has the potential to lead to a beautiful life.

Eva

Thanksgiving Day

Eva sets the table as she listens to her favorite B.B. King playlist. Kyle loved the blues, and despite his deafening absence in the house since his exodus, she still loves the music. Some people can't listen to music that reminds them of old lovers, but Eva doesn't subscribe to that theory. Maybe it's because she officially has the blues and finds it therapeutic, she chuckles to herself, sensing the irony of the lyrics. She places the napkins next to the plates, and then the silverware on top. Emily purchased the centerpiece flowers from her favorite flower truck, which includes colorful autumn mums, some deep russet colored roses, and greens. Lastly, Eva retrieves six stemmed wine glasses and puts them in the right corner of each place setting.

She surveys the table. She thinks it looks okay.

When Kyle was here, she would have been obsessed with getting the table just right. She would have been making herself insane attempting to create just the right menu for Thanksgiving. She hasn't seen her parents since February. When they first moved and sold her the house, they rented an apartment down the road and spent six months here and six months in Florida. Two years ago, they decided to make Florida their primary home. All their friends are there, and despite that Eva and Amelia had decided to stay in Maryland, the trade-off for not living in the same state was that they came here for holidays, at least for now while they are still in good health, and Eva and Amelia have a vacation spot to visit in Naples.

Unlike in past years, Eva's heart just isn't in it.

The doorbell rings, and Amelia, her husband, and their five-year-old daughter, Jilly, are standing on the front porch. They named her Jillian, but no one calls her that. She is Jilly and always will be Jilly. Eva smiles when she sees Jilly's soft, light brown curls and blue eyes as she walks through the door with her favorite doll, the one Eva gave her for her birthday last year. Amelia had told Eva that the doll was the biggest hit ever, and as an only child, that doll goes everywhere Jilly goes, kind of an imaginary little sister. And now, they are both here.

"Hello, Jilly!" Eva says, as her niece leans in to hug her. Eva bends down and meets her eye to eye. "I see you brought Dolly with you."

"She's not Dolly anymore, though," Jilly says. "Her name is Ariana."

Eva looks at Amelia, who mouths *"after Ariana Grande."*

"Oh, I see," Eva says to Jilly. "Well, welcome to Thanksgiving, Ariana."

Jilly immediately drops Ariana on the sofa when she sees Brownie come in from outside with Emily. "Brownie!" she exclaims, and then heads back outside with the squeaky toy to play with the dog.

"Are Mom and Dad here yet?" Amelia asks.

"No, but I expect them any minute."

"I have all the pies, Cool Whip, and other treats. I'm excited for Thanksgiving, even if you didn't go all out this year."

Eva gives her a look, because she knows she's being funny. She's the best sister a girl could ask for, and Amelia has had to listen to Eva moan about Thanksgiving this year. Eva feels bad about that, too. She recognizes that she's been wrapped up in her own sorrow.

When her parents come through the door ten minutes later, it's a big Levoni family reunion. Everyone is hugging and kissing and catching up. Eva still feels as if she's in a fog. As much as she wants to get over stupid Kyle, she seems to make progress one day, and then has a total setback the next. The three sessions she has had with her therapist, Janice, a younger, intellectual type who says the words "think deeply" too much, have been minimally helpful. She knows it will take time. Janice said something along the lines of "it takes people who lose a loved one to death nearly three years to get over the horror of that; people who are in relationships and break up? It can take a good while to get over it as well. And some people never fully recover."

That was encouraging, Eva thought at the time.

Eva checks the turkey. She had put the huge bird in the oven promptly at eight-thirty, knowing they were going to have a Thanksgiving lunch and then binge all evening on pies, desserts, and then maybe turkey sandwiches later in the evening. Her parents stay at the hotel on the water downtown, so as not to inconvenience either daughter, and no matter how much they plead for them to stay at the house, they claim they like the freedom of not having their girls feel like they have to tend to them every second.

Emily, who decided not to go home to Virginia for Thanksgiving, is celebrating with Eva and her family. At first, Eva was surprised she accepted her offer, because she didn't know how comfortable she would feel with her family, but then was thankful she decided to share the day. Last night, they drank wine and made the sides for the turkey.

As Eva, Emily, her mother, and her sister prepare the food in the kitchen while the men watch football, Eva feels her cellphone vibrate in her pocket. She sees his number. She hesitates a moment, and then, hesitantly, she picks up the phone.

"Hello?"

"Hi Eva," he says.

"Hi." She can feel her mom and sister looking at her.

"I just wanted to wish you a Happy Thanksgiving. I know you're probably entertaining or going to your sister's place, but I wanted to wish you well and say I'm sorry once again. I'm sorry for how it all—"

Eva turns her back to her family, as she hears Kyle talking, but soon remembers the tip Janice gave her during the last session. Kyle wants to be forgiven. He wants to be let off the hook. He wants her to say everything is okay, so that he can move on guilt-free into his new relationship. It's how it works. Her therapist said as much.

"You know, you're right. I have a house full of company—turkey's coming out of the oven now. Can't talk. Another time," and she hangs up, remaining calm and staying cordial, even though she wants to tell him to go screw himself. The good news is, she asserted herself. She wonders if Janice will think she handled it well.

Her sister eyes her, and Eva just shakes her head as they continue to place everything on the table and her family gathers around the table. Eva's dad decides to say the blessing, which Kyle had done for the last several years when they hosted Thanksgiving here.

"Thank you, Lord, for bringing us all together once again on this gorgeous Thanksgiving Day. We are thankful that we can all be together to share this blessing, and cheers to our wonderful host, Eva, for hosting the day."

"Amen," everyone says.

Eva can't swallow and she fights back tears. She can feel it all rising within her. The wine last night. The lack of sleep over the last several months. Jilly and that blasted, sweet doll that she loves. And seeing her parents, who after all these years, are still madly in love with each other. It is enough to make anyone have a meltdown.

And a meltdown she has.

She can feel herself begin to hyperventilate, and in order to not scare the living daylights out of Jilly, she excuses herself into the kitchen. Emily follows. Of course, Emily follows. That dear girl has been with her through it all. She has lived here on site. Has known Kyle. Has seen Eva relegated to being a hot mess. Has brought her flowers regularly, for God's sake.

And as Eva falls into Emily's arms, the tears flowing down her face, Eva has a good Thanksgiving Day cry.

Before long, she feels both her sister and her mother wrap their arms around her.

Her dad stays in the dining room with Jilly and George.

"Just breathe," her mother says. "Breathe."

Eva takes breaths as the three women look on, not really sure what to do except to give her a hug and offer support.

"Kyle just called. Right before I took the turkey out."

"Such a bastard move," Amelia says. Eva loves when she gets pissed on her behalf. She finds it hilarious. "Can't he leave well enough alone?"

"He is a jerk," Emily chides in. It is the first time Eva can recall her saying anything bad about Kyle at all. She has been so supportive and has always tried to stay neutral. But now she makes her feelings known.

Eva grabs a tissue and pulls herself together. She winks at Amelia, and begins to laugh, a sort of crazy laugh, but a laugh nonetheless. Then Amelia starts to laugh, then Emily, and finally her mother.

"Thank you all," Eva says, drying her eyes. Then, for Amelia's sake, she says, "I'm not letting that idiot ruin my Thanksgiving. Let's go eat."

With bloodshot eyes and a puffy face, Eva walks out of the kitchen, back to the dining room table, plunks her ass down, and begins to drizzle gravy all over her turkey without saying another word about it.

＊

Later that night, after her mom and dad return to their hotel and Emily returns to the cottage, Eva is alone with Amelia, George, and Jilly, who packed their bags to stay the night with her. She plays with Jilly for a while and reads her a bedtime story.

"Will I see Uncle Kyle again?" Jilly asks innocently, as Eva tucks her into her bed.

"I don't think so," Eva says, gently. "He had to go home and take care of his own mom and dad."

Jilly thinks for a moment, a long pause filling the air.

"Will I have to take care of Mommy and Daddy one day?" Jilly asks.

"We all have to take care of each other," Eva says. "That's what families do."

"That's good," Jilly says, "because I like our family. I don't want to take care of another family."

"Well," Eva says, "we should always take care of people we love, whether they are family or not, right?"

"Right," Jilly says. She hugs Ariana, and Eva helps her snuggle in for sleep.

"I love you, Jilly-girl," Eva says, kissing her on the forehead.

"I love you, Aunt Eva," Jilly says back.

*

When Eva walks downstairs, she sees George sprawled across the couch. He's watching the football game.

"Good Thanksgiving dinner, Eva," he says to her, patting his stomach. "You out-did yourself."

"Thanks, George," she says, hitting him in the arm. "You've got a good kid up there."

"Yes, Jilly's a keeper," he says, smiling.

"Want to get some fresh air and sit on the porch for a little bit?" Amelia asks Eva.

"That would be nice," Eva says.

They wrap themselves up in two plaid lap blankets and sit on the front porch. There is nothing like the smell of autumn in the air. Eva loves it—has always loved fall ever since she read a book when she was younger about a high school student who goes back to school in September and what happens in her life that year. She can't remember the name of the book, but it made her love school and hearing stories. She felt a connection with that independent character, and it may have been the book that made her fall in love with reading.

Her sister sits beside her, each of them in rocking chairs, and they watch people stroll by. The bars in Eastport are open, and people come down to drink and hang out in the city during Thanksgiving weekend.

"Are you okay?" Amelia asks her.

"I guess," Eva says. "Sorry about the meltdown."

"Ah, no worries. We all have them, as you probably remember."

"I do."

"Do you remember how hard we both cried when Tom died?"

"Yes. I've never seen so many tears. I don't think you have, either," Eva says.

"Nope. I don't think so. It's probably why it takes a lot for me to cry these days. I think I used up most of my tears back then."

"We're both lucky to be alive, you realize. I'm thankful every day," Eva says.

An older couple holding hands walks by on the sidewalk, and they wave to them. Eva looks at her sister, and they nod to each other.

"If Tom had lived, do you think you would have ever met George?" Eva asks her sister.

"I don't know," Amelia says. "But I do know the hurt goes away little by little, although we never forget."

"I know how much you loved him," Eva says. "We all did."

"And I know how much you love Kyle."

"Loved."

"No, love. You still love him. That's why it hurts. And it's okay. But there will be a George for you. You know that, right?"

"I can only hope he'd be as great as your George," Eva says, looking at the moon high in the sky across the street as it brightens the darkened street.

Lily
Friday after Thanksgiving–Black Friday

After working at the boutique all day, Cora and Lily return home. They had arrived at the shop early before the crowds came and stayed late to straighten up after the crowds left. There was an unrelenting stream of shoppers for Black Friday, and a consistent wait for the dressing room that Cora monitored. The store had a good day financially. Maria had gone down the street to pick up sandwiches from the deli, but Lily was only able to sneak a few bites during a short-lived lull. Cora, Maria, and Lily made a good team, and Lily was thankful that her daughter was willing to come in and help, turning down an invitation to a friend's house for Friendsgiving.

Cora immediately flops onto the sofa and begins to scroll through her phone, while Lily tosses her keys onto the counter, grabs the Thanksgiving leftovers, and piles turkey, stuffing, sweet potatoes, green beans, and cranberry sauce onto each of their plates and heats them in the microwave. Since that day in October, Cora hasn't eaten much. She blames herself entirely for the cancellation of her father's wedding, and for the breakup of her father and Melanie.

Lily is still struggling with the way it all happened, as well. When Lily fled the scene and ran after Cora, Brad had found Cora first. Lily and Brad sat with her, as Cora was crying on a bench under picturesque trees, where she had taken refuge. Lily listened as the two of them talked. After a short discussion, which consisted of Cora telling her father that he was an idiot for "thinking of marrying that woman," Brad looked as if he'd been slapped in the face. Lily will never forget how his tanned face went pale—the embarrassment of the unfolding events taking a toll on him.

"I thought you liked her," he said to Cora.

"She's a little older than me, Dad, and I like Mom a lot better. And I think she just really, really, only likes your money and the lifestyle you can give her."

The words of a seventeen-year-old truth teller. This is what emerges when you raise your child with the notion that telling the truth is always better than pretending, faking, or lying. Lily guessed that Cora simply couldn't hide her feelings any longer.

Brad had whispered, "I can't do this today," loosened his tie, and looked at Lily and Cora, then marched away, down the path back to the Calvert House, leaving them both agape. As he walked away, Lily figured he was done with the two of them, and that he was off to make a new life with Melanie.

Lily never expected him to make a different decision, to return to the venue, explain to his bride that he couldn't go through with it, and then make an announcement to the guests inviting them to enjoy the party, but that the wedding was canceled.

From what Lily heard later, it was all quite dramatic, and there were tears and sighs of disbelief. The groom's father had the audacity to call Brad a weasel. Of course, Lily didn't see or hear any of this for herself, because she remained on the bench with Cora until they decided to go home. More in-depth details of the afternoon came later that night from Charmaine, who watched the antics in the back of the room like a fly on the wall and even recorded a short clip of the speech on her phone so Lily could hear it.

But Lily couldn't bring herself to listen to what Brad had said. As much as Charmaine wanted to share Brad's speech with her, Lily declined to see it. Surprisingly, it affected her in a way she didn't quite understand.

Cora came home and spent two straight days in her room. She refused to come out, feeling far too humiliated by the drama she had caused, blaming herself for ruining the wedding. Lily had to place food outside her bedroom door for her to eat, and she ate very little.

Brad called Cora and talked to her on the phone. He reassured her that, while he was upset for the way it went down, he was neither angry nor was he holding a grudge against his daughter, someone he loved dearly and protected with vigor. Melanie packed her bags the next day and caught a flight to Florida with her parents, who decided to return home immediately. They were none too pleased with Brad.

No one was.

No one except Lily.

And not for the "I told you so" reasons, or because she wanted to get even with him, which at one time, even a few months ago, she very much did want to do. She was pleased because it may have been possible that perhaps Cora, in her teenage wisdom, had communicated something to her father that no other person had been able to do since this charade with Melanie had started: that it probably was not going to be a long-term relationship if all that Cora had shared with Lily about Melanie were true.

Cora, it seemed, just wanted the best for her father, despite being angry at him, and was less than enthralled with his choice of a lifetime partner. She saw things that were troubling to her. Perhaps all the years Lily and Cora had spent watching schmaltzy Hallmark Christmas movies opened Cora's eyes to what a "happily ever after" should look like. Cora could not imagine that kind of happiness for her father with Melanie. It bothered Cora to watch Melanie use her dad's credit card as if it were hers. She bought herself expensive things. And yet, she still went to bars with friends her age and partied. Cora had spotted Melanie out one night at a bar on Main Street when she was eating with friends. She watched Melanie from across the room that night and wondered why in the heck she would want to marry her father when she was out on the town flirting with men her own age. But Cora had kept this to herself and hadn't even shared it with Lily. Clearly, she had kept it all to herself. But there was no hiding her feelings on the wedding day. Cora hit a breaking point and finally spilled the beans.

"Why didn't you share any of this sooner? It might have been helpful," Brad had asked Cora days after the canceled wedding.

Cora knew why, but the problem with young people is that they don't always know how to articulate their insights. So, she kept it all inside and let it fester.

And now, weeks later, neither of them has heard back from Brad, despite leaving messages on his voicemail yesterday wishing him well on Thanksgiving.

All of that to say, Brad is probably feeling as lost as Lily had been after he left their marriage.

Lily places the plates on the table, feeling famished with sore feet from standing all day, and she hears her cellphone ping. She picks up her phone. The text is addressed to both Lily and Cora and reads: "I'm fine. Just needed to get away. Staying with my brother for a bit."

Cora enters the room having received the message as well and holds her phone in the air. "He can't even wish us a Happy Thanksgiving a day late," she moans. "Ugh. He's never going to forgive me!"

"He already has," Lily says, finding herself defending her ex-husband. "That's the thing about being parents—we don't stay mad for too long."

"But I've ruined his life, Melanie's life..." Cora's voice trails off as she picks a piece of turkey off the plate with her fingers.

"Look at it this way. Maybe you didn't ruin his life. Maybe you saved it. Now, get a drink, sit down, and stay a while," Lily teases her. "Food tastes better when you sit. We already had to stand to eat once today. Believe me, both Melanie and your dad will be fine."

Cora gets them both glasses of water, and then sits across from her mother at the kitchen table in the cottage-style home Lily bought in the neighborhood near the Naval Academy stadium. Grey siding with white trim and a perky orange door, the house oozes with charm. The gardens are filled with hydrangeas that bloom all summer and vines that climb along the white picket fence. There's a screened-in porch on the side of the house, and it's Lily's favorite. She bought at the right time and got a good deal on it, thanks to her realtor friend. She was lucky the property had been lovingly refurbished just three years prior, so it was in move-in condition. Cora went to the Catholic high school in town, so the home was convenient for both of them, and in good weather, their bicycles are often their favorite mode of transportation. Brad kept the old house in Pendennis Mount, a large craftsman-style stunner with views of the Severn River. When the divorce happened, in Lily's fragile state, she knew she could not stay in the house she shared with Brad and let him keep it.

"Well, did you hear from your friends? How is Friendsgiving going?" Lily asks Cora as she toys with her food.

"Still going. They want me to come over."

"So go," Lily says, meaning it. She believes her daughter needs to get out of this depressed rut she finds herself in presently.

"I don't want to leave you alone," Cora responds.

"Since when?"

"I don't know. It's a holiday weekend, and I hate to leave you by yourself."

"I'm fine. I don't need you to babysit me. I'm tired. I'm going to curl up on the sofa and read a good book."

"Are you sure?" Cora asks. Lily can sense a hint that she really does want to go over and see her girlfriends.

"Positive. I won't wither and die while you're out. I promise."

Cora laughs and gives her mother the Cora look—the one that means a combination of "are you kidding me?" and "you're so funny, Mom," and then trudges upstairs to her room to change. Fifteen minutes later, she reappears, looking cute in her new sweater from the boutique, jeans, and black booties. Her brown hair is pulled into a high ponytail. She looks adorable.

"Have fun," Lily says, and then begins to clean the dishes and put her kitchen back in order. She plays her favorite Chris Botti CD to relax (yes, at home, she still loves her CD player and has quite a collection on disc), and pours herself a glass of wine. A tall, cold glass of white wine.

Lily picks up her new book and her favorite fuzzy white blanket, and gets comfortable on the sofa, her wine glass next to her—along with a good-sized piece of pumpkin pie. She's tired of counting calories. She's exhausted from trying to please everyone in the store and being "on" all the time, doting on everyone but herself. Well, not tonight. Tonight, she's on her own, and being on her own means reading a good romance and eating the pie. She even tops it with whipped cream. A lot of it. She takes a big bite.

Alone again, she thinks. And she's happy for the quiet evening at the moment.

Reid

Thanksgiving Day

Reid stretches out in his bed on Thanksgiving morning and turns to see the blonde hair of the woman he met at the bar the night before. It's coming back to him. She flirted with him after his set, and he flirted back. When he finished playing, he stayed too long, drank too many beers, and talked with her. He was feeling unusually lonely, and although he pledged not to involve himself in any woman's life, he had broken his own promise to himself. She was funny and attractive, but not someone he saw himself getting into a long-term relationship with at all. She giggled far too much and seemed unable to make idle conversation. She played on her phone like a teenager. Looking at the backside of her now, her naked body draped with the sheet, he wonders how they both allowed themselves to become this entangled. He also wonders why she wouldn't have any place to be on Thanksgiving morning. He didn't want to think too hard about that question.

He clears his throat and looks at the clock. She stirs and turns to look at him.

"Morning," she says, mascara blotches smudged under her eyes. Seeing people in the light of the morning is always sobering.

"Morning," he says, as he puts his feet to the floor, his back to her, and pulls up his boxers.

"Oh, and Happy Thanksgiving," she says.

"Same to you. Which, speaking of, unfortunately, I have to get ready to visit my sister and her kids, so I've got to get going."

He figures, why pretend their interlude is something it will never be? Reid's done this a couple of times before, and he knows the drill and the simple explanation for it: loneliness. She was lonely. He was lonely. He'd had too much to drink, and so did she. They found themselves naked in a bedroom thinking only of the momentary pleasure. Reid always forgets about how awkward it can be waking up next to each other the next morning.

Reid can tell by her expression that she feels used. Frankly, he does, too, in a weird sort of way.

"Oh, yes, sure. I've got to go, too," she says, reaching for her undergarments and beginning to dress. He looks away. He feels like a shit for allowing last night to happen. Shame on him. Must stop drinking, he thinks briefly.

Since his relationship with Lexi ended, he hasn't felt anything for anyone, and if truth be told, he hasn't really wanted to look for anyone else. He does his best to shut down his emotions, and resorts to an occasional hook up now and then to fill any physical voids he may be missing. He's only human, after all, but even the worst humans can feel empty when it's over. And today of all days—Thanksgiving—he feels like a real asshole.

"So, are you playing at the bar any time soon?" she asks, attempting to make conversation.

"Actually, yes. I'm there later tonight for a couple of hours, which is why I have to go now to spend some time with my family before I need to get to work."

"Got it," she says. She's younger than he is, he can tell, and probably not too street smart, but she gets the message he is sending. She grabs her purse and takes out her phone when she buttons the last button on her white, feminine blouse that shows way too much cleavage on Thanksgiving morning. She walks out of the bedroom and into the living room to call an Uber to come pick her up. She had been with friends, but she left them behind to walk home with Reid.

She's still pretty in the morning light, but Reid knows this isn't going anywhere. He felt little connection with her both mentally and physically. He prides himself on his instincts about women. He has a tendency to know right away if there's anything at all to pursue. He's quite certain there's nothing here he wishes to continue.

"Well, um, thanks for the night. My ride is going to be here in a minute."

"Okay, well, have a good day today," he says.

"Yeah, you, too," she says, as she opens the door and begins to walk away.

"Take care," he says, closing the door firmly behind her.

*

Guilt and shame are funny things. He's learned to live with them for so long. He can't imagine waking up in the morning and not feeling them daily as his constant companions. The feelings have been with him for so many years at this point that he's afraid it's become a tireless trait. No matter how many times he's tried, he keeps running in the same hamster wheel and can't seem to get off it. Ever since he dropped out of college, made stupid decisions, and disappointed himself and his family, he's been trying to put things right but has so far been unsuccessful.

Sure, he works hard now as a laborer, building decks and refurbishing old homes, but it's not what he'd wanted to do, although he and his partner have done pretty well. But with a two-person business and only a handful of part-time workers they can count on, it's tough to schedule enough projects in order to earn the money he would like. He had it all going for him in college. He would have graduated with honors, would have had a senior internship with a financial company that may have set him on a course of success. But he got stupid. He sealed his fate in his junior year when he was kicked off campus for alcohol violations, and then, after that, was arrested for driving under the influence. All the scholarships he earned were gone. His father, who had paid the balance of his education and who had hooked him up with the internship, was more than disappointed.

The arrest for driving while intoxicated affected his relationship with his father more than anything. His father's dad had been an alcoholic, and Reid had heard all the stories. His father swore off drinking altogether in his life, hoping his son would do the same. After the college fiasco, and after his father bailed him out, Reid's relationship with his father deteriorated. Reid's lawyer was able to get him off with only paying a hefty fine and attending substance abuse meetings. Due to findings in the drunk driving case, Reid's lawyer found that the breathalyzer test may have been misread, so his punishment was lessened. His license had been revoked, and Reid was without the ability to drive for a while, making his working life a challenge. When he was able to drive again, Reid had saved enough to buy a used truck, and he connected with his partner, Don, an old friend, to start their business. His father had loaned him money to get the business off the ground, despite their strained relationship. But more than anything, over the years, it's been his mother who has made every attempt to repair the relationship.

Regret. It's the overriding emotional feeling that haunts him every day. You would think he'd start doing something about it instead of just wallowing in the way his life has unfolded because of his dumb decision-making.

*

Reid enters his dark, small apartment after spending the day with his family. The meal was tasty, and Emme's kids make him laugh. He spent most of the time on his sister's carpeted family room floor playing with the kids. Bernice, who's five, with red hair and freckles and seems to be a little intellectual, and Mason, who's two, with his throaty laugh, who only wants Reid to sit on the floor and play with trucks all day, help him feel a sense of normalcy. They are adorable, and he wants to be a good uncle to those kids.

He wants to hide his head in shame when he thinks about his behavior the previous evening, hooking up with a woman he'd never met before. What was he thinking? How would he feel about someone doing that to Bernice when she grows up? He'd want to kill the son-of-a-bitch. How much lower can I go? he thinks. When he analyzes the situation from that perspective, he hates himself for what he's done.

Reid makes a quick change into jeans and a long-sleeved black tee, sees the unkempt bed from this morning, and scratches his head. He's been actively looking for other rentals and wants to get the hell out of this crap apartment, but he's been too unmotivated to make the effort.

He grabs his guitar. It's an acoustic session tonight. He looks forward to getting lost in his music for a couple of hours, and promises himself not to bring anyone home from the bar tonight.

He hopes he can keep that promise.

Dimitri

Thanksgiving Day

Dimitri carries the pre-cooked small turkey he ordered from the supermarket in one hand, the remaining groceries necessary for a somewhat decent Thanksgiving dinner in a recycled bag in the other hand. His father fell in October and fractured his right foot while simultaneously spraining the other. Therefore, Dimitri decided it was best if he brought dinner over to his dad's place.

It's a sunny early afternoon, and Dimitri can tell that the neighbor's kid probably raked all the leaves in his dad's yard. The leaves are bagged and set at the side of the house. His father's green house with dark brown shutters in Edgewater isn't big, but it's kept up well. His father is a proud man, and someone who takes care of his property and his belongings. He always feels a twinge of guilt as he pulls up to the old house, primarily because he knows he hasn't cared for his dad to the best of his ability. He often blames it on being busy or working too hard, but the truth is, his father lives so close to him, and no excuse is ever good enough. Dimitri remembers feeling ashamed of his home when he was a kid, embarrassed that it wasn't large and on a big plot of land. But the water and dock were right down the street, and his father always kept a small boat that he allowed his children to take out on the South River once they learned to drive it at sixteen. His father had taught them all the ways of the river, red-right-return, and how to use a depth finder. Dimitri remembers fondly his days spent on the river with his siblings and friends, and he gives his father credit for having the trust in them all to keep the boat intact and treat it with respect. Which they did.

Still embarrassed by being fired and knowing how hard his dad worked to put him through college, Dimitri can't bring himself to tell his dad about losing his job. He's been interviewing and sending off resumes, but everyone knows that November and December are the two worst months to look for a new job. His severance will run out before he knows it. He knows the clock is ticking.

Dimitri raps on the front screened door which his father had left open since the day's weather is in the high-sixties, a beautiful day to celebrate Thanksgiving and watch football.

"Hey, Baba," he calls to his dad. His mother, who tried to keep some of her Greek traditions, had insisted that Dimitri call his father "Baba," the name she called her own father.

"Hey, Dimi." His dad has called him the shortened version of his name since he was a young boy. "I see you still haven't cut that hair." It's a long-standing joke between them. Dimitri wears his wavy hair to his shoulders and pulls it into a ponytail for work. He often receives comments like "you don't look like an accountant" when people first meet him. He is proud of that.

His dad sits upright in his reclining chair with his feet up, his salt and pepper hair catching the sunlight. "I'd get up to say hello, but I'm afraid my body wants me to be in this chair. Looks like you bought out the store."

"I figured we might as well eat well while we watch the games."

"Did you get my favorite?" His dad peeks at the bag.

"Yup. Two cans of sweet potatoes and cranberry sauce to go

with the turkey."

"Good job. Stuffing?"

"Of course. At least I know how to make that."

Dimitri moves past his dad, giving him a pat on the shoulder, and sets up in the kitchen, where he begins to organize the things he bought. He opens the fridge and sees a big bowl of fruit salad.

"Did you make this fruit salad, Baba?"

"Nah, Ilene next door brought it to me this morning. She put it in the fridge for us to have. And the pumpkin pie."

"Where's the pie?" Dimitri asks.

"I think she set it on the back porch."

Dimitri steps onto the back porch, still with its green, Astro-Turf carpet and small table, and sees the pie. It's homemade and full. Dimitri is thankful for Ilene, who often tends to his dad and seems to enjoy cooking for him. Dimitri had forgotten to pick up dessert when he was in the market, though he did pick up a pack of Marlboro Lights, which he left in the car. His dad hates the smell of smoke, having given up the habit after nearly twenty years in the early nineties. He'd probably be pretty disappointed to see Dimitri has picked up the habit again.

From the right drawer, Dimitri removes the pot he'll need to make the stuffing. It's not difficult, and Dimitri can handle himself okay in the kitchen. He's not a chef by any means, but he knows how to make the basics, and it doesn't get any simpler than stuffing out of a box. All morning, he's been trying not to think about the lingering feelings of humiliation from losing his job or his ex-wife and where she is at the moment, although he knew that she wouldn't be the one making the Thanksgiving meal. She was a lousy cook. With her boy-friend's money, she probably hired a chef to make the whole dinner for them, and an interior designer probably set the table so it's perfect for her Instagram account.

He doesn't want to feel full of anger this morning for her. Honestly, he doesn't. It's Thanksgiving. He is here with his Baba, something he doesn't spend nearly enough time doing, and today he just wants to watch football and not think about anything—his boring and limiting former job, his cold, emotionless ex-wife, his siblings who rarely travel for holidays, or the compulsion to play the Blackjack table. Screw all of it, Dimitri laughs to himself. Today it is all about his father, football, and food.

*

After eating their meal in front of the television while watching the Washington vs. Dallas game, Dimitri feels pretty pleased with himself for throwing together a decent meal for two bachelors on Thanksgiving. Dimitri's phone vibrates. He is expecting a return text from his brother, Sam, who is in California. But it isn't from Sam.

It is from his ex-wife.

He pulls the phone away from his eyes to read it more clearly.

"Is that from Sam?" Baba asks.

"Nope," he says, trying not to have to relay this one.

"Who's wishing you a happy Thanksgiving, then?" Baba asks.

"It's not about Thanksgiving," Dimitri says. "It's from my ex-wife."

Dimitri swore when she left that he would never say her name aloud, ever, ever again. So far, he's kept that promise.

"What's that witch want?" his father asks, using the remote to click between games.

Dimitri is taken aback. He's never heard his father call her a name, although he knew they weren't fond of each other. Dimitri explodes into laughter because the insanity of her question in conjunction with his father's reaction causes him to spit his beer all over the card table and his meal.

His father looks at him inquisitively, and then a little wicked smile creeps across his face, accentuating the lines around his eyes and near his mouth.

When Dimitri finally stops chuckling, he answers. "The witch wants to know if she can stop by and pick up some things she forgot to take with her that I tossed into the basement."

"Tell the witch that her millionaire boyfriend can buy her whatever is missing," he says, a twinge of mischief in his eyes. "Then, take the rest of her crap to the dumpster and dump it." Dimitri loves his approach to her request and that he is standing up for him in this situation.

*

After Washington loses for a second straight week, Dimitri cleans up the kitchen for Baba and helps get him up the stairs for bed. Baba's still a little wobbly, although Dimitri thinks he's making a pretty strong comeback for someone who just turned seventy-three.

"You good, Baba?" Dimitri asks before he heads home.

"Good, Dimi."

"You need anything else before I go?"

"Nope. Just fine," Baba says.

"Okay, then. I'll give you a call in a couple of days to check on you."

"Might be nicer if it were sooner than that, being that we have a lot of leftovers and more games on Sunday," Baba says.

"Okay, Baba. I'll try. I'll call you tomorrow," Dimitri says.

As the sole caretaker of his father, Dimitri feels a certain amount of resentment toward his brothers and sister. They got as far away from Annapolis as they could once they married. He doesn't know why he feels this way about his own flesh and blood, except that they rarely fly home to visit. Baba's only seen his two sets of grandkids twice in two years.

Fed up with thinking about all of this, Dimitri pulls out of the driveway and turns onto the road. There are a decent amount of people out and about for Thanksgiving night, and as the night is still young, and as Dimitri absolutely dreads the idea of going back to an empty house, he makes the decision to stop into the corner pub off Route 2 before returning home.

Meg

Hope comes in many forms, and Meg knows all too well what a lack of hope feels like. The morning is bright, but crisp, and a strong, cold breeze indicates that winter is soon to arrive. Meg decides to make the walk to work today, bundled up in her puff coat, hat, and gloves, and wears her leather backpack as she walks. She typically only drives to work in bad weather, especially when it's pouring down rain. It costs money to park in the historic district, and she truly loves walking. It awakens her spirit and keeps her in touch with nature, the earth. She loves the smells of all seasons: forsythia in spring, roses in summer, leaves in autumn, and snow in winter. And while she appreciates all the seasons, she misses the warmth of the summer most of all and the feeling of the grass between her toes or dipping them into the creek. Walking makes her feel grounded in ways that driving or riding in a car never do.

On the route to the bookstore, she crosses over the Eastport Bridge, and passes the waterfront hotel. Her strides bring her past the waterfront hotel, toward the circle, and then she crosses the brick street that meets the sidewalk and takes her up Main Street toward Church Circle. Her store is only five down from the circle, and she loves taking in the sights of other shops and peeking in their windows, especially when they're dressed for the season. There's a spirit of community among the storeowners, and they regularly check up on each other. Annapolis is charming in its greens, its twinkle lights, and the newly lighted snowflakes that dangle over the alley near the state capital. Decorations hang in windowpanes. Meg spent all week preparing for the holidays, running garland along the shelves and in the front window. She put gingerbread houses with books in the front window as a display, and there's an enormous Santa on the second floor of the bookstore that houses the coffee café and small stage. All of these great finds were from the Christmas store a few doors down from hers on Main Street. Before she makes her way up the sloped street to her store, she dodges into the coffee shop for a minute.

When she reaches the front door to her shop, she takes a deep breath, and touches the door handle. Wait, she thinks. I need a photo of this moment. She is trying to juggle the drink, bag, and her phone, and decides to place the bag and the drink on the sidewalk for a moment to capture the photo of today. She had pledged to take photographs and document her experiences, because journaling has always allowed her to tell her own story, even though the journals may be for her eyes only. As she walks through the door, pleased with herself, she's thankful to see a small crowd in the store, even before all the "madness" of the night actually begins around five o'clock. This is the second year she will experience Midnight Madness, one of her favorite traditions whereby shops stay open until midnight for all the Thursdays in December leading up to Christmas. Tonight launches the first of three scheduled.

Meg surveys the place and walks up and down the few aisles, straightening up the books here and there. In her opinion, a bookstore not only has to exude the smell of paper and cardboard, which heightens the senses and awakens the feelings of nostalgia and comfort, but each book must be properly placed and displayed so that customers feel compelled to pick up and peruse a book before they decide to walk out of the store with it.

Meg's intuition is strong, and it has carried her through to today's job of being an entrepreneur. It's a small bookstore, she knows, but she promised herself to become a part of the town—the city—and that she has done and continues to do each day. She cares about the people and has an extraordinary amount of empathy for almost everyone who walks into her shop. If there's one thing she's learned over the last several years, it's that people who love bookstores love stories, and everyone has a story to tell.

"Morning, Meg," Clarke calls to her when she sees her. She is restacking the books in the children's section. It's a small area, but Meg has made sure to carry all the best books for kids, the ones she believes will help them grow into caring adults. Clarke wears her hair in a wavy bob, and she always has a chain on her eyeglasses that she drapes around her neck. In her sixties, she is tall and lanky, but agile and spry. Since Ray left for Japan, Clarke's been her right hand person, which allows Meg a little freedom to sleep in every now and then as Clarke is an early-bird and loves opening the store for her.

"You've been the biggest help to me, and I can't thank you enough," Meg says, handing Clarke a brown bag and the smoothie.

"What's this?" Clarke asks.

"Your lunch," Meg says. "I'm tired of you not eating properly. Now, take a break and eat something. And enjoy your Acai smoothie."

Clarke blows Meg a little kiss, smiles, and goes upstairs to the coffee bar that two new employees, Jordan and Briana, manage for her. It's a pretty basic coffee bar, with four tables and chairs, and offers cookies, muffins, and coffees and teas.

Meg takes her purse up to the front register and organizes the items she has brought with her. A woman with a bandage across the bridge of her nose walks up to the counter with a book in hand.

"I've heard good things about this novel," she says to Meg. "Do you recommend it?"

"I do, actually. It's a sweet read, and it will leave you feeling happy at the end of it."

"Ah, perfect," the woman says. "That's just the type of book I could use right now."

"Something to lift the spirits?"

"Exactly," she says.

Meg watches the woman intently as she fiddles with her purse, her hand trembling slightly, searching for her wallet.

"If you don't mind my asking, what's happened that you need that bandage?" Meg asks. She knows that if she asks the right way, people tend to respond kindly, and often with the truth.

"I was in a car accident two weeks ago. Slammed my face into the steering wheel and fractured my nose. It's not a pretty story." The woman looks down and fiddles with a book ornament on the counter.

"Oh, I'm so sorry. I can imagine that must have been frightening for you."

There's something in the woman's tone of voice that leads Meg to believe that she is not being entirely truthful, and that's okay. Not all people have a desire to tell their stories, especially troubling ones that put themselves or others in a bad light. Still, Meg plays along, and smiles at her.

"Yes," the woman says, continuing to justify the situation, "but even more frightening for the steering wheel. The car was totaled. And now, I walk everywhere or get a lift. I hate the idea of buying a new car right now."

The woman places the book on the counter and Meg begins

to ring her up. Behind the counter, Meg processes the credit card payment, grabs one of the letters she had placed in her backpack earlier, and puts it in the front of the book without the woman seeing what she is doing, and then places the book in one of the store's pretty shopping bags. The woman signs her receipt and thanks Meg for her help.

Meg can feel something deeply concerning about the woman's story; as an intuitive empath, she has the ability to not only read situations, but to feel them on another level. It took her years to understand her innate skill and how to manage it, and when she came to fully comprehend her gift, her life changed. She pledged to do good with it. Meg is neither a witch nor a fortune-teller nor a clairvoyant. She is a full-blown empath who can sense other people's emotions and energy, often "hearing" the most important thing: the words that people don't say. More often than not, she feels things first—has strong instincts—then attempts to rationalize or understand the logic that surrounds them. It's the ability to recognize the feelings she senses from others that has set her on the trajectory of helping others. As well, empaths have a need to be connected to the natural world. Being near the water and being able to take out her boat does wonders for Meg's empathic needs. She understands that this connection to the water is crucial to her health.

As she learned several years ago, having a big heart comes with the territory when you are an empath. She firmly respects and embraces her calling to invest in people.

*

As the night progresses, and the shop becomes busier with the Midnight Madness shoppers, Meg is energized and feels a sense of wonder. She has spent many summers in Annapolis over the years—from the age of ten until twenty-five—and got a sense of the rhythm of the place. Spending those summers with her aunt and uncle and living down the road from the marina they owned and managed was so special to her. Uncle Ben, her mother's brother, treated her like a daughter. Uncle Ben always cared for her, and when she was here, she felt a sense of purpose. And that purpose brought her back year after year.

"Meg, do you want us to set up outside on the sidewalk?" Jordan asks her.

"That would be great. Put that tablecloth I brought with me on the table outside, and you all can set up the hot chocolate and candy canes," she tells him.

It's almost five, and Jordan greets people at the door, Briana manages the coffee bar upstairs, while Clarke and Meg manage the downstairs. All four of them begin to get into place, as the crowd begins to pick up.

By eight o'clock that night, five of Meg's letters have been given to customers who needed them. Figuring out who will be the recipients of the remaining five letters is part of the role she plays as shop owner. Bookstores, you see, require more conversation, whether it's about a particular book, the type of book someone wants to read, or a personal story that has led that person to choosing a particular book. That's where Meg's intuition comes in, and it is precisely how she determines who is in need of a letter.

In the full spirit of the season, carolers stroll the streets, Santa's workshop on a float rides by the store, alpacas are featured in front of a store a few down from hers, and people wearing Santa hats stroll by and stop into the store.

Clarke brings Meg a cup of coffee from upstairs after she sees her yawn across the room as Meg remains at the checkout, talking with customers and ringing them up.

"You might need this," she says, handing it to her. "Three hours still remain."

Meg nods, accepts the coffee, and takes a sip. The sixth letter has been placed inside a man's book. She feels a little guilty that Clarke has spent so much time at the store today. Earlier, Meg urged her to go home for a two-hour break, and she was glad she took her up on that offer. Clarke lives within walking distance in an old, historic, but beautifully renovated home near the water that she shares with her husband. When Clarke returned at four-thirty, she told Meg, "Don't give it another thought! I'm invigorated by all of this. It only happens three times a year. I love being here for it."

About forty-five minutes later, a petite brunette in a gorgeous brocade coat with fur at the collar approaches the checkout counter.

"Have you heard if this book is helpful?" the woman asks Meg.

"I've heard good things about it, yes. It seems to help people with moving on from difficult situations," Meg says back.

"Good. I need all the help I can get," she says, grinding out the words with a little slur. "It's been a hell of a year."

Understanding that the book is for her, Meg reaches for one of the letters and slides it into the front of the book behind the counter where the woman can't see what she's doing. She hands her the package.

"I wish you a happy holiday and best of luck with the book," Meg says.

*

There are three letters that remain for the night. Meg is hopeful they will all land in the hands of their rightful owners tonight. She also notices a couple of people placing letters in the gold mailbox that is affixed to the back wall on the first floor. She had a sign made that sits above the mailbox that reads "Letters of Response." There is no explanation, just the mailbox with the sign. It's been interesting to see the feedback over the last several months. A few days ago, she received a phone call from a reporter who got a whiff of the letters in the books and wanted to write a story about it, but she declined the interview and asked him not to cover it. She doesn't do what she does for publicity. She wants it to remain clandestine. It is just something she feels she needs to do for others, when she, herself, has felt the benefits of receiving such a letter many years ago.

Meg senses the blonde woman at the counter may be in need of one of the three remaining letters.

"Wonderful book! Are you planning a visit to Paris?" Meg asks her, making conversation as she takes the book from her.

"Oh, no," the woman says. "That chance passed a couple of years ago." The woman tries to chuckle and make light of it as she says it, trying not to make Meg feel uncomfortable.

"Maybe you'll get there sooner than you think. You never know, right?" Meg says, making idle conversation.

"Not with my luck with blind dates. Anyway, the book's not for me. It's a gift."

"Well, that person is very lucky. This is a gorgeous book."

"It is. And believe it or not, it's for the person who was supposed to take me to Paris." The woman rolls her eyes.

Meg senses there's an interesting story here. Intuitively, she knows the letter must be placed inside this book.

"Any chance you can gift wrap it?" the woman asks.

92

STEPHANIE VERNI

"Happy to do it," Meg answers.

As Meg begins to wrap the gift, she hears the woman mumble "*I'm an idiot*" to herself. Meg doesn't let on that she heard her say this, and finishes up by tying ribbons around the gift, the letter tucked tightly inside the book's front cover.

"I hope the recipient appreciates this thoughtful present," Meg says, handing over the gift from behind the counter.

"That makes two of us," the woman responds.

*

A little while later, Meg senses something familiar about the man who approaches the counter.

He's wearing a leather jacket and a scarf, and his dark eyes are slightly glazed. His longer hair is pulled back in a ponytail, and he appears tan despite it being winter in Maryland. He has squared shoulders and a chiseled face. She feels as if she's met him before, yet there's something mysterious about him, too.

"Merry Christmas" she says, as she begins to ring him up. He can barely look her in the eyes. "Is this a gift?"

Embarrassed, he replies: "No, it's for me." It's a book about finding a new career, and how to know if it's the right one for you.

"Well, I've had a lot of people tell me this book is quite useful," she says. "They've said it's helped them figure things out."

"Let's hope so," he mumbles, and displays a half-grin. "I've lost my job and am about to start over," he explains.

As he signs his receipt and puts his credit card back in his wallet, Meg strongly believes he should receive the second to last letter between the pages of the book he's purchased. Her senses are heightened with this one. She smiles at him warmly, and hands him his bag.

"I wish you all the best," she says.

*

As the clock edges closer to midnight, the crowds begin to thin out, and Meg cleans up the counter area. She tosses remnants of ribbon clippings into the garbage and organizes the "book pick up" shelves behind her. It's been a whirlwind of steady customers, and sometimes the checkout line is at least ten people deep.

She adjusts her reindeer antlers that she's been wearing all night. It's the least she can do to get into the spirit and make people laugh. Bing Crosby sings *White Christmas* from the bookstore's speakers.

A man places a book on the counter, and she turns to smile at him.

"Is this all?" she asks.

"I also have a book on hold," he says, gruffly.

"What's the name?"

"Reid," he says.

She knows exactly where it is because she just saw the name on the book when she straightened up the bookshelf moments ago. She finds his name and withdraws the book from the shelf.

"This one?" she asks, holding it up for him to see.

"Yes," he says. He gives her a small smile.

"Is this one a gift, too?"

"Nope. That one's for me. Recommended by a friend."

She sees the guitar across his body and makes the connection.

"You play at the tavern down the street, right?"

"I do," he says. Meg notices he's a man of few words.

"I've heard a set or two. You play a lot of sad songs," she says to him, making conversation as she processes his order. "But I do love listening to acoustic guitar."

He's caught off-guard by her remark and doesn't respond. *Sad songs. A lot of sad songs.* She smiles at him, and he smirks back.

"I may have to rethink my playlists," he says, still puzzling over her comment.

She fiddles with his package and places the last letter of the day inside the front cover of the book that's meant for him. She then hands him his bag. He thanks her and walks away. Meg watches him walk out the door, package in right hand and his guitar slung across his left shoulder.

*

When Clarke closes the door at midnight, the four employees spend about ten minutes cleaning up.

"Hey, Jordan, would you mind dropping me off at home? I forgot I walked here today," Meg asks.

"No problem. Gotta go that way, anyway," he says, holding the door open for her. He's tall and muscular with a scruffy beard that he swears he'll shave off when he marries Elena, his fiancée. Meg feels tiny next to him. She locks the bookstore door behind her, taking a quick look at the sign, lit brightly for all to see. She couldn't be prouder of this bookstore, of Brodie's Books.

As they take their steps into the night air, Meg is delighted and feels giddy. The snow has covered the sidewalks, and as they approach Jordan's car, she twirls and catches her first snowflake of the season on the tip of her tongue.

Meg's Letter

Dated August 20, 2008

Dear Miss Meg,

As someone who has watched you grow up and has gotten to know you over the years, I hope you will allow me this opportunity to write you a letter. As a longtime neighbor of your Uncle Ben and Aunt Nancy, I've enjoyed watching you grow up. Additionally, your uncle and aunt have taken very good care of Stella and me, even though they had so much on their plate already. I've learned to become a good letter writer, you see. I have become good at it from all the practice I've gotten over these many years. From the time I went to war and was deployed overseas at eighteen, I vowed to write letters. They kept me sane, and still do to this day. I wrote letters to my parents, to my brothers and sisters, to the dearest of friends, and to the love of my life. I write anonymous letters to strangers I meet, drop them in mailboxes, in books at the library, or leave them under rocks or behind trees.

Some of my letters from the war never made it home to Stella. I would anxiously wait for a letter from her. My letters were sent, yet sometimes never received. She presumed I was dead for an extended period of time, but she stayed devoted to me and trusted in the love we had for each other. By the stroke of a miracle or a higher power, somehow, we found each other when I was sent home after the war ended. I'd lost a little of myself over there, you see. Part of me died along with some of my fellow soldiers. Stella had so much love and faith in me, and though we were thousands of miles apart, her love sustained me, and I believe once I came around, mine sustained her, too. I know this because she's told me so, in words, in cards, and in letters. I'm eighty-five years old now, and am thankful we are both healthy and together, although we move much slower these days, and my handwriting isn't as steady as it once was. I take great joy in the letters I write to strangers, to acquaintances, or to people I know. When I first began writing the letters to lift others up, it was because it helped to guide me out of darkness. The mere act of letter writing was therapeutic for me. The thousands of letters I have written over the years have saved me, letter-by-letter, word-by-word, and sentence-by-sentence. In turn, I hope they have helped someone else in the process. I believe that's what love and kindness and a generosity of spirit can do for people, even with the horrors, loss, guilt, or feelings of hopelessness we carry around with us.

For a young lady, you are mature beyond your years. You have such compassion and empathy. When I saw you break down in tears at the funeral, I knew I had to try to help in some way—to reach out to you. This is the best way I know how.

Stella and I have watched from afar and marveled at the way you have taken such wonderful care of Brodie over the years. From the time you were ten, you have doted on him, loved him, and been his summer companion and friend. He adored you. Watching you two together as you pushed him in his wheelchair or sat under the tree and read to him gave Stella and me hope in the human race, especially after the atrocities I have witnessed in war. When you graduated from college and continued to come for extended stays in the summer, Brodie's face would light up knowing that his beloved Meg had come to spend time with him. You devoted your summers to taking care of Brodie. In a world where there are a lot of rotten ones, you are a good egg, Miss Meg.

Knowing how much you must be missing Brodie, I hope you do not find this is too forward for an old man who still tries to find the good in the world. If you'll permit me to continue, I'd like to share a letter that my mother had passed on to me when I enlisted, and then when I served. She would write to me often, sometimes every day, and I saved every letter I could. I found comfort in her words when I was away, fighting, not knowing if I'd ever come back. And so, I'll share with you the letter my mother wrote to me, the one I found most touching and uplifting, and the one I forced myself to memorize forward and backward and backward and forward in the cold days of war when life felt hopeless. There were so many days I wondered if I'd ever make it home. These words carried me through the war, and they continue to inspire me even today. She wrote:

To My Dearest John—

You were brought into this world to do good, to love, and to be loved. I know full well that there will be times of immense struggle. There will be times when you will doubt your full potential. There will be times when you'll face an enemy, or perhaps someone who is simply unkind who pretends to be a friend but is not a friend. I will pray for you and always do. You will have to ask yourself if you believe in yourself, in love, in goodness, and in all that will help lift your spirits. Dearest—you will have to find the path to your own survival, your happiness, and your future. You are fighting for all of us, but also for yourself. We are frightened for you, yet we carry hope in our hearts. Dark days find all of us at various times of our lives, and I am so sorry that you have to endure the darkest of days. I assume the struggles you face may be overwhelming and lead you to despair. They may bring tears, leave you feeling worthless, leave you wondering what all of this fighting is for. Believe me, your father and I often wonder the same sometimes. Missing and worrying about you is painful.

I hope you can hear my voice through these words imploring you to be strong, to be brave, and to believe that from the moment you entered the world, you were destined to be exactly who you are, without pretension, without apology. Remember who you are and what you stand for. Continue to be yourself: kind, loving, and determined. You certainly have brought joy to your family. Make no apologies. Be you, my darling, in every sense of the word. God loves you and so do we.

You have brought light and love to so many others, some of which you may know, and others that you may not know, or others you have yet to know and affect. This is your gift.

Know that there are people who care. Know that there are people who love you. Know that you always have us, your family, your friends. You are not alone, my sweet boy. You are never alone.

We love you with all of our hearts, forever and a day, for all eternity.

Love, Your loving mother

And to you, Meg:

I'm not sure why I felt compelled to share my mother's words with you. She has long passed, but her words live on. Perhaps I figured her words will continue to live on if I pass them along to you to do with them what you will.

Please know that your kindness towards Brodie was not lost on me, Stella, your uncle, your aunt, and especially not on Brodie. I saw the heartbreak in your face when we all had to say goodbye. He lived, he loved, you loved him. This is what life's all about.

Let your continued kindness seep into all those you know. There will be others who will need the compassion that you shared with Brodie. It seems to be your gift.

This is my letter to you, sweet girl. We are so glad we have had the opportunity to get to know you. You are a light. Continue to be a light.

Your friend,

John E. Anderson

After the Letters

Later that Year

Eva

Thursday, December 13

Eva folds the book neatly and places the letter back inside the cover. She hasn't stopped thinking about its contents since Sunday morning, when she actually took the book out of the bag to read it and the letter dropped to the floor.

She had picked it up gingerly, wondering if it had been intended for her. As she looked at it, she marveled at the lovely stationery, the handwriting, and the way the letter read—it was so beautiful and eloquent. She loved the story that was contained in the letter and the way it made her feel to read it. Reading the letter also left her feeling completely useless as a person, as she's been so focused on herself over the last several months since Kyle left, and not in a good way. She'd failed herself by engaging in detrimental self-talk that affected her self-worth. Month after month since he broke her heart, all she's done is harbor anger and frustration, ambling through the days, counting down the hours until she could leave work and go back to her house and mope around. She also recognizes that she probably had one too many drinks during that period of time.

As the letter said: *Whether you need to change your course, let go, forgive, find your value, or see this as the push you need to be brave and figure something out, please know you have what it takes to do it. Do what it takes to find the strength and courage.*

Since reading the letter, she's thought about things, reflected, and has decided that she needs to do better—that she can do better. The letter made her think about changing her perspective. Not at first when she read it, but as she thought about it more over the course of the day, she let her guard down and made room for self-awareness, allowing emotions to not just come, but to go. There were things she needed to let go of, and although it still isn't easy for her, the letter brought new ideas to light. It's funny how hearing someone else's words can clear out the cobwebs—or at least allow you to be open to change.

She walks around her downstairs straightening everything up. She's already eaten dinner, cleaned the kitchen, and is waiting for the guy to arrive. With Emily's departure at the end of the week, the cottage will be vacant, and she's started interviewing possible tenants for the rental. Because the cottage sits on her property, she has to get a sense of who might be a good fit. The woman she interviewed yesterday morning was okay; she was young like Emily, talked too much, and Eva got the impression that she might party too much and have her friends over constantly. Eva likes the quiet life she leads and doesn't want that interrupted. Eastport is already alive and kicking on the weekends. And in the summer months, because of the access to the water and the marinas that surround the peninsula, it becomes much busier with cars and foot traffic, not to mention the crowded bars.

Promptly at seven-thirty, she hears footsteps. She neatens up the magazines on the coffee table and adjusts her skirt. She had decided not to change out of her outfit for work—her straight skirt, emerald green blouse, and tall black boots—so she will look professional for the meeting. Her hair is still up in a high bun from her day at the office.

Eva opens the paned front door before he can knock. She has

a few decorations up already, and earlier she hung the huge evergreen wreath she bought from the market. She smiles at the casually, but well-dressed man, in front of her. By the sound of his voice, she expected someone much older for some reason—he's much more handsome than she expected, maybe a little younger than she is, and he looks vaguely familiar.

"Hi," he says, extending his hand. "I'm Reid Jones."

"I'm Eva Levoni," she says, offering her hand for a handshake. "Come on in. Let me take your coat."

He enters the room, and Eva notices his big, brown puppy dog eyes as he looks around at her place, taking it all in, and hands over his coat. "I'll just put it here because we may want to throw our coats back on to walk to the cottage. It's bitter out there tonight. Feel free to sit down. Can I get you anything hot to drink?" Eva asks.

"Water's fine," he says. She walks into the kitchen and returns with two glasses of water, which she places on the coffee table, and sits in the chair across from him.

"Beautiful home you have here," he says. "It's been renovated well."

Eva loves when someone compliments her home. She took great pains to make sure it was lovingly restored from when her parents owned it and helped her out with the changes. Not a lot needed to be done to it, but the small alterations she made from the days of her parents' ownership had made it feel more like hers with the painted white shiplap and feminine chandeliers. Kyle had tolerated her taste in decorating, and when he moved in, she promised to keep the master bedroom more neutral, and decorated the living room with a nautical theme to please him. She's started to overhaul that room completely over the last few months to please herself, rather than him.

"Thank you," she says. "So, tell me a little bit about yourself and why you would be interested in renting the place."

Reid shifts a little in his chair, but keeps his eyes on Eva as he talks. "It's a long depressing story, and if by the end of it you just want to toss me out of here, I won't blame you a bit."

Eva crosses her legs and leans back, intrigued. "That's an attention-getting opener," she says.

Working in public relations for so many years has given her the opportunity to finesse her people skills. She knows how to relate to people—people of all walks of life. In high school, she never fit into any one clique; she had friendships with everyone. She was voted "most likable" in the senior superlatives, and continues to take pride in that moniker, even all these years later. She enjoys witty banter with people. Honestly, she feels most let down by Kyle for that very reason. All the time they were together, she thought their conversations and wit suited each other. Go figure.

"Well, while it may be intriguing, you may not want me around when you hear my background, but I won't lie to you, so here goes," he starts. "I grew up here in Annapolis in Murray Hill. My parents just sold the family home, and I'm devastated by it. I was a great kid in high school. Played sports, did well in school, and earned a couple of scholarships. In college, I disappointed my parents by partying too much and getting kicked off campus for alcohol in my room, so I dropped out, never finishing my senior year, and I'm still trying to work my way back from that. I'm a hard worker, a contractor who has a business with a partner, and I just can't stand to be in the sad, dingy apartment where I live any longer. It's time I tried to save some money to buy a place of my own. I also need some breathing room. I wish I could have afforded to buy my parents' house, but I can't. I play guitar and sing on the side, often in town. That's me in a nutshell," he says.

"Wow. Brutal honesty. That's rare."

"Well, years of living with disappointments will do that to a person. And truthfully, recently, I was encouraged by someone to start fresh."

"Now that I look at you, I know why you look so familiar. Did you just play last Thursday night for Midnight Madness at the tavern?" Eva asks. "I thought I recognized you."

"That's me," he says. "Guilty as charged."

"Good music. A couple of songs you sang made me want to cry."

"Yeah, I've been told that before," Reid says. "So, why do you have a place to rent?" he asks.

"My tenant, Emily, is moving on to get a Ph.D. in New York City, and she leaves on Friday, so I have a vacancy. She's been great. I'm not sure I can replicate the kind of renter she's been," Eva says with a wink. Reid catches her meaning and smiles.

"Well, you never know. I may be an even better tenant she is. I do come with a lot of handy-man skills."

"True," Eva says, knowing she already factored his aptitude for that into the equation.

"I also work a lot. I'm out a lot. And I don't typically have people over. I'm kind of like an extroverted hermit. I'm a dream come true."

Eva raises an eyebrow, and a smile creeps across her face. She's impressed with this potential tenant, much more so than the woman, Kelly, she met yesterday.

"So, tell me about you," Reid says, matter-of-factly, as if Eva has no choice but to fully answer the question.

"I thought this was my interview," Eva says with a wink. "I'm kidding. I'll try to be as forthright as you were. I've lived here for over eight years," she begins. She remembers the letter she read yesterday morning and decides to spill her guts without caution. "The man I lived with for all of that time, someone I loved and thought I would spend forever with, left me earlier this summer for his high school girlfriend, whom he neglected to tell me he'd been communicating with on Facebook for over a year. He went back to his hometown in Kentucky, and on New Year's Eve, he'll marry her and inherit her five kids, which he said he never wanted, by the way. I work in town for a communications agency, and I've been working there for as long as I've lived here. I walk to work often because I hate driving cars. I have a sister who lives on the Eastern Shore with her family. My parents are in Florida most of the time, I'm an adoring aunt, and I love to read, hence all the books. I'm kind of like a dream come true," she says, cleverly borrowing his words.

He laughs. He actually chuckles. "This feels more like a dating app interview than an interview to rent a place, but I'm enjoying it."

Eva blushes. "Still interested in seeing the cottage?" she asks. He nods. She's relieved she didn't scare him away with her frankness. Emily is out for the night at a goodbye party with friends, and Eva had asked her to keep the place tidy because she was showing the rental.

"Sure thing," Reid says, as Eva flicks the flood lights on in the back, casting the light onto her gardens.

They slip into their coats and exit out the patio door that leads to the painted trellis.

"This is beautiful," Reid says, examining the exterior of the cottage and the landscaping.

"Not so great in winter, but in summer, yes. What do you do as a contractor?"

"I build decks and renovate kitchens and interiors, mostly. My partner and I have been doing these types of projects for three years."

Eva puts the key into the cottage's front door. She turns on the light in the main living area and tells Reid to step inside as she closes the door behind them, attempting to keep the chill away. He looks around the place and walks around, inspecting it.

"Seems like it gets some nice, natural light," he says.

"It does," Eva says. "That's what Emily loves most about it. And we share the yard and the dog."

"Whose dog?" Reid asks.

"My dog. She's up in my bedroom now."

"I didn't hear her bark," Reid says.

"She's not much of a barker, thank goodness. She's sweet, but beware—she'll become attached to you. It's in her nature."

"I like dogs," he says. "May I look at the rest?"

"Sure, of course. Let me get the lights for you."

Eva walks ahead of him and turns on the kitchen lights and the bedroom and bathroom lights. It's not a big place—it essentially has four rooms: a kitchen with a small table, a small living room, a bedroom, and a bathroom. She watches Reid look around, taking note of the construction more than the actual place itself. Then, when he's finished taking a gander of it all, he turns to Eva.

"I'd really love to live here," he says.

"I didn't mention that it comes furnished, too. I own all the furniture and decorated it neutrally so that it feels welcoming to any renter, but feel free to add your own personal touches."

"Not a problem. I hate all my things. They're all hand-me-downs and seriously just a bunch of crap. I actually don't want much of what I presently own. I'm kind of looking to start all over, save a lot of money, and move toward owning my own place in the near future. Basically, it'll just be me, my clothes, my guitar, and my books. And I do own a flatbed truck due to my business."

"You have a collection of books?"

"Not like yours, but yes, I have some books. They'll fit well on those shelves over there," he says pointing to the bookshelf behind the swivel chair that faces the television. "When will you make a decision on who will get the place?"

"After I check the references," Eva says. "Probably in a couple of days."

"How many people have you interviewed?"

"Two. I have one more tomorrow."

Reid remembers that he left his references in the car. "I need to grab my reference sheet for you from the truck before I go."

"Great," she says.

He seems fine, but she'll know better after she speaks with his references. He was honest up front. She has the feeling he's trying to get his life back on track—there's something in his eyes—and she appreciates that. As her letter said when she read it, a little kindness can go a long way.

As they lock up the cottage and walk back toward the house, Eva turns to Reid. "So, do you want to meet her?"

"Who? Your tenant?"

"No," Eva laughs. "My dog."

*

"How was the guy?" Emily asks, when she raps on Eva's door after returning home from her night out with friends.

"He was good. You might know him—or know of him. He's the guy who plays at the bars in town. The dark-haired guy who plays at the tavern—"

"The acoustic guy who plays all that melancholy stuff?" Emily looks astonished.

"You know him?"

"No," Emily says, "but I know he plays all that mellow crap that makes you want to cry into your beer." Emily prefers EDM and grunge music.

"So, what you're saying is that he's good at his job?" Eva teases.

"Ha, ha. Very funny. Did he seem nice? Did you tell him not to play all that sad stuff in the cottage with the windows open?"

"Good point. I'll have to make him sign a contract never to play anything that will make me cry. Anyway, he liked it. Said it was well made. Called himself...what was it? An extroverted hermit."

"Whatever that means," Emily says. She is too smart and has no time to try to figure this guy out. She'd rather talk about Aristotle or Plato. Seriously. The Greek rhetoricians played a key factor in her master's thesis that she just finished writing. Eva can't remember the title of the paper, but she'd helped Emily proof it several times.

"Well, I liked him better than Kelly who talked too much."

"So, you're getting somewhere then. Does he have a gun?"

"A gun? Jeez, Em, I didn't ask him that question."

"You know, just in case someone tries to rob the house or steal Brownie."

"Because you had a gun and that kept us safe," Eva says, laughing, knowing Emily does not have a gun. Even Emily begins to crack up at her ridiculous question.

"Well," Emily says. "Either way, you should probably take some karate classes or self-defense classes, just in case."

Eva can't stop giggling at Emily, who has always been able to make her laugh.

Eva's going to miss her when she's gone.

*

By the end of the next night, Eva has made her decision. She had called the references and is feeling good about her decision. She isn't going with Kelly, the talker and partier, and she isn't going with Sammie, the artist.

She's never had a male tenant in the cottage. Before Emily, there was Suzanne, a recently divorced mother of grown children who needed a year to figure things out. She ended up moving to Miami to be near her parents, who had retired there five years prior. Before that was Cassie, a barista who thought she was going to marry a midshipman and move all over the country. She lasted the year, but her midshipman was shipped off, and the relationship fell apart. Cassie left the area and moved back to Mobile, Alabama. She'd met the guy on a trip to Annapolis and thought it was the real deal and love at first sight.

Now, Eva is going to offer the cottage to the singer of sad songs.

His references were glowing. The man who owns the bar where he primarily sings gave him rave reviews. "He's been playing for me for two years, at least once a week. He's reliable and has never taken a sick day. Plus, I think the ladies love him." His contractor/ business partner said, "I couldn't ask for anyone better. He's trying to make things work, make things successful." And his current landlord said he'd never been late on the rent or missed a payment.

The guy checked out.

She picks up her cell and dials his number.

"Hello?" she hears him say at the other end of the line.

"Hi, Reid, it's Eva Levoni." She can hear the noise in the

background. "Did I just interrupt your gig?"

"Nope. I'm on break, so happy to get your call, I think." He's shouting into the phone.

"Well, I'll keep it short and sweet. The place is yours if you want it," Eva says, mimicking his shouting so he can hear her.

"Let me think about it," Reid says. Eva can imagine him grinning on the other end of the line.

"Oh, okay," Eva replies. "Take your time."

"I'm only kidding. I'd love to take it. Can I swing by over the weekend and pay the deposit?"

"Of course. Emily moves out Friday, so feel free to stop by on Saturday. I'll be here."

"With the dog?"

"Yes," she says, smirking to herself. "She's excited to see you again."

Lily

Friday, December 14

"Just go," Cora says to her mother, pushing her out the door of her own store. "Go out with your friends and let Maria and me lock up tonight. Try to have a good time."

The store was unusually busy earlier, and Lily recorded one of her best days of sales. Clothes flew off the racks, and handbag sales were extraordinary. It is convenient that a new shipment of merchandise arrives in the morning, so that she can replenish the racks.

Lily leaves Cora and Maria to lock up the store. During the holiday season, Lily likes to keep the shop open later on Fridays, as opposed to the normal six o'clock closing time, and they'd been there all day.

"We've got this," her daughter says, kissing Lily on the cheek and holding the door open for her as she exits the shop. "You have done enough."

"Yes," Maria echoes. "Go have some fun for once."

Lily has agreed to meet several of the former neighbor friends at a bar in Edgewater where they would often go to hang out and be silly, sometimes even getting crazy enough to sing karaoke. She's also supposed to participate in an ornament exchange and realizes she needs to pick up an ornament on the way. Sitting beside her on the seat of the car is the book about Paris she purchased for Brad as a gift on the evening of Midnight Madness. She's toyed with the idea of holding onto it until Christmas. Who gives their ex-husband a gift that harkens back to something they both dreamed of doing together while married not long after he left his young bride-to-be at the altar?

As vicissitudes of emotions clog Lily's brain, she decides not to wait until Christmas Day to give Brad the book. She's afraid she will lose her nerve. She had seen his face drop the day of the wedding when Cora ran out the door, and she understood the depth of his love for their daughter. Despite recognizing the insanity of the gesture, and wondering if cold feet will lead her to chicken out, she turns her car in the other direction, and drives to the house they used to share together with Cora. It's his house now. Lily hasn't spoken to Brad in weeks. And his bride-to-be apparently moved to Florida. Cora filled Lily in, and Brad told Cora that he's laying low at home trying to deal with everything that happened. Cora quoted him as saying he "feels like a heel on many levels."

Months ago, Lily felt nothing but rage for her ex-husband, the man she loved so fully and unabashedly. She was bitter and hurt. She resented him. She was so crushed by the divorce that she had trouble wrapping her head around their relationship's demise, saying often to anyone who would listen that she didn't see it coming. And yet, here she is, feeling like a complete lunatic and driving to his house—their former house—to drop off a Christmas gift for the man who wrecked her heart and made her doubt the existence of a solid, long-lasting love.

As she pulls up the street in Pendennis Mount, she notices the lights are on in the house, but she doesn't see anyone inside. She doesn't want to interact with Brad, doesn't want to have a conversation with him, and doesn't want him to see her. She simply wants to leave the gift on the doorstep for him to find. The gift tag reads: "Don't open until Christmas." Knowing him as she does—or at least as she used to know him—she wonders if he'll have the willpower to wait.

Instead of pulling into the driveway, she parks two houses down in front of the Richards' home. She hopes they don't see her, either. She has no interest in making small talk or blowing her cover. She turns the headlights off and grabs the package, walking toward her former home. Her heart races, and a sinking feeling fills her stomach. So many memories in this place—memories of bringing Cora home from the hospital, of the many celebrations and holidays they spent around the fireplace or in the big kitchen, of Saturday mornings packing the cooler with drinks and food to take on the boat, of entertaining their family and friends on the large, back patio, and of a general feeling of love in the home. Of course, they bought the property when they were young and didn't have two dimes to rub together. Over the years, with the expertise that Brad gained as an architect, they had reconstructed and expanded the house to the beauty it is today. The vast windows across the back with views of the water were her favorite feature of the home. She misses it. All of it.

Lily tip-toes up the walkway, and leans the package up against the front door. She had stuffed the bag with even more tissue paper in an attempt to disguise that it's a book.

She darts away from the house, moving quickly, yet quietly, back to the car in her heels as they click the pavement. Hopefully, no one has seen her come or go. Lily has to get to the Hallmark store immediately and then to the bar or her friends will wonder where she is, though they are used to her insane hours in retail. They've accepted the fact that she's typically the last to arrive.

As she turns the keys to the ignition, a chill running up her back, she takes a deep breath and hears a voice in her head asking her just what in the hell she thinks she's doing.

Reid

Saturday, December 15

Reid looks around his sad little apartment as he begins to pack up his items. He's already visited the local dump twice this morning to dispose of the things he no longer wants and dropped off a big load at Goodwill.

When he first saw the ad for the cottage that Eva posted, he had saved it for over a week before he finally got the courage to reach out and call the number. Meeting Eva and getting the call from her that he could have the place brought him a sense of contentment he hadn't felt in a while. Happy to know that he will live somewhere else while he strives, once again, to pull it together this time, he reaches again for the letter—the one he found inside his book. In this day and age of instant text messages and digital everything, he can't remember the last time he received a letter, never mind the last time he wrote one himself. He found it uplifting, and ultimately, inspiring. Had it not been for the handwritten letter, he may not have had the nerve to take the step and make the call.

As Reid's life seems to have been a continual act of rebounding to correct some of his past mistakes—and some current ones—he sits on the arm of his sofa and unfolds the piece of stationery again. He takes a moment to read the letter he found inside his book one more time. He loved the words that prompted him to move to Eva's cottage in Eastport, and the message that seemed to come at exactly the right time:

Dear Reader,

If you are receiving a letter in your book, it is because I sensed you might be in need of encouragement. Whether your problem is big or small, it is not insurmountable, and you have the capacity to get through tough times.

It may seem strange to receive a letter from someone you don't know intimately, so let me briefly share why I am writing to you. I am carrying on a tradition that a very dear friend of mine, who passed away recently, began. When he returned from World War II, he wrote letters to strangers, leaving them in odd places all over for people to find, to both heal himself and help others. He did this for sixty years. Learning about his commitment to helping others, I promised myself that I would attempt to do the same to carry on his wonderful tradition of writing to people who may need a pick-me-up, a sign of understanding, or just a friend at the other end of the pen. If you are not in need of this letter, perhaps you can pass it along to someone who might need a reminder that they are valued and loved. If you might need a letter of encouragement, please read on.

When I hit a rough patch in life, my friend's letter reminded me of what I am capable of as a person. Now, I hope to do the same for you. To remind you that you matter, that you have the power to be what you want to be and to lift others up, and to strive to be the best person you can be. You have the power to change anything about your life that doesn't feel right. Whether you need to change your course, let go, forgive, find your value, or see this as the push you need to be brave and figure something out, please know you have what it takes to do it. Dig deeply and find the courage.

One thing I've learned in life is that we can't do these things alone. We need support. And so, reader and friend, I am here for you, just to remind you that any obstacle you face is worth striving to overcome. Reach out to people and connect with those who can best help you find your way. Do not be afraid to be vulnerable. We've all been there and know how it feels.

In the meantime, have faith in yourself. Look your challenges in the face and let them know they have not beaten you. Continue to find hope and be hopeful.

Be well, and remember your value,

Brodie

P.S. If you wish to write back, there is a mailbox in the back of the bookstore where you can drop off a response letter. I am happy to correspond with you!

*

"You made it!" Eva says, bundled up in her black jacket, with jeans and little booties, as she opens up the door to his cottage and places a fresh vase of seasonal flowers on his kitchen table. It's a beautiful sunny day, but cold. "I know flowers are a little feminine, but I wanted to welcome you properly. And I'm ordering lunch for us. Take a peek at this menu," she says, handing it over to him.

Reid smiles at her. "If you saw the apartment I just left, you'd know that they're already brightening my day," he says.

"Good. Can I help you with anything?"

"Nope. I've got it, but I appreciate you asking. As you can see by the back of my truck, there's not too much to move in. It shouldn't take me more than an hour or so. Maybe you could help me organize my books later? I loved the way yours looked in the house."

"Organized by color?"

"It looks cool," he says. "But you can arrange them using any method you want."

"Okay. It's a deal. I'll order lunch and help you with your books. See one you like?"

Reid glances at the menu, but it doesn't take long. "A Reuben, with extra dressing," he says.

"A man who knows his sandwiches—I love it," Eva says, and disappears through the door.

Reid spends the next hour walking back and forth from the truck to the cottage unloading his belongings. Eva had moved her car to the street, which allowed him to back the truck all the way into the driveway to make it easier. Reid already has a positive impression of his landlady—she seems sweet and wants him to enjoy living on her property. And she can't be that much older than he is, which makes him wonder how she can afford such a beautiful home in a pretty expensive part of Annapolis.

When he places the last box inside the cottage, he shuts the door behind him and takes off his coat. He lights the gas fireplace, and he sits down in front of it for a moment to get warm. It's definitely December, and it's been a colder one than normal. Working as a contractor outside a lot, Reid prays for good weather. The weather gods have not cooperated lately. The phone rings.

"Are you settled yet?" his sister, Emme, asks on the other end of the line.

"Boxes are everywhere, but I'm here," he says. His sister has always been good about checking on him, even when things looked the bleakest. He acknowledges that he doesn't give the same effort to their relationship that she does, mostly because she's always had it all together. But today, he feels bad about the lack of reciprocity, as he looks out the windows of the cottage.

"Well, that's good. I'm glad you got out of that other place. It gave me the willies."

"Whatever the 'willies' are, it gave me them, too. How are you?"

"Oh, I'm fine. Minus the lump they found in my breast yesterday."

"What?" Reid feels his heart sink for a moment. He runs his fingers through his hair. "What's happening?"

"I went for my routine breast exam, and they found something iffy. I have to go back next week for another scan. As you can imagine, my mind is going in a hundred different directions, and I'm a little petrified, but I can't be too weird because of the kids. Which brings me to my question that I have to ask you: If something happens to Andy and me, can we put you down in our wills as the guardian for the kids? We realized we need to update the wills immediately. The kids would mostly be taken care of monetarily, but we can't ask Andy's sister, because she's a loon, and we can't ask our parents, because they're aging, which leaves you to be the one we would burden with the request of raising our children."

"You know I would do anything for those kids. I'm just sorry I'm not on the best financial footing." He feels honored that she would ask him, considering the current state of things.

"You will be, though," she says.

"And how do you know this?"

"I have a good feeling in my body that something good is going to happen for you, even if part of it's a lump."

He laughs. Leave it to his sister to still have a sense of humor even when she's clearly unnerved and scared.

"You know I'd do anything for you," he says. He doesn't often utter these types of words. "So, I guess it was the perfect time for me to quit drinking since you're asking me to take care of your kids in case of an emergency."

"What?" his sister asks.

"I got brave. I'm off booze, that's it. End of story. It's taken me down some dark paths, and I have to try to straighten my life out now. Drinking never got me anywhere. It only got me into trouble.

Plus, I got a letter."

"A what?"

"Never mind. Let's put it this way: I got the push I needed to take matters into my own hands and stop making excuses and wishing things would change. I think I have to be the change."

"Wow. Impressive. That's a good reason. I'm proud of you. Stay strong and stick with it. Call me whenever you feel you might feel tempted to drink."

"I will. I promise," Reid tells her.

"So, how's your new landlord?" Emme asks, changing the subject.

"It's a great property. The cottage is clean and well-built and the rent's affordable," he says.

"I didn't ask about the place, although I'm glad it's nice. How's the landlord?"

"She seems nice. She's not much older than I am and had a recent split from someone she was with for ten years. She put a fresh vase of Christmas flowers in the place this morning as a welcome, and she's picking up sandwiches for lunch. I asked her to help me organize my bookshelves, and she said she would."

"Sounds like she's more than nice," Emme says.

"Maybe," Reid says, and he hears the knock on the door. "I have to go—she's back. So, now that I'm straightening myself out—or at least attempting to—count me in on taking care of your kids for the rest of my life in case of an emergency. But I know you will be fine. Keep me posted. No worrying until we know what it is."

Emme sighs. "Right. Thanks, Reid. Have fun today!" she says, mischievously.

*

"Did you get everything in?" Eva asks.

"I did," Reid says, unburdening her arms of the bags she's carrying. "What is all this?"

"I figured I would get you some basic groceries from the market. It's all part of the Welcome Wagon. Just some milk, eggs, bread, fruits, a couple of amazing croissants, and a few other things you might need to get through the day."

"That's very nice of you," he says, placing the bags on the counter.

"Well, let me know if you need anything else. The sandwich is in the smaller bag."

"Oh, I thought you were staying to eat?"

She stops and looks at him. She's petite, but he can sense a big personality. He could tell the night he met her. Plus, there's an ease of conversation he feels with her, something he hasn't experienced in a while. Maybe he's been too closed off. Maybe he hasn't associated with the right people. Maybe his frame of mind is changing. For a moment, he feels off kilter.

"I can stay if you'd like company. I didn't want to invade your new space," Eva says.

"Did you invade Emily's space when she was here?"

"Only intentionally once in a while," she said, smiling.

"Then, let's have lunch."

He steps over some boxes and begins to unload the groceries into his kitchen. He likes the place so far. It's spacious—and perfect for him. She walks over and sits down at the kitchen table as Reid stretches across and sets their sandwiches and the chips in front of her. She arranges the plates, and he grabs two waters from the fridge that he put in earlier.

"Well, cheers to my new landlady," Reid says, raising his bottle of water to hers.

"Ugh. That makes me sound really, really old," she says, laughing. "I just conjured up an image of Ma's Boarding House from *It's A Wonderful Life*."

"Good flick," he replies, not wanting to insult her. "Okay, so here's to the new place - to Eva's cottage."

"Here's to having you here," she says.

After making a lot of small talk about where they grew up and how they lived in the same town for most of their lives but never knew each other, they realized they had a couple of connections in common. Nobody they know extremely well, but peripheral people who also live in Annapolis, and have for a long time.

Eva moves over to the tall bookshelves she had built in behind the sofa and begins to open the boxes of Reid's books as he works to put things away in the kitchen and elsewhere in the cottage.

"Did you love this one?" she asks him, holding up a copy of a Tom Clancy novel.

"He's one of my favorites. I love spy novels. Do you?"

"An occasional one. I like mysteries and romances and a good fantasy story every once in a while. You seem to enjoy reading biographies."

"I do. The Steve Jobs one is my favorite."

"I liked it, too. And Katherine Graham's autobiography about her life as the publisher of The Washington Post when it was an objective paper."

"Oh, harsh. I've never read it," Reid says.

"Also loved David Ogilvy's book on advertising. It's a game-changer for people in marketing, advertising and public relations. Like seriously, it made me look at the advertising world differently. Have you ever read something that's changed your perspective on work or life that much?"

Reid remembers lots of books, but for some reason, the letter he read earlier comes to mind. It has given him a feeling of hope in people and in himself that he hasn't had in some time. "Yes," he says. "I have."

"It's such a great feeling, isn't it?" she asks.

"It is."

About an hour later, Eva surveys her work on the bookshelves. Reid has some cool pieces of memorabilia that he's had framed or saved, and he hangs them around the cottage, while Eva places a couple of collections of concert tickets on the bookshelves.

"You've seen Eric Clapton seven times?" Eva asks, looking at the framed ticket stub.

"He's my favorite guitarist. He's amazing," Reid says.

"And John Mayer five times? He's one of my favorites."

"Yup. I'm afraid so. Totally underrated as a guitarist. He's incredible."

"Do you write your own music like he does?"

"Sometimes. I've written a few decent things. I've never done anything with them."

"Why?" she asks, looking intently at him.

"I'm not sure."

"Do you play your songs at the bar?"

"No, no one ever really wants to hear your own songs. They typically want to hear songs they know and can sing along to, you know?"

She nods. Reid can tell she's probably one of those people.

Reid moves next to her, and they stand back and examine the decorated and organized bookshelves. She brings her hand to her chin and thoughtfully surveys her work.

"You may have missed your calling," Reid commenting on the display she created. "Interior design may have been your thing."

"You think?" she asks. "Hmmm...well, if you're happy with how it looks, my work is done here. I have to take Brownie for a walk. Is there anything else I can help with?"

He smiles at her again—his good smile. The one that means he's actually momentarily happy. The one he promised himself—and secretly to the letter writer—to find again.

"I think the Welcome Wagon brought its A-game today," he says.

She puts on her coat, gives him a 'thumbs-up,' and walks out the door. For the first time in a very long while, a sense of calm and contentment washes over him—until he remembers his previous conversation.

Before he lifts another finger, Reid takes his phone from his back pocket searches for the number of a florist. He orders a bouquet of flowers to be sent immediately, with a note that says, "Thinking of you. I love you," and asks that it be delivered today, if possible, to his sister Emme.

Dimitri

Sunday, December 16

Dimitri stretches out on his bed, his morning coffee by his side, and folds the letter back up, tucking it inside his nightstand's top drawer. He folds his hands over his chest and takes a deep breath, closes his eyes. Time to move on. Time to stop wading in all this anger.

Last night, when his buddies came calling to go to the casino, he said yes at first, and then recanted, thinking about the words in the letter he received inside his book. *Be kind, and kindness will find you. Be good, and goodness will find its way to you, as well. And take care of yourself and others.* He's a pretty smart guy, and he knows right from wrong and good from bad, although he probably hasn't exactly allowed his conscience to be his guide. He recognizes a lot of his bad habits: the drinking, gambling, and anger at the world. He has a father who needs him—who has asked Dimitri to take him shopping today because he still can't drive himself—but his walking has improved. Dimitri understands he has a responsibility to his father, to a man who raised him right, and who would otherwise be incredibly disappointed to learn that his son is not only a divorced man, but a man without a job, as well. He still hasn't told him, but he knows he needs to do so.

The book he's been reading—the one he purchased the night of Midnight Madness—is also helping Dimitri figure things out. Previously, he felt stuck in a rut. He couldn't make a career change because he had a wife and bills to pay. Without her running up the credit cards, he's a freer man. If there were ever a time to make a career change, now would be the perfect moment, or at least somewhat soon before his severance package ends. He's been reading the book and taking career assessments online to try to figure out his next move.

With one last deep breath, he plants his feet firmly on the floor and stretches. It's off to the shower and then to pick up his father.

*

"Hey, Dimi," his father says as Dimitri walks through the door.

"Hey, Baba. How are you feeling?"

"Much better. Look—no cane. I can manage without it finally."

Dimitri watches him walk across the living room floor as if there had never been an injury. He's walking well and is steady on his feet. Dimitri raises his eyebrows in surprise.

"I'm impressed, Baba! You're doing well."

"I've been doing my exercises every day, religiously. The physical therapy seems to be helping."

"So, where are we headed today?"

"I need to go see the woman at the bookstore. She has ideas for books for the grandkids we can buy and mail out."

"The woman at the bookstore?"

"Yes, you know, the bookstore on Main Street I told you about. Her name's Meg. She's delightful. She's so helpful and suggests the best books to read. I just finished this one. It was good." Baba holds up a British mystery. He's always been a fan of suspense.

Dimitri's ex-wife judged his father because he worked with his hands. She believed him to be unintelligent, when in fact, most of what Baba has learned comes from reading—newspapers, magazines, and books. Educating his kids well and making sure they received a proper education was important to both his father and his mother. They instilled a love of reading in him at an early age. Has he ever thanked his father for that?

"Okay, that sounds good. Where else?"

"Well, we could head to the barber and get that hair of yours cut." Baba gives him a little dig. He's been wanting him to get rid of his longer locks for years, but Dimitri has worn it long since college, except for the brief period when he cut it off to find his accounting job. Once he secured it, he grew it out again. It's been this way since then.

"No barber today, Baba."

"Soon, though, right?"

"Maybe. We'll see," Dimitri says. He does often wonder why he is so attached to his hair. Who knows? Maybe a new mindset, a new look? He'll think about it.

"Well, I thought we could go to lunch downtown and then stop to pick up some Christmas decorations. Sound good?" Baba asks, giving up on the haircut.

Dimitri thinks it all sounds good. What else does he have to do on a Sunday? He's looking forward to spending time with his father. It's rare that they go out and about like two bachelors.

He helps his dad with his coat and hat, reminds him to grab his wallet, and the two of them walk out into the crisp air to tackle the day.

*

Luckily, just as they arrive by car to Main Street, they snag a parking spot a few doors down from the bookstore. Dimitri waits as the person exits the tight spot, and then eases his car into it.

He helps his father out of the passenger side, locks the car, and they walk a few steps up the street to the entrance of the bookstore. He wonders if the woman will remember him—remember that she placed a letter in his book. Could she remember? She couldn't possibly remember all her customers, could she? He wonders how many she writes a day and how randomly they are placed. Regardless, he is happy to have received one.

"Mr. Vassos!" Dimitri turns quickly, thinking she is addressing him, but in fact, she is addressing his father. "So good to see you!" She gives him a little hug, and his father blushes a little.

"Hello, Meg," Baba says. "Happy holidays."

"And to you! How are you feeling?"

"Much better. I'm getting around much better, right Dimi?" Baba says, turning to Dimitri.

"Much better," Dimitri says.

Meg extends her hand to Dimitri as she looks at him with a puzzled brow. "Nice to meet you, Dimi, although I feel as if we've met before."

"It's Dimitri," Dimitri says, giving his dad a rap on the arm and clarifying his name to her. "My father's nickname for me is Dimi. I've been in a couple of times and recognize you."

"Oh, wonderful. Then, welcome back, Dimitri," she says, correcting his name. "What can I help you with today?" she says, turning her attention back to Baba.

"I need books as Christmas gifts for the grandkids who don't live in the area, and they're easy to ship. Any chance you can help me out with that?"

"Of course," she says. "Kids books are now upstairs. We can take the elevator."

"I can manage the stairs," Baba says boldly.

"Okay. I'll lead the way," she says, heading for the stairs.

Dimitri and Baba begin to climb the stairs, his father taking one step at a time, and the smell of freshly brewed coffee hits Dimitri's nose. He realizes he hasn't had anything to eat at all this morning, and he even forgot to make his cup of coffee for the road.

As Meg leads Baba around the children's section, Dimitri orders a coffee and a croissant for both of them. He waits at the small table that is adjacent to the coffee bar and watches Meg help his father. He knows she wrote the letter. He is certain. Maybe it's a team effort and the staff is involved, but his hunch is that she is the writer of the letters, and because he is a curious person by nature, he wants to know why.

Piled high with many books, Meg and Baba return to the table and place the books in front of Dimitri. "Looks like you picked some winners," Dimitri says.

"I'd like to think so," Meg says, with a big smile.

"I notice you have a piano up here. What's that for?" Dimitri asks, surprised at himself for being so bold.

"I try to host events up here when I can. I have found that when someone plays music in the store, people linger longer and often buy something. It's an interesting correlation, but when it's quiet like a library, folks tend to feel a bit intimidated and don't stay as long to peruse the shelves. That's why I try to play music through the speakers. But when I have someone playing piano, it livens up the place. It's wonderful background music."

"Sounds fun," Dimitri says, meaning it.

"Do you play?" she asks him, leaning in.

"I do. Not professionally, but I do play."

"What kind of music?" she asks. Dimitri notices how bright her eyes are.

"Anything. I'm trained, but I also play by ear."

"That's fascinating. I wish I had a talent like that."

"Something tells me you have a talent. Perhaps it's a hidden talent," Dimitri says. Meg shoots him a look that indicates there is an understanding between them. That perhaps Dimitri knows more than—

"Were you in the store the night of Midnight Madness?" Meg asks.

"I was," he says. He thinks something has clicked with her.

"I knew you looked familiar," she says, clapping her hands together. "And you definitely resemble your dad. So, how about you play a little for us now, like an audition of sorts," she says, with a wink.

"Right now?"

"No time like the present," she says.

Baba is watching this interaction between his son and Meg intently, like he watches his Sunday football games, and chimes in: "Go ahead, Dimi. Play a little for Meg." Baba always loved having the piano played in his house when Dimitri was growing up. The simple things continue to bring him the most joy.

Meg pulls out the piano bench and motions for Dimitri to sit and play. The sound of the piano—of Dimitri's fingers moving across the keys—begins to fill the store. He chooses to play an assortment of old Ella Fitzgerald and Louie Armstrong songs, a Sinatra classic his father loves, and a John Mayer tune. He moves from one song to another seamlessly as Meg and Baba watch as Dimitri's fingers glide across the keys and his body bends to the rhythm of the music and to reach for the keys. One of Meg's assistants bounds up the stairs to see who's on the piano.

"Who's playing?" Dimitri hears her ask Meg in a loud whisper, as Dimitri continues to play.

"Dimitri," Meg says, proudly. "Isn't he wonderful?"

"Amazing! Is he hired?" the assistant asks.

"We're about to find out," Meg replies.

*

Later that night when Dimitri is back home and alone, he thinks about Baba buying all those gifts for his grandchildren. Dimitri never interferes in the lives of his brothers and sisters, but tonight he will make an exception. He dials his brother's number.

"Hey, bro," Eric says when he answers Dimitri's call, "this is a surprise."

"Hey, Eric. Do you have a minute? I wanted to talk to you about Baba and possibly visiting this Christmas," he begins.

Meg
Sunday, December 16

Almost everyone who purchases books mentions something about the piano player to either Clarke or Meg. Dimitri's father beams as Dimitri plays, and settles himself into a chair near the piano with a cup of coffee. Dimitri just keeps on playing. When Meg talks with him about possibly playing and getting paid to do it, he hesitates at first, and then accepts the invitation. Meg gives Dimitri her business card and asks him to play on Friday. Dimitri's music has filled the bookstore with songs that people know, and that Sunday afternoon quickly becomes one of Meg's favorite days in the shop since she's been open. The bookstore feels alive with people, books, and music.

Later, as Meg walks home that night after closing up, she feels a sense of accomplishment. She recalls seeing Dimitri the evening of Midnight Madness. It is difficult not to forget two things about him that night: first, that he is a very handsome man, with chiseled features and bone structure, and second, that he seemed like one of the unhappiest people she talked with that night. Everything about him that evening, from his posture to his lack of communication and eye contact, to the book he selected at that late hour, indicated a sadness or depression. This, Meg remembers. This, Meg could feel.

With only nine days until Christmas, Meg enjoys strolling the streets at night, bundled up in her coat, drinking the hot chocolate she made herself for the walk back to her condo. The only problem is, Meg doesn't feel like going home and being alone. Spending the afternoon at the store and some time with Mr. Vassos and Dimitri makes her miss family time. She wishes her parents lived closer, and sometimes regrets being so far away from them.

As she sees some of her fellow shop owners are staying open an hour later tonight, Meg has stuck to her regular Sunday hours for the bookstore, not wanting to exhaust her employees or make them work so much that they couldn't enjoy the holiday season themselves. She feels restless as she passes the t-shirt shop and the boutique she loves. When she reaches the tavern, she pauses for a moment and attempts to peer through the window. She wonders if the guy who plays the sad songs is playing tonight. Without a second thought, she turns and walks through the tavern doors and heads to the bar area.

With the guitar strap strewn across his body, she sees him playing, and moves closer toward the area where he is seated. There is one table with two seats open, so she sits down. His songs lilt in the air. Meg looks around as people are singing along as they drink their beers, tapping their feet under tables, and some are engaged in conversation talking over the music. The singer's eyes close as he hits the high notes, and Meg marvels that both this guy and Dimitri have the ability not to look at the instrument while they play it. As someone who can't play an instrument or carry a tune, she is in awe of the musical talents of others.

"By any chance, is this seat taken?" a woman asks Meg, raising her voice loudly enough so Meg can hear.

"Oh, no. Feel free," Meg responds. She recognizes the coat. The gorgeous coat with the fur collar. She's seen this woman before. She's been in the shop.

"Thank you," the woman shouts back. "It's crowded in here

tonight. Did you come to hear Reid play, too?" she asks.

"I actually did," Meg says, incapable of fibbing at all to any-one at any time.

"Me, too," the woman says. "I just met him. He's renting the cottage on my property. I'm Eva, by the way."

Meg nods and smiles. "I'm Meg."

When Reid finishes playing the song, he looks over and ac-knowledges Eva with a wave. He then looks at Meg sideways. He must remember me, Meg thinks, because he then nods at her with a grin. Eva sees the interaction, and her face looks puzzled. She turns to Meg.

"Are you a friend of Reid's?" she asks, innocently.

"No, not really. I met him in the bookstore I own up the street. He came in one night." Meg doesn't let Eva know she recognizes her, too, the coat a dead giveaway, from that same night. She decides to let her do with the information what she will. It doesn't take Eva long to make the connection.

"Oh my gosh! You're the woman with the reindeer antlers! I almost didn't recognize you."

"I could pull them out of my backpack and put them on if it will make you feel better," Meg says, trying to be funny.

"Oh, no, no. That's not necessary, but hilarious! I love your bookstore. And I especially loved the letter you gave me inside the book."

Meg looks at her squarely and smiles broadly. She loves when people tell her they love the letters they receive. It makes her feel as if she is carrying on the good work of John. For every letter she sends and receives feedback, there are hundreds from which she hears noth-ing. Yet, the mere notion that someone takes the time to read the let-ter fills up her heart with so much good energy, she can hardly stand it. There are so many letters she has given to others that have never been acknowledged. It's nice to hear one that is.

"I'm so glad," Meg says, reaching over and tapping Eva on the arm.

"It's helping me move on from a pretty shattered broken heart," Eva admits. "It came at the right time."

They both turn their heads back to the small stage area to focus on the remainder of Reid's set, and they each take a sip of the red wine they ordered. The song list has changed since the last time Meg was in here a couple of months ago. While he plays an occasional emotional love song, Reid's replaced a majority of the melancholy stuff with contemporary, upbeat music that he's adapted for acoustic guitar, as well as a holiday song thrown in now and then for fun, just as Dimitri did earlier in the bookstore. The people in the bar seem to enjoy his playing, especially tonight.

Something seems different with Reid—now that Meg knows his name—than it did the night she met him. She remembers him being a little drunk and wrapped up in his own world. Likewise, something seems different with Eva. Meg wonders if they've each shared that they received letters in their books with each other or talked about it, although Meg never writes two letters in exactly the same way. Nevertheless, the messages of hope and love may often be similar.

When he completes his set, Reid pulls up a chair and joins the women at the table.

"That was great," Eva says, smiling at him.

"Thanks," he says, and then, turning to Meg, "better selection of music tonight?" He's clearly looking for approval from her for some reason. It's his way of letting her know he remembers their conversation.

"It's making me feel happy, so yes," she says.

"I'm Reid," he says, extending his hand to shake hers.

"Meg."

"So, you two know each other?" he asks Eva, motioning to Meg.

"No, we just met," Eva says. "Well, not exactly. We have met before. Meg owns the bookstore up the street, and I've been in the store before."

"So have I," Reid says. "Great shop."

"Thank you. I just closed up and happened to be walking by, so I thought I'd pop in for a minute before I head home for a glass of wine. I'm glad I stopped in tonight," she says.

"Thanks for coming," he says, and she nods back to him.

"By any chance," Meg says, directing the question at Reid, "do you know a guy named Dimitri Vassos?"

"I don't think so, why?"

"He's an amazing pianist. I should introduce you two in case you ever want to play together. I just hired him to play our upstairs piano in the store. It's his first time playing anywhere in public."

"Cool," Reid says. "I'd like to meet him. And I didn't know you had a piano in the store."

"I could do better hiring people to play it. It's upstairs where the coffee bar is. Dimitri will be there Friday night, and Saturday and Sunday afternoons for now."

"Sounds good. I'll have to drop by sometime."

Meg takes her last swig of wine and places tip money on the table for her server. She puts her arms back into the sleeves of her drab coat, fastens her backpack, and stands up to leave.

"Going already?" Eva asks Meg.

"It's been busy at the store this week, and I'm pretty tired. But I look forward to seeing you both soon. It's been great meeting you," Meg says, buttoning up her coat for the walk home.

"You, too," they both say.

To Eva, Meg says, "And I love your coat, by the way."

"Oh, thank you. My ex—," she begins to say, and then quickly corrects the sentence. "Someone gave it to me as a gift. It's from the boutique on State Circle."

"I'll have to check it out sometime," Meg says.

Meg makes her way to the door as Reid heads back to the stool to play, and waves goodbye to her as she heads out the door and back into the night's chilly air. Out of the corner of her eye, Meg sees Eva cross her legs and get comfortable as she stays to hear Reid play his next set.

*

When Meg returns to her place, she climbs into the bathtub full of lavender—the best herb to fully relax a person—and turns on her little CD player she keeps in the bathroom for just these types of moments. When she's in the tub, she plays only classical. Brodie loved classical music, and his love of it made Meg love it, because he always wanted to listen to Beethoven or Mozart. Aunt Nancy always said it calmed him down when he would become anxious and when they needed to work on his motor skills. She had taken him to music therapy sessions, which was important to helping Brodie's muscular function. Cerebral palsy can be such a frustrating condition, mostly because in Brodie's case there was a fully-functioning mind trapped in a body that walked only a little and spent the majority of time in a wheelchair. During Brodie's birth, oxygen did not flow properly to Brodie's brain, and the result of an umbilical cord wrapped around Brodie's neck affected him for the rest of his life. Meg tries not to think of what he would have been like had the emergency situation not happened, and poor Aunt Nancy still beats herself up about the incident in private.

Despite his condition, Brodie had been a blessing to them all, though. While his life may have been a short one, everything Meg is and has is a reflection of Brodie's time with all of them. She thinks of Uncle Ben's kindness in giving her the money he had saved for Brodie to give her a life that Brodie never had the chance of living. Brodie had helped Meg in so many ways that Uncle Ben and Aunt Nancy became another set of parents to her. They are both good, hard-working, decent people, and she loves them dearly. Adding a little more bath salts to the water, Meg allows herself to remember Christmases past, of jolly times when they were all together. She can picture Brodie getting excited about Christmas morning and of all of them sharing a meal together on Christmas Day.

Meg is lost in thought when her phone rings. She steps out of the tub and wraps herself in a towel, reaching for the phone.

It was a number she didn't recognize.

"Hello," she says, trying to towel off.

"Hi, Meg. It's Dimitri. Sorry to bother you this late. I saw your number on the card, and I had a quick question. I was just wondering if there's a particular song list you'd like me to put together for the weekend. I want to practice this week so I'm ready for you."

Meg smiles. She's pleased with herself. She can hear by the tone of his voice that he's embracing his new role as a musician in the bookstore.

"That is entirely your call. You know way more than I do about any of this."

"What's that music I hear in the background?"

"Classical," she says. "I just got home, and it relaxes me."

"I'll throw in a few classical pieces then," he says.

"That would be great," she says. "And some holiday favorites."

"Got it. And thanks for taking good care of my dad. He appreciated the gifts you chose for his grandchildren. That was very nice of you."

"Well, he's a really nice man and has supported the store ever since I opened."

Meg senses a pause on the other end for a second, and then Dimitri speaks again.

"I'm glad to hear it. Thanks for the opportunity. I won't keep you. Have a nice night, and I'll see you on Friday."

"Thanks, Dimitri. And thanks for entertaining everyone today. It was so fun to hear you play. Have a good night, and I'll see you soon."

As Meg hangs up the phone, she thinks of sweet Mr. Vassos and how proud he must feel to have raised a person like Dimitri. Whatever Dimitri's backstory is, whatever Dimitri's going through that has him feeling down in the dumps, noticeable enough for Meg to have placed a letter in his book, she hopes he is on his way out of it, much as she had been able to rise above her own circumstances not too long ago.

Eva

Friday, December 21

Brownie wags her tail as Eva comes through the door after her last client meeting of the day. She's exhausted from designing the public relations campaign for a local food distributor, and she had to create the holiday posts for the social media team before she left the office. It's always frenetic at work right before the holidays hit, especially when most of Eva's clients are retailers, restaurants, and food and grocery chains. She's looking forward to the break.

She lets Brownie out of the house, places the leash around her collar, and takes her for a stroll around the block for some exercise. Eva could take the easy way out and allow her to run around the fenced backyard, but she believes she needs more exercise than that. Plus, the winds of the last week have subsided, and the weather is cooperating. With a coat on, it's quite pleasant for a December evening.

She walks down to the water where the marina is and lets Brownie sniff around. Four days until the holiday, and she's still not done shopping. She needs a few more things, and then remembers Meg's bookstore. Didn't she say there's a guy on piano playing tonight? She wonders if she should head up to the store and to see what's happening.

Eva finds Meg naturally pretty, but more than that, she finds her mysterious and intriguing. She imagines she must have a line of men wishing to date her. Her long, brown hair is naturally wavy, and when she smiles, you can see her set of perfectly aligned white teeth. Eva's always had to work hard to be beautiful; she maintains her straight hair beyond her shoulders, exercises every day, and always wears a little makeup every time she leaves the house. Meg had mentioned that she liked her coat, and it makes Eva wonder if she ever splurges on something expensive for herself. Eva's job requires her to dress professionally, and she drops a lot of money on clothes, from designer suits and blouses to outerwear and shoes and boots. Her petite stature is also a challenge, as she often has to have clothes tailored to fit her frame. Meg, who is several inches taller with that 'girl next door' look can get away with looking radiant in a pair of jeans and a Boho top.

After talking with Meg at the tavern, Eva decides that she wants to get to know her better. They are close in age, and as she closely examines the letter she received from 'Brodie," there's got to be a reason why she does what she does. She wonders how many other people receive letters. Everyone? A select few? How does she decide who needs a letter? And how does she know if the letters ever make a difference in someone's life?

As Brownie and Eva approach the driveway, Eva sees Reid pulling into the spot across the street. They've been two passing ships in the night this week; he's been working a lot, and so has she. Twice this week, Eva didn't get home until eight.

"Hey," Reid says. Brownie sees Reid and runs toward him, wagging her tail.

"Hey, Brownie."

Brownie is happy to see him, and Reid crouches down to pet her. Eva takes note that her dog likes him. The dog was never too fond of Kyle.

"How was your week?" Eva asks.

"Good," he says. "How was yours?"

"Busy. Insanity. It's always like this right before Christmas," she says.

"Me, too. What are you doing tonight?" he asks her.

"I was actually thinking of heading up to the bookstore. Meg had mentioned that guy who is playing piano tonight."

"I was thinking the same thing. Want to go together?"

Eva is thrilled to have company, and once she gets Brownie settled, she slips into jeans and her low boots to hoof it to the bookstore since it's a pleasant December night. They walk over the Eastport Bridge, the full, yellow moon hanging in the sky, the Christmas lights adding to the city's warm glow. Eva carries a large bag with her for shopping.

"Since you and I have both grown up here, have you ever thought about packing it in and moving somewhere entirely different?" Eva asks, making conversation as they walk together.

"No," Reid says, matter-of-factly. "I never have. You?"

"After Kyle left, I tossed the idea around. My parents live in Florida, so the thought crossed my mind. Plus, I don't like to drive, in case you haven't noticed. I only drive when absolutely necessary, so living here suits me. If I moved, I'd have to live and work in the same city because I value being able to walk most places."

"And where does this fear of driving come from?" Reid asks gently.

"From a deadly car accident I was involved in when I was in high school. My sister's boyfriend was driving, and we were hit on the driver's side. She and I were badly injured and he died on the scene. Call it a bit of a phobia, or a lot of phobia, but I've had a hard time shaking that from my memory. My sister adored him. They most likely would have stayed together forever and ever. It was the worst thing I've ever been through. We were trapped in the car for a while before the paramedics could get us out."

"I'm so sorry."

"My sister—well, something in her died that day, too. She's never been the same since, and I would suppose all of my fears about cars began on that day."

"Understandable," Reid says.

Eva hates telling this story, and typically only tells it to people she knows well, which makes her wonder why she's telling the man who is renting her cottage. There's something about talking to him that makes her feel as if she can say anything she wants, and he won't judge her or mock her or hold anything against her.

When they arrive at the doors of the bookstore, they can hear the sounds of music floating out of the upstairs window, which is slightly cracked. Eva guesses Meg does this on purpose to draw people into the store, a good marketing ploy. When Reid and Eva step inside, they are surprised to see such a big crowd. Meg catches Eva's eye from behind the counter, smiles at her, and points to the antlers on top of her head.

Eva and Reid pass the long line of customers at the checkout and find the stairs in the back of the store, making their way to the piano player. As she walks among the books and arrives at the stairs, she sees a gold postal mailbox mounted on the wall. Above it is a sign that reads POST LETTER REPLIES HERE. Eva smiles and understands Meg even more, connecting the dots. Not only does she write the letters, but she willingly becomes someone's pen pal. Eva feels her heart skip a little to know that someone would take the time to do something like this, and it reminds her of how she loves the idea of the owls bringing letters to people in *Harry Potter*. The difference here is, Meg disperses the letters, becomes a pen pal, and continues to correspond as needed. At least that's what Eva surmises.

As they reach the top of the stairs, the piano is in full view, and the man sitting at the piano is playing without any sheet music. He is intently playing, as his fingers move swiftly over the keys. He's not singing, only playing. Reid takes note and folds his arms as he watches. Eva watches Reid watching the piano player. Something about the expression on his face suggests that he thinks the guy is good—not just good—but very good. At the end of the song, Reid claps loudly. There is not enough time for introductions, as he launches directly into another song, so Eva and Reid pull up two chairs and sit for a moment and listen.

"Hot chocolate?" the guy behind the coffee bar counter asks Eva. "It's free. On the house tonight."

"That's very nice!" Eva says, and the guy puts two cups of hot chocolate with whipped cream in front of them. It's only days before Christmas, and Eva likes the vibe of the place.

When the pianist takes a break, Reid and Eva walk up to him and introduce themselves.

"Are you friends of Meg's?" the pianist asks them.

"Sort of," they say. "We've only just met her recently."

"Same here. My father actually introduced me to her, but I've been in the store before."

"Good playing," Reid says to him. "You've obviously been playing for a while?"

"Since I was a kid. I've just never done anything with it. You play?"

"I dabble in piano, but I'm not that good. I play guitar."

"Really?" Dimitri asks.

"He plays at the tavern down on Main Street," Eva says. "He's really good, too," she says, realizing she sounds a bit too eager to prop up Reid, like a crazy fan or stalker, just by uttering those words.

"When do you play?"

"Typically, I play one night on the weekend and one day during the week. It's my side gig."

"Me, too," Dimitri says. "Actually, I don't know what I'm saying. I'm currently unemployed and this is the first time I'm getting paid to play anywhere."

Eva and Reid look at him and almost feel badly for him. He could use a confidence boost.

"What's your day job?" Eva asks.

"You mean what was my day job. Boring. Totally boring. Accounting. I was let go a few weeks ago and am still looking for a job. Then, this opportunity came along."

Just then, Meg appears and joins the three of them as they are talking.

"I see you met some of my new friends, Eva and Reid," Meg says, showcasing that brilliant smile of hers. "I'm glad you all met. Reid plays down the street. You two would make a great duo. This is Dimitri."

Dimitri and Reid look at each other and shrug their shoulders simultaneously.

"What are you?" Eva says, teasingly. "The Music Matchmaker?"

"I don't think so, but it would be great if there were such a thing," Meg says. "I'd totally be into that." They laugh and begin to make idle chit-chat and talk while people continue shopping. Meg begins to excuse herself, saying that she needs to return to the register because the store is so jammed.

"I'm so glad you all came out tonight," she says, looking each one of them in the eye, before she gets back to work.

"We are, too," Eva says, speaking for the group. And she truly means it.

Lily

Christmas Eve
Monday, December 24

Lily awakens before the sun is up. She has to work at the store until three o'clock when she will close for Christmas. She's tired. The time leading up to Christmas requires late hours and a lot of work. She feels the ache in her feet, her back. She's been standing and bending and reaching for items all week for customers, and she promises herself that she will get a new pair of shoes for herself for Christmas, a flat pair with an arch for support.

She tiptoes out of bed and past Cora's room. Her door is cracked, and she can see her sleeping in her bed, curled up underneath the covers. Cora will spend Christmas Eve with her father and Christmas Day with Lily. Lily forced herself to come to terms with the results of their fractured family traditions months ago. She never wanted it this way, but as the Rolling Stones sang, *You Can't Always Get What You Want.*

Lily turns the coffee pot on and sits at the kitchen table looking out at her backyard. She misses looking outside the windows of their home in Pendennis Mount and seeing the river. Her current house is adorable and convenient and perfect for two people, but her heart aches when she thinks about how she and Brad lovingly restored that old house over so many years. Being married to an architect made it easier. Renovating it was the pet project that they did together, and truthfully, they made a good team. They rarely fussed or argued over things. People always say if you can survive building or renovating a home together, your marriage can survive anything. This wasn't true in their case. It ended regardless of the lack of fights and camaraderie. At the end of the relationship, when Brad said that he felt they'd become more like roommates and less like two people in love, it devastated her. How could one person feel that way but not the other? It's taken a long time to come to terms with the unraveling of a relationship that meant the world to her.

Could she have done things differently? Of course, she could have. Could he have done things differently? Of course, he could have. Could they have worked harder to fix what was broken? Maybe. If only Lily had known Brad was feeling these things, maybe the issues could have been addressed. But, as with most marriages, the demise can rarely be pinned on one person; it often takes two people to make a marriage fail. Lily is mature enough to understand that part of the blame must fall to her. It's taken her a while to be able to think it, let alone say the words aloud. As Brad had said, they drifted apart, perhaps unknowingly.

And yet, she realizes now, in hindsight, that giving that book about Paris to Brad for Christmas may have been a mistake. A huge mistake. She is questioning the choice of the gift. What prompted her do it? Her emotions had been running high. It's the holiday season. She's alone. No blind dates ever work out. She is simply feeling sorry for herself, and so much more. The list is long. Lily chastises herself, and in the quiet hours of the early dawn, she wonders why she still loves a man who no longer loves her.

*

"So, Cora's out with her Dad?" Marie asks, as they work side-by-side taking care of the morning's shoppers. Customers buy last minute gifts for their loved ones. Scarves and hats are flying off the racks, and the new cashmere black sweaters are nearly gone. Several red blouses have sold this morning, along with an assortment of bracelets and bags. Lily is always amazed at how many people wait until the day before Christmas to shop.

When the last customer has left the shop, she locks the door and begins to tidy up. Marie begins to make her sweep around the shop as well.

"That's it," Lily says to Marie. "You're done. Go enjoy the holiday with your family, and I'll see you on 'Return Day.'"

Marie and Lily had always called the day after Christmas 'Return Day'. There really is no need for further explanation, except to say that for some reason, people want to exchange their items immediately after Christmas, especially if they want to wear something right away and it doesn't fit. It's hectic—almost as frantic as Black Friday. She's not looking forward to it.

After she closes down the register for the day, she slumps in one of the two chairs she has in the store, the lights having been turned off. Only one light in the back of the store remains lit, and Lily takes a deep breath in and looks around this store she has created and maintained all these years. Brad had helped her build it. He had supported her need to do something besides staying home with Cora. When Cora turned eight, she began to think seriously about the place. Now, it's been almost ten years and it's a big part of her life—her livelihood and her passion. She'll leave the decorations up until the second week of January. Cora will help her take everything down the following weekend. She's good at organizing, and Lily is thankful for her help.

A knock at the door startles her, and she sits straight up to see who it is. Cora is knocking on the door and yelling through the glass.

"It's me, Mom! Open up!"

Lily walks toward the door and unlocks it. "You nearly gave me a heart attack," she says, pounding her chest where her heart is. "Oh my gosh!"

"What are you doing sitting here in the dark?"

"Resting," Lily says, "and thinking."

"Well, think no more. Dad wants to take us both out for Christmas Eve dinner. He made reservations at Harry's, so you only have to walk about sixty steps to have dinner with us. We already parked. He's getting the table."

"What? I'm tired. Plus, I'm not really dressed for it."

"I think you have a store full of solutions to that problem. Besides, you need a good meal, it's Christmas Eve, and it's a chance for us to all be together. It's been a while, in case you don't remember. I don't think you're going to say no to me, right?"

Lily looks at her daughter and squeezes her face with two hands. "Are you sure he wants me to come? This was supposed to be your father-daughter time together."

"He asked me to invite you. He was worried you'd say 'no' if he asked."

"It's an unusual request at this point in our relationship," Lily says, placing her hands on her hips.

"Not really, Mom. It's the holidays, you're my parents, and no one should be alone."

Lily looks at her smart, kind daughter and smiles. "Give me a minute, and I'll be over."

*

The restaurant is beautifully decorated for the season, and the smell of food wafting in from the kitchen makes Lily realize how hungry she is at the moment. She is escorted to the table, where Brad stands and pulls out her chair. Lily takes note of his good manners and sits down. The gesture feels awkward and comfortable at the same time.

"That's one of my favorite dresses in the store," Cora says. "It looks so good on you."

"It does," Brad says, looking Lily in the eyes.

Lily smiles and doesn't know quite how to handle the compliment.

"Thank you both. And thank you for inviting me to your dinner."

"We're glad you came," Brad says, cheerfully. If Lily weren't so tired, she might have said he was trying too hard.

The server comes over and describes the specials on the menu. Once they make their decisions, Brad orders a bottle of wine for the table.

"Are you going to let me have some? It is Christmas," Cora says, looking from parent to parent.

"Christmas Eve," Lily says, correcting her. "But maybe a sip or two," Lily says, looking to see if she and Brad are in agreement. Brad nods. Lily loves how Cora desperately wants to move from being a teenager to being a grownup, even though she has repeatedly said that wine tastes "yucky."

The bread arrives at the table, and Cora dives in first. Brad attempts to make conversation.

"So, how's the store doing?" he asks Lily.

"Good. It's been a solid quarter. Everything is going well. This past week has been particularly good. How's your job?"

"It's all good. I've gotten a lot of new clients lately. People want to design their own homes—or redesign them like we did—so I suppose that's a good thing."

"I'd say so." Lily can feel her eyes linger on him for a second too long.

Music plays lightly in the restaurant and Lily takes note of it. Bing Crosby sings a Christmas song, and then the music transitions to Louis Armstrong's version of *La Vie En Rose*. Lily shifts in her seat, fidgeting a little; her face feels flush. She's been anticipating Brad making some sort of comment about the book—about why in the world she would have given him a gift—and a sentimental one at that. She keeps looking down at her plate, smearing a little butter on her bread.

"Cora, did you know that one thing your mother and I never had the opportunity to do while we were married was to go to Paris? It's your mother's favorite city. She went for a long weekend years ago with friends from college, and I couldn't go with her. I promised her I'd take her one day, and we never made it a priority."

Lily looks up from buttering the bread. Cora looks from one parent to the other.

"I didn't know that. When did you go to Paris?"

Lily adjusts herself in her seat. "It was such a long time ago. It was spur of the moment, and I went with a friend of mine who had studied abroad in France the year before. We hopped on a plane and went during fall break. Your father was playing football in college, and there was no way he could get away to go with us. I spontaneously went with my friend and her boyfriend. More fun for them than me, I would say. But I fell in love with the city and always wanted to go back."

"I've never seen any photos from the trip," Cora says.

"That's because I don't have any. I left my camera in the cab on the way to the airport to come home and all the photos I took vanished along with it."

"She doesn't need the photos. All her memories are up here," Brad says, pointing to his temple. "I really would like to go sometime. To see the architecture and walk the streets."

Cora pipes in, dismissing her dad's comment and feeling bad for her mom. "Well, I'll go to Paris with you anytime you want, Mom. Anytime." But Lily heard his comment.

"Thanks, Cora. Maybe we will one day."

"I hear the shopping is amazing," Cora says.

"It's all amazing," she says. "It's certainly a special place."

Brad looks at her from across the table, and no words need to be spoken. This is his way of recognizing the gift, Lily thinks. This is his way of letting her know he got it.

Lily is aware that they will always have a connection, a history, though hers would always be much deeper than his, she is certain. She didn't leave him. That should speak volumes. She remembers something her mother said to her once when she was a teenager, before she met Brad: "Make sure the person you fall in love with loves you more." Lily never quite understood what that meant, but now she understands it completely.

All this time, she's loved him more.

*

As they walk out of the restaurant into the night air, Cora receives a call from a friend, and asks if she can answer it. Lily and Brad tell her she can, and they are left together on the sidewalk outside the restaurant, as Cora takes several steps away from them to talk on the phone.

"I'm glad to see you are doing well despite—" Lily begins.

Brad puts up his hand to stop her from talking. "It's over and done with now. And honestly, I can't say that I'm upset about the wedding not taking place, about Cora's reaction, and about her saying how she felt. I think it's a blessing. I'm seeing things more clearly than I have in years," he says. "I needed the time to think and be alone." There's a pause, and then Brad continues, saying, "It's Christmas Eve. How many Christmas Eves have you and I spent together?"

"A lot," Lily says.

"Yeah, a lot. And because of that, I want to tell you—I need to tell you—I'm sorry for being a complete shit of a husband. I wish I never let you down."

Lily sees the regret in his face and nods, just listening to him talk.

"And I know the gift left on the front porch is from you. I can tell by the handwriting on the gift tag. I haven't opened it yet, but I will tomorrow before I head to my brother's house."

"You haven't opened it yet?"

"No," Brad says. "It said not to open it until Christmas Day. I'm abiding by that command."

Lily mentally rewinds all of what happened inside the restaurant in her mind. If he's being honest, he doesn't know it's a book about Paris, and yet he mentioned their trip that never happened to Cora and about her love for Paris. They talked about the very subject at the table, and yet Brad hasn't opened the book?

Lily's head begins to reel as Cora finishes her call, walks over to them, and casually says, "Did I miss anything?"

Reid

Christmas Morning

Reid puts the key into Eva's front door. He hears the pitter-patter of doggie feet running on the hardwoods as he turns the knob. Brownie is excited to see him, and he grabs the leash and places it on the dog's collar. Eva had asked him if he could let Brownie out before he leaves for Emme's house for Christmas dinner, because Eva had to leave very early in the morning to be with her family on the Eastern Shore at her sister's house. He decides to do one better and takes Brownie for a walk around the neighborhood streets as he sees her do every day.

Eva had to drive over the bridge and navigate the highway, as it takes about an hour from here. She didn't mention that she was nervous or anything about the trip. He heard her car start at about seven o'clock in the morning, and then she was gone. She had let Brownie out, and now it was nearing noon, and Reid needs to get on the road himself soon. Christmas dinner is at two o'clock.

As he walks through the streets of Eastport on Christmas morning, he takes a deep breath and feels a sort of contentment that he hasn't felt in a while. He's also interested in meeting with Dimitri again. After talking to him for a while at the bookstore, and after hearing Meg's suggestion that they play together, they made plans to meet at Dimitri's house after Christmas to jam a little and see how that goes. After listening to him play, Reid was intrigued. He's been going it alone for months—years—by himself. He wonders what it would be like to play along with someone. Maybe it would up his game.

When he returns to Eva's, he lets Brownie inside, walks over to the dog's food and water bowl to make sure it's sufficiently filled, and notices Eva's white kitchen is spotless, albeit for some books stacked on the kitchen table. Curious as to what she is reading, Reid walks closer to the pile, feeling a little like a snoop, to take a look. Hanging from the pages of one of the books is a letter that looks similar to the one he received. As he leans in for a closer glance, he can see the familiar stationery, the handwriting, and the beginning of the letter that says, "Dear Reader." It takes everything in his power not to pull the letter from the book and read it in its entirety. It takes all the self-control he has to step away.

This new observation has piqued his curiosity. The fact is that Eva got a letter in her book, too. The question is, when? Why? And what, exactly, does her letter say?

He considers reading the letter, and then thinks better of it. Being willing to change means attempting to make all the right decisions and ethical choices in these types of circumstances, so Reid leaves the letter exactly as it is, untouched, and walks out the door, back to his cottage. Another battle won, albeit a small one. He is adding them up, one by one.

*

Reid grabs his bag of gifts from the car. For the entire hour drive to Towson, he's been thinking about this bookstore owner and her letter writing. He wonders what drives her to write these letters.

He wonders how she has so much time to do it. He wonders how many people get letters each day. He knows there are answers to these questions, but he is uncertain as to whether he will ever know the answers.

Unless he writes back.

That is a possibility.

There's that mailbox he saw in the back of the store for correspondence. He knows it's there. And he knows that may be the first action step he needs to take if he wants to learn more. He's not sure.

As he turns onto his sister's street, his thoughts drift to his sister, and he realizes that he's most excited to see her, and wonders if the results of the second breast scan have come back. Emme had said she would call as soon as she knew something.

As he walks up the slate walkway to her Towson home, she opens the door before he can ring the doorbell. She is holding a glass of Champagne for him to take.

"Coca-Cola would be better," he says to her with a wink.

"Right," she says back, smiling. "We're toasting because I'm fine," she says. "Bad scan."

Reid's eyes grow wide, and he realizes he just received the best Christmas gift he could get—that his sister will be fine. His mother and father, who had been standing in the foyer, open the door wider and step outside onto the front porch to join them, and it's the first time in a long time that his immediate family is together, sharing a tender family moment to celebrate his sister's good health. They spontaneously embrace in a group hug, his sister shedding a few tears of happiness, along with his mother.

Reid thinks about the letter he found inside his book, and begins to make sense of things that felt fuzzy before. It may have taken a while, but Reid senses that his sister's scare helps them all realize what is truly important in life, and it's not about how many mistakes someone makes, or how long it takes to get one's life together. It's not about holding on to past resentments. It's not about wishing someone could be something they're not. And it's not about holding on to guilt or shame.

What it's about, Reid thinks, is about loving each other, despite all those things.

Dimitri

Thursday, December 27

At Dimitri's urging, his brothers and sister and their families had agreed to come for the holidays for a couple of nights. Spending Christmas with his whole family ended up being the best thing for all of them. Plus, Dimitri was able to see the joy on his father's face as he spent time with his grandchildren, and Dimitri reconnected with his brothers and his sister.

Dimitri relished seeing his nieces and nephews, and his dad spoiled them all with gifts. Earlier, Baba had demonstrated his pancake-making skills to his grandchildren, and they cheered him on when he flipped the pancakes in the air. His sister captured it all on video and posted it to her social media pages. Everyone was laughing as the kids chanted, "Baba, Baba, Baba," as he let the pancakes fly in the kitchen. Dimitri noticed how much Baba's face lit up when the kids were around. He looked so much younger. At night, when the kids were tucked in, the adults played cards and shared some laughs. Throughout the holidays, Dimitri let go of things that had been dragging him down.

He believes he is making progress.

When he hugs his brother Eric and family goodbye at the airport two days later, he feels a pang of happiness mixed with a little sadness at having to say goodbye. It's been a great Christmas, and he's sad to see it's over for now.

Of course, Dimitri won't deny that the letter he received has had an effect on him. He had been on a path to mental self-destruction and misery for a while, hating his ex, hating his job, resenting his siblings, and resenting people he deemed as happy. Getting a letter of encouragement from a relative stranger was just what he needed. There was something about the words that were so carefully chosen and thoughtful. Then, when Meg asked him if he would play the piano in her bookstore, something began to come alive in him. At first, he was upset about losing his job, but now he has embraced the notion as a chance to rethink things, to allow himself some time to figure things out a bit. Life is short, and way too short to be miserable most of your waking existence.

He straightens up the place when he gets home, making sure it's tidy from all the company he's had. Some of his siblings stayed with him and others stayed with Baba. He takes the trash out and wipes down the counters.

When the doorbell rings promptly at eight, Dimitri jogs toward the door and opens it. While he doesn't have a lot of Christmas decorations up, he did hang a wreath on the front door and put up the old, sentimental ceramic lighted Christmas tree his mother had made years ago on the table in the dining room. He also put some lights across his fireplace mantle. But that was about it.

"Hey, man," Dimitri says to Reid, opening the door and feeling the cold. "Good you could come."

"Yeah, I'm looking forward to it," Reid says, his guitar across his shoulder. "Nice house you've got here."

"Thanks," Dimitri says. "I think I pissed my neighbors off by not hanging any lights outside. And the inside needs redecorating. It reeks of my ex-wife's taste."

Reid chuckles. "I know someone who could help you with that. Eva—the woman you met the other day at the bookstore—has really great taste. I'm renting the cottage on her property in Eastport."

"Oh, cool. I didn't know that. I thought you two were a couple."

"No. We just met a couple of weeks ago. She's nice, though."

"Well, I just may give her a call. This place is in desperate need of some pink detoxing. Would you like a beer?"

Reid replies honestly, "Actually, I'd prefer water or a soda."

"No problem," Dimitri says. He pours both of them Cokes with lots of ice, and they head toward the piano. "I've been trying to lay off the booze myself."

"Nice piano," Reid says, tickling the ivories. It's a black baby grand, and it takes up a third of the living room.

"Thanks. Yeah, I bought it when we moved in. It's probably the only thing in here that really feels like mine. Well, that and the TV. The ex didn't play, so it's all me."

Reid removes his guitar from the case and sits in the chair beside the piano. "It was good of Meg to introduce us."

"So, now that we have the time, tell me about your playing," Dimitri says. "All the details."

"Well, I've been playing almost all my life. I feel like I've had a guitar in my hands ever since I can remember. My dad encouraged it at first, and then worried I'd try to make a living as a musician, which I kind of do now, to be honest. It helps with a little extra cash, and my day job is pretty taxing. I'm a contractor, and I work outside in all kinds of weather."

"Don't knock it. It's better than sitting at a desk punching numbers all day. The most un-sexy job in the world."

"I wouldn't say that," Reid says. "Money matters."

"So does happiness." Dimitri checks himself. Did those words actually just come out of his mouth?

"You are right about that, the trick is, how do we combine the thing we love doing with earning a meaningful income? It's the biggest challenge of all," Reid says.

"It is, and now that I'm unemployed, I'm trying to figure out what that next thing is for me. I'm taking it day by day." He knows Reid's right, and he senses under all that self-deprecation, Reid's a pretty good guy. He's a few years younger than Dimitri, but he seems to have a good head on his shoulders. He's excited to see what happens when they play together.

"Alright, well, why don't we give it a whirl and see what this sounds like?" Dimitri says.

They start off by playing a couple of easy Beatles tunes, just instrumentals first. Then, as they begin to gel, they take a crack at *Eleanor Rigby*, and Reid begins to sing. Dimitri hears Reid's voice and then it hits him. He remembers seeing him perform at the tavern on the night of Midnight Madness. It's a good voice, Dimitri thinks. It's got great quality and his pitch is perfect. It's got excellent range, and the tone is versatile, perhaps with the ability to perform various genres of songs.

"*Ah, look at all the lonely people,*" Reid sings. Dimitri loves the way the piano and guitar sound together on this tune. It almost gives him chills. Reid knows the lyrics by heart. They play the song all the way through, with Reid singing the lead part. When the song is over, Dimitri looks at Reid and asks, "Can we give it another try? I would like to try harmonizing with you."

"You can sing?" Reid asks, his eyes wide.

"In middle school, I accompanied the chorus and sang along. I don't have a voice like yours, but I may be able to give it a try," Dimitri says, not sure where the courage or confidence to try this is coming from, exactly. He hasn't sung in front of anyone in, well, years.

They play the song again. Dimitri harmonizes. He has a few little slip ups as he works at finding his own tone and range to match Reid's notes, but it sounds decent for a first attempt. The two like the way it sounds—they like the way they sound together. They even grab their phones and record a couple of songs, just to hear the harmony, then analyze what needs some work. As they continue trying different songs, from John Mayer to Prince to attempting a Kenny Chesney song, they muddle through, see where they can improve, and enjoy jamming. By the time they look at the clock, it's midnight.

"Wow," Dimitri says, as they call it a night. "That was a hell of a lot of fun."

"It was," Reid says. "So maybe we should think about taking the show on the road?"

"Really?" Dimitri says.

"Well, I don't literally mean on the road, but let's see if we can work toward playing in town and see what happens. I mean, what have we got to lose? I've been solo for a while. It will be fun to do it with someone else. A new challenge."

Dimitri looks around the room at all the shit that used to be his ex's, the things she no longer wanted. It reminds him of all that he did for her, and how little he's done for himself. His dad may think this opportunity is pretty cool, as well. Baba always loves to listen when he plays.

"Sure. Why not?" Dimitri says, and they shake on it.

Meg
Friday, January 11

Meg arrives at the bookstore two hours before the store is to open at nine o'clock. She has some work to do, and she wants to take a look at the letters that have come into the mailbox in the back of the store. She doesn't often get a lot of responses, so there's no need to check the box every day. But twice a week, on Tuesdays and Fridays, she collects any letters that have been dropped off, and responds to any that require it. Occasionally, she sees someone head toward the mailbox. But there are times when Clarke is managing the store, and Meg has no way of knowing who is dropping off letters. It's her pet project, and no other employees are involved in it.

As a psychology major in college, Meg always knew she wanted to help people in any way that she could. She was an active member of the psychology club, and she went on to earn a master's in Social Work. She worked in social services for a few years, but as a full-blown empath who experiences deep feelings and a high sensitivity to others, she took way too much to heart, and while she knew she was providing support and counseling for others, it often left her feeling drained and exhausted. While still feeling the need to be connected to people, she wanted to do something different after Brodie's death. Uncle Ben had offered her the opportunity to live in Annapolis—something that she had told him she wanted to do for years, because of her love of the water and the way of life—and she decided to move to Annapolis permanently.

Her mother's good friend, Mrs. Marshall, had owned a bookstore in their hometown when Meg was in high school. When Meg closes her eyes, she can still smell the mustiness of the store, see the red and white striped awning that had hung over the door, and remembers the dimness of that old-fashioned bookstore. Meg loved perusing the aisles of books and could often be found in the shop doing homework after school. One day, Mrs. Marshall approached Meg and asked her if she wanted to work two days a week in the store during the school year, and so Meg did. It was her love of stories and people, along with her psychology degree, her relationship with Brodie, and the letter from Mr. Anderson, that prompted her to follow her own dream. And while she initially felt awkward taking the money that was meant for Brodie, Uncle Ben impressed upon her that he wanted her to do with it what her heart intended. Meg spoke with her parents about the decision to move to Annapolis, and they supported her choice. They understood how much she had loved her summers in Maryland, and her need to feel connected to a community.

With her purse filled with ten new letters, Meg opens the door to the bookstore. It's a little after seven. She turns on the lights and powers up the computer. She tucks her purse and the letters behind the counter, and takes a quick spin around the store, straightening up anything that looks unkempt. A large delivery of books from various publishers is scheduled to arrive around eight o'clock, and she's thankful she'll have lots of help this afternoon to unpack and get the merchandise out on the floor. Her storeroom isn't too large, so she has to be careful about just how much inventory she keeps.

Finished with her morning roundup, Meg goes to the backside of the mailbox from the storeroom and opens the door to see what's in there.

Three letters.

She opens the first letter and reads it.

Dear Brodie,

Thanks for the support and the letter. It gave me just the courage I needed to leave my abusive husband. I am living with my sister now, and am feeling much better. I've started divorce proceedings, and you will no longer see me with bruises on my face. Not ever again. Many thanks, Tia

The second one reads:

Dear Brodie,

Thanks for the letter inside my book. I'm starting to muster up the courage to do something brave. I'll let you know when it happens.

—Lila

The third, and last one, reads:

Dear Brodie,

I'm not sure how intentional the plan was for me to find the letter inside my book, but I want to believe it was intended for me. My letter was placed inside the front cover of a book about Paris that my ex-wife gave me for Christmas. Recounting how I came to receive a gift from my ex-wife makes me feel ashamed, but I have to begin here. I left my wife a few years ago. This past November, I was going to marry someone else, but my 17-year-old daughter, who was a bridesmaid at the wedding, ran out of the service before it happened, and I left my bride at the altar. My daughter was not happy with my future bride, and after some soul searching, I realized that I wasn't either.

My daughter saved me from making another mistake. The thing is,

I feel awful about that situation, but I feel even worse about something else. I had personally invited my ex-wife to the wedding and asked her to come for our daughter's sake. I hurt her pretty badly, and she said she didn't want to come, but then found the courage and came anyway. I have to give her credit for agreeing to attend. I know it was difficult for her. When I saw her that day, standing on the other side of the room, looking as beautiful as she did when we fell in love in high school, I realized how much crap I've put her through, and even more than that, I realized that I still love her. But now, everything is a mess. She bought me that book about Paris because I had promised to take her there (well, we actually promised each other to take that trip), and we never did.

Anyway, when I received the letter inside the book, there was something about reading the words on the page that helped me see everything more clearly. Did she ask you to put the letter in the book, or was it your choice to do so? Did she share any information with you that led you to put the letter in the book? Or is it a totally random act? I'm curious, and I'm wondering if she knows about the letter at all. As you can imagine, if I have any chance at repairing a damaged relationship and broken trust and letting her know how I feel, I might need to know more about how the letter found its way to me. It has helped me to see what I've done and given me hope that perhaps I have time to repair what's been broken. I have no idea, really, but it may be worth a try.

If you could let me know whether she knows or not about the letter, that would be most helpful. Thank you for helping me see what's important, and I look forward to hearing from you soon.

Signed,

Brad Webster

555 Avenue on the Point

Annapolis, MD

Meg remembers the woman. She remembers the story of Paris. And now, he's gotten the book as a gift and read the letter. He received a letter about fixing things that are broken. She is excited that maybe, just maybe, these two will find their way back to each other. Forgiveness and love. Love and forgiveness. And a daughter who recognizes something that maybe neither of them do, Meg thinks.

Each day during her writing process, Meg crafts letters that cover topics such as being resilient, knowing you are not alone, forgiving yourself and others, and setting things right. So, on any given day, she writes ten letters. So far, her methodology has worked out.

And she always responds when someone asks or reaches out. This letter from Brad Webster deserves a response.

She walks over to the counter and puts the letter in her purse. Could it be possible that Brad Webster and his ex-wife could find their way back to each other?

Meg's always been a sucker for happy endings.

*

At two o'clock, the door to the bookstore opens, and Meg is delighted to see Mr. Vassos walk toward her. She smiles at him as she finishes up with a customer, and he waves to her, then begins looking around. He's by himself, and she wonders if Dimitri is with him.

She walks over to the stacks where Mr. Vassos is reading the back of a book.

"Good to see you today, Mr. Vassos," she says.

"I think we can dispense of the Mr. Vassos stuff, Meg," he says. "You can just call me Nicholas."

"Okay, Nicholas. I think I can do that. Is Dimitri with you?"

"No. You'll be pleased to know that I'm healed enough to drive myself now. Got the doctor's blessing this morning."

"Wonderful," she says. She knows she will be seeing Dimitri

later tonight. He's scheduled to play from six until eight when she closes.

"Are you looking for something in particular?"

"Nope. I just like being here," he says. "But something will catch my eye, I'm sure."

"Well, have a coffee or tea on me upstairs, will you?"

"I will," he says. "And good of you to introduce Dimitri to the fella Reid. They've been playing together, practicing."

"They have?" Meg's eyes grow wide.

"Yup. It looks like they have their first performance in a few weeks, at least that's what Dimi said."

Meg clasps her hands together. "You just made my day, Mr. Vassos—Nicholas," she says. Knowing that she had a little hand in getting those two guys together fills her with joy. She remembers Dimitri's face the night of Midnight Madness—how he looked so despondent and downtrodden. She remembers the look in his eyes as she rang up his purchases. And she knows he got a letter. He seems to have come a long way since then.

"Has he found a new day job yet?" she asks.

"Not yet," Nicholas says. "And if you ask me, I'm happy about that. He needs some time to figure life out. He isn't getting any younger, and he needs to have some happiness, he's been miserable for so long. That ex-wife of his left him reeling."

Meg doesn't know the whole story but hates hearing this. She is hopeful that something will change for him for the better. She likes Dimitri. He's nice, kind, prompt, plays the perfect kind of music for her store, and seems like a pretty amenable guy. She's glad she hired him to play, although she doesn't have enough money to pay him well, and the feedback has been terrific. He doesn't seem to mind the pay—it's what she can afford. In fact, Dimitri told her he would play whether he got paid or not, because it gave him the opportunity to do something he loved. She admires him for that.

"This one looks good," Nicholas says, holding up a World War II two-part series.

"You'll like that one. A lot of the midshipmen who come in here say it's their favorite."

"Done and done," Nicholas says, as she takes the books to the counter for him and shoos him upstairs to have that coffee on her.

*

Dimitri walks through the door at five thirty, a little earlier than usual, and says hello to everyone. Meg sees him and waves. She's busy helping a customer. In fact, the store is unusually busy for a Friday in January, not that she's complaining. She's helping so many people because Clarke has the flu. The day is flying by, and she never gets to formally say hello to Dimitri until she hears him play.

He starts off with a classical piece by Debussy, one that she knows well. Music has always had an incredibly calming effect on her, and she believes it has added to the atmosphere in the store. She may even go so far as to say that it's drawing people in to shop. She always leaves the window upstairs slightly cracked a little so that the music can flow out into the streets.

At seven fifty-five, Meg closes the door to the shop, as it's time to wrap up. She's starving and is desperate to go home and get something to eat.

Dimitri wraps up at eight, and Meg rings up the last few customers. Jordan closes up the coffee bar, and Meg hears Dimitri coming down the stairs, his leather briefcase slung across his shoulder. He looks happy and content. A little smile moves across his lips as he sees

Meg. She smiles back.

"I saw your father today," she calls to him across the store, as he makes his way closer to her.

"What? He drove himself here?"

"He did. He said he got the doctor's clearance to drive." Meg powers down the computer and slips into her coat.

"He told me it looked like it was happening, but I didn't talk to him today. Where are you headed?" Dimitri asks, as she grabs her purse.

"I'm starving and my feet are tired. I need to go home to eat and sit down for a bit," Meg says.

"How about if we eat together? I haven't eaten either."

Meg feels something shift inside her when he asks her this question. By her own doing, she has sworn to herself that she would never allow herself to get close to another man after Will, someone she was with for over two years. Ever since, she's held true to that promise. When she gets something in her mind, she's stubborn, and ever since Will, she's learned how to keep intimate relationships at a distance.

"Just a quick bite," she says. "How about the Irish Pub?"

She promises herself to keep to small talk. She hopes he doesn't ask her about the letter she slid inside his book. Anything but having to talk about why she does what she does. She never expected to get this close to a recipient of a letter. Usually, it's all done from afar. But this one—and a couple of the others—sort of happened by chance. So far, the letters have allowed her to be a behind-the-scenes type of gal, or a pen pal.

"Sounds good to me," Dimitri says, holding the door open for her as they walk out into the night air.

As they cut through the alley to State Circle and walk toward Maryland Avenue, Meg sees a blonde woman coming out of the clothing boutique. She pauses outside to put the key in the door and lock it up. This is the boutique Eva had told her about, the one where she bought that gorgeous coat. And then she realizes something else, as she begins to mentally put the puzzle together.

That's her, she thinks to herself, remembering. That's the woman who bought the Paris book.

And now, feeling utterly satisfied, she has all the information she needs to respond to the letter from Brad, the ex-husband who received the letter.

Eva

Eva stretches as she wakes, and Brownie, who is curled up at the bottom edge of the bed, raises her head to look at Eva.

"Morning Brownie," she says, and the dog gets up and wags her tail, moving closer to Eva. She pets her head and Brownie snuggles in closer.

She reaches for her cellphone, and sees she's missed a phone call. As she scrolls, she also notices a text message that's come in.

Hi, Eva. Reid gave me your number and said I could call. Not sure if he mentioned that I could use a little help redecorating my home. He said you have a good eye. Willing to pay you to help me. Perhaps a little side gig? Let me know if you're willing. I stink at this. Dimitri

Eva laughs. She knows Reid and Dimitri have been spending a lot of time together lately, practicing in the evenings and figuring out song playlists. Reid also mentioned that next Saturday night they have their first paid gig at the tavern where he normally plays. Because of Reid's long-standing relationship with them, the tavern even adjusted the payment for a duo, and Reid felt proud that he got it done. According to Reid, Dimitri bought a pretty elaborate portable keyboard and amp that he will be able to take with him on the road.

Despite only knowing Reid for a month and a half, Eva's gotten to know him pretty quickly. In their spare time, they sometimes hang out, either in Reid's cottage or her family room. When they're really bored, they play cards. He's also great about walking Brownie when she has a late night at work and can't get away to let her out. All she has to do is send a quick text to Reid, who leaves very early in the morning and is home around four in the afternoon on most working days. He is always willing to help her. In a very short time, she's become accustomed to having him around. He's also super handy when something goes wrong with the house, like last weekend when her kitchen sink pipe was dripping inside the cabinet. In a matter of moments, the thing was fixed.

Eva has to respond to Dimitri but decides to call him instead. Sometimes she's just too damn lazy to punch the touchscreen and invariably makes a lot of typos. She misses her old Blackberry with actual keyboard buttons.

"Good morning," he says, when he picks up the phone.

"Good morning. I hear you may need some help decorating."

"Yes," Dimitri says. "I know we only met that one time, so feel free to say if this is really awkward, but would you be willing to help a man with absolutely no decorating skills? I'm just so sick and tired of being reminded of my ex-wife every waking hour."

"I can relate, and I'm happy to help," Eva says, chuckling. "I was thinking I might need to see your space first, and then we can figure out a strategy."

"Sounds good."

He gives Eva his address, and they plan to meet at eleven. She's got nothing else to do today. Why not? Sounds like fun. And she actually likes figuring things out, playing with design and colors. It's a lot like crafting a visual PR campaign. And while she has absolutely zero training in it, her mother always said she had a good eye for design.

After she lets the dog out, eats, and has her morning coffee, she showers and dresses for the day. She puts on a little makeup and grabs her coat. Tomorrow's the Super Bowl, and she was asked by some of her co-workers to come over to watch the game. She's not entirely up for that, because she spends so much time with them, including attending happy hours and birthday celebrations, but she told them she would play it by ear. Working in the fields of public relations and advertising, she enjoys watching the Super Bowl commercials more than the game itself, especially when her team's not in it.

"Where are off to?" Reid calls to her, as she walks toward her car and he's about to get into his.

"Well, thanks to you, I'm going to Dimitri's to help with a redecorating task you set me up with."

Reid looks at her, and for a moment, he doesn't seem to know what to say. "You're not upset that I told him he could call you, right?"

"Not at all. It should be fun."

"So, what are you two going to do today?" Reid asks.

"I just want to see his place and see the space and its current state. You realize I have no expertise in this whatsoever, so I hope your friend isn't disappointed."

"Nah, he won't be. Wait until you see it. It's so pink."

"What? You're kidding!"

"Nope. His ex-wife apparently loved all pink things." Reid is laughing, but Eva can tell he's completely repulsed by the decor.

"Well, okay. I'll see what I can do."

"When will you be back?" Reid asks, leaning in toward her.

"I'm not sure," Eva says. "Why?"

"Just wondering, that's all," he says.

"Are you going somewhere?" Eva adjusts the cashmere scarf

around her neck.

"I have to run out and spend about an hour on one of my client's jobs. I have to install some things that weren't delivered yesterday, and the client called and said they arrived on his front step."

"Okay, well, good luck with that. I'll see you later, then?"

"Yup. Sounds good," Reid says, with a wave.

Eva walks toward her car and clicks the remote to unlock it. She can feel Reid is still watching her as she opens the driver's side door.

"Hey, Eva?"

"Yes," she says, turning toward him.

"Got any plans for the Super Bowl?"

*

"Well, Reid was right. There is a lot of pink going on in here," Eva says, as she places her purse on the chair and takes a look around. Dimitri takes her coat and drapes it across the back of the chair.

"I know. I can't believe I've let it stay for this long. I think I just get more pissed seeing it, you know?"

"I would get pissed looking at it whether there was a broken relationship or not." She walks over to the living room where the baby grand sits. "Is this where you guys practice?" Eva asks.

"Yes. Among all the pink."

"Okay. We definitely need to do something about all this, pronto."

Eva surveys the space and talks with Dimitri about what he likes, doesn't like. She removes her notepad from her purse and takes notes so that she remembers. The house is pretty big, and Eva surmises that Dimitri must have made a good living as an accountant.

"So, any news on the job front?" she asks him.

"Not really. I have a couple of interviews, and truthfully, it's not that I can't find a job. Good accountants are in need everywhere. It's just that I'm not entirely sure that's what I want to do for the foreseeable future. I'm exploring another idea, but I can't tell you about it just yet."

"Will it require more decorating?" she teases.

"Actually, it might," he says, raising his eyebrows. Eva's intrigued.

As she looks around and takes a peek at the other spaces, including the dining room, kitchen, and family room, she knows she could transform this place into a space that is warm and cozy and not frilly with a minimalist feel. She takes note of Dimitri's bookcase in the family room and sees that half the shelves are empty.

"Do you have any memorabilia or collectibles that we could fill these shelves with? Maybe even stuff from college?"

"Down in the basement, I have boxes of stuff. I've loved baseball my whole life and have a collection of cards and baseballs—signed ones, too. I also have a ton of albums—like real LPs. My ex-wife wouldn't let me put out any of my stuff. We can certainly go through those boxes to see if anything would work for you."

"No, you mean work for you! It's your place. It should feel like your place. What are your favorite colors?"

"Good point," he says, laughing. "Blue, yellow, and green, but no pastel shades. No oranges or reds, either."

"Got it," she says.

They walk down the stairs to the basement, and Eva's eyes grow wide at just how many boxes Dimitri is talking about. There are so many. So, while his ex-wife decorated the house with the Pink Panther in mind, any representation of Dimitri was left stuck down here in boxes.

"Here's a box of my books. This one has my baseball stuff. This one has all my music memorabilia."

Eva knows this task is going to take hours to go through, so she gives Dimitri a job.

"Okay. Here's what I want you to do. I want you to pull out all your favorite things. It doesn't have to be today, but over the next couple of weeks, attack a box at a time, and see what you have that you love. Once you select all your favorites, I'll figure out how and where to display them. Sound like a plan?"

Dimitri agrees, and they go back upstairs where Dimitri brews them each a cup of coffee and they talk about their new project.

*

Later, after Eva returns from Dimitri's place, she puts on the kettle for a cup of tea. It's frigid today, and she can't seem to get warm. Even Brownie wants to spend as little time outside as possible, barking to come in after she relieves herself in the yard and plunking herself in front of the fireplace.

It's three o'clock, and Eva opens the book she's reading and stretches out on the sofa. The house feels quiet. It feels empty and quiet a lot. When Kyle was here, it was never quiet. He was always doing something, listening to music or one of his favorite podcasts. When she wanted to read back in those days, she would have to find a quiet spot in the house.

Now, the whole house is her quiet spot.

Startled by the knock on the door, Eva removes the lap blanket she had placed across her body, and gets up to go to the door.

Reid is standing on her front porch holding up two bags of

groceries. She opens the door.

"Super Bowl party for two tomorrow?" he asks, smiling a mischievous smile.

Lily
Sunday, February 3

The snow flurries begin to fall early, before the sun even starts to rise. Lily checks the weather on her phone; it's supposed to get to forty-six degrees by the afternoon. Cora is sound asleep, and Lily told her not to worry about working at the store today. Cora's friends are having a Super Bowl party, and Lily encouraged her to go and make her signature homemade pizzas to bring to the event. Cora loves to work in the kitchen; she's always cooking or baking up something new, often leaving the kitchen looking as if a tornado has blown through. She loves that her daughter has found a passion for it, and wonders if it will be a career she pursues after graduation. Cora's mentioned it a couple of times. Nevertheless, Lily wants her to go to the party and have fun with her friends.

As she flicks the back porch light on, she squints to see the snow falling. Lily brews her coffee, adds creamer and sugar to it, and sits at the table looking outside. Unfortunately, her body seems to wake up at six no matter what. She'd give anything to sleep in like she used to when she was with Brad. Sometimes, she'd wrap her legs around his, feel the warmth of his body, and place her head on his bare chest. In no time, she'd fall back to sleep. She loved listening to him breathe softly as he slept. It calmed her and made her feel whole. She misses those moments with him. Those intimate moments when it was just the two of them snuggled up in bed on a Saturday without a care in the word. That was so long ago.

Now, it is just Cora and her, and before long, it will be just Lily in the house once Cora goes to college in the fall. Lily's dreading the idea of her only daughter being gone, dreading the thought of her only child leaving the nest to find her own way in life. She can't help but wonder just how much damage she and Brad have done to her. Will she fall in love and marry, or has their divorce ruined all the magic that marriage can potentially offer? At least it felt magical to Lily for a while.

Lily scratches her head and tells herself that these are way too many questions to be having at this ridiculously early hour, but her brain is wired that way. She second-guesses everything. She specializes in analyzing nuances and words and actions. And sometimes, when she really wants to drive herself crazy, she analyzes what is NOT said. When the coffee is gone, she heads upstairs to take a shower and dress. She even decides that she may have to bundle up and walk it today; it wouldn't do her any harm to move the legs and buns and walk to work. She works so much these days, she finds it difficult to get a workout in among all her responsibilities.

Chilled from the walk, she opens the front door to the boutique and checks the heat. She decides to tackle her least favorite things to do—pay the bills and get her inventory in order. Lily's not the best at keeping track of things, and she hired a new service to help her with the computer that took the place of a register years and years ago.

At nine fifty-five, Lily opens the door early for her standard ten o'clock store opening time. She fiddles with a couple of the mannequins she has on the floor and straightens up the racks of purses and scarves. At precisely ten on the nose, she hears the doorbells chime, and she turns to see who her first customer of the day is. Lily recognizes her right away—she's the woman from the bookstore.

"Good morning," Lily calls to her across the floor.

"Oh, good morning!" Meg says. "Just the person I was hoping to see. A new friend of mine told me she bought her gorgeous coat here and sent me to have a look."

"Do you remember what it looks like?"

"Yes, I do. It's stunning. It's tailored, deep navy brocade with a fur collar and tie at the waist. Ring any bells?"

"I know the one. I don't think I have any left in blue, but I'll show you what I have," Lily says, and walks Meg over to where the coats are displayed.

"Oh my gosh, I love the camel shade and the dark fur!"

"It's really elegant," Lily says. "That color will look good with your coloring. Do you want to try it on?"

The woman nods and Lily notices how eager she is to slip into it. Lily watches her examine herself in the mirror once she gets herself zipped up and tied.

"Oh my. It's perfect on you. Just stunning. And the color brings out your eyes," Lily says.

"I like it, too," the woman says. "Do you remember me from the bookstore? I own Brodie's Books."

"Of course, I do," Lily says. "I'm Lily."

"I'm Meg."

"We talked about that book I was buying that night," Lily says, testing to see if she actually remembers.

"The one about Paris, right? Did you give it as a gift?"

"I did." Lily has to give her props. She did remember.

"Anything come of it?" Meg asks.

"Oh no. It was just a gift, nothing that would warrant anything happening because of it. So no, I'm still here in Annapolis and have yet to board a jet bound for Paris with any sort of Prince Charming."

"Prince Charming is highly overrated for independent, entrepreneurial women like us," Meg says, with a smile. She makes Lily laugh, which is a good sign.

"You may be right about that," Lily says.

"How long have you lived here—if, indeed, you do live and work here in Annapolis," Meg asks her.

"Oh, I've lived here my whole life. Grew up here. Met my ex-husband in high school and raised Cora, my daughter, here. I've owned my store for ten years now, and I've been divorced for two. I live near the Navy Stadium in a small Cape Cod. That pretty much sums up my existence. My daughter is off to college in the fall."

"You're far too young to have a daughter about to go to college," Meg says, surprised.

"Thank you, but it's true. She'll be gone, and it will be weird." Lily adjusts the collar on Meg's coat, as it wasn't completely straight. Meg turns to the side and glances in the mirror.

"You know, I've only lived in Annapolis for less than two years. I work so much, I rarely have time to socialize and make friends. This morning, I was moaning to myself about it. I know I need to connect with people more. Are there any groups you would recommend I join?"

"I'm in the same boat as you. I don't know of any women's groups per se, but I'm still friends with a few of my former neighbors, and we do a girls' night out once a month. Feel free to join us," Lily says, meaning it. "And I'm always available for dinner after we close our stores. You and I are probably on similar schedules."

"You know, that sounds great. In fact, I came in here at this hour because my colleague, Clarke, is covering the store for me right now. I know material things shouldn't make us so happy, but the idea of owning this coat is making me very happy."

"Who in the world said material things can't make us happy? Your books make me very happy. Besides, sometimes material things are the only happiness I can find in one day," Lily says, in a self-deprecating way.

Meg laughs. "I think you're speaking the truth," she says, a twinkle in her eye. She walks toward a tailored red dress that hangs on the rack next to the mannequin that is wearing it. "In that case, I might just need this red dress, too," she says, removing the dress from the rack and holding it by the neck of the hanger in front of herself, looking at it in the mirror. "I just remembered that next Saturday night, I'm going to see a new friend of mine play at the tavern on Main Street in a new duo he's in, if you'd like to join me."

Lily is happy to be invited somewhere. She loves live music. It only takes her seconds to respond.

"Count me in," she says.

*

At the end of the workday, and after reading a text message from Cora saying she was off to be with her friends for the night, Lily takes the walk home. She is tired, it's chilly, and her feet hurt, but she makes the walk anyway, tucking her large bag over her shoulder, the snow flurries long gone. The sun is lowering in the sky, peeking through the clouds. All day long, she kept thinking about Meg—the woman who bought the coat and the red dress who owns the bookstore. She seems like a genuine and caring person. Lily wonders if people perceive her the same way she perceives Meg—as exuding a sense of warmth when her customers walk into her store. She needs to reflect on that.

As she makes the left onto her street, she sees a familiar car parked in front of her house. She stops for a second to see what is going on. Lily is several houses away from her own house. Not wanting to be seen, she steps behind a pine tree, like a kid playing hide-and-seek. She watches him walk from her front door back to the car. He starts the car and drives away in the opposite direction.

She walks quickly toward her house, her curiosity piqued. When she hits the front walkway, she notices an envelope wedged into her front door. She bounds up the steps and retrieves it, her name written on the envelope in familiar script, takes off one of her gloves, and opens it. Inside are two tickets to see a film at the Young French Cinema next Sunday evening in Baltimore, with a note inside that reads, *A belated Christmas gift. Take yourself to Paris next week— and bring Cora. XO, B*

Lily stands motionless and befuddled on the steps, feeling anything but cold.

Reid

Saturday, February 9

Reid catches himself whistling the song he and Dimitri will play tonight as they make their debut together as a duo. He's impressed with Dimitri's ability not only to play by ear, but also to improvise. He reminds him of a 1940s jazz musician, someone who can feel the music and just go with it. Improvisation is clearly Dimitri's thing, and Reid has to admit, Dimitri challenges his musicianship in ways that it hasn't been challenged before. He is really enjoying jamming with him and putting their own spin on contemporary songs. They're starting to find their own sound.

Additionally, his newly acquired good mood causes Reid to acknowledge a couple of things about himself: first, he catches himself whistling happy tunes, something that's been lacking for many, many years, and second, he admits to being a bit jealous of the time Dimitri and Eva have been spending together planning the décor for Dimitri's house. It surprises him to feel this way.

When he brought the bags of food over for the Super Bowl and asked Eva to watch the game together, he realized he just liked being around her. Eva's five years older than he is. She's mature and put together. He admires the wisdom she often shares with him. Since college, she's been working in an industry that's fast paced and changes constantly, and she's had to adapt to that change. She was also in a steady relationship that lasted ten years—and she wasn't the one to opt out. Her boyfriend was. From the stories she's told Reid, she seems to be someone who is loyal and kind, loving and dedicated, all qualities to admire in a person. At the same time, she seems fragile and vulnerable, much like he is, and he's skeptical at the thought of putting himself out there at the moment; neither of them seems to be at the right juncture in their lives to become involved. They both have so much baggage. Plus, if they were not compatible, it would make for awkward living arrangements, seeing as how Reid lives on the grounds of her property. If anything went awry, it could affect their good landlord-tenant relationship and lead to the end of their companionship.

Despite rationalizing all of this, he genuinely enjoys hanging out with her, and finds himself becoming creative about ways to spend time with her.

"Did you always want to own this house?" he asked her, as they watched the game.

"Always. I've loved this house since I was a teenager. Of course, it looks a lot different than it did in those days."

"The updates are great. It feels like you," Reid had said.

"What, exactly, does that mean?" she asked, with a smile.

He was forced to reply and did so honestly. "It's just really pretty."

Stunned by his words, she looked down at her wine, and replied softly, "Thank you."

He knew he caught her off guard, so he quickly switched the subject, not wanting to make her feel uncomfortable or as if he might make a move on her.

"One of the biggest disappointments in my life was not being able to buy my parents' house last fall. I don't have the money for it. And so, it went to someone else."

"You'll have to show me the house sometime, so I can see where you grew up," she said.

There was something in the way she said those words, a glint of hope that she might actually care about him a little, a hint to let him know they might be on the same page. Tread lightly, he thought to himself. Take your time with this one.

After Reid found the letter in the book, he began to do things differently. Namely, deciding to move to a more pleasant locale, teaming up with another musician to stretch his talents, and keeping a daily journal topped the list of things he's actively initiated to help himself. He even bought himself a new pair of sneakers and has started running again. No one would expect this of him, but he got the idea to keep a daily journal after seeing someone post about its benefits on social media. Sometimes, his journal includes a lot of chicken scratch or bulleted items, and other times, he writes full paragraphs. Sometimes, he scribbles possible lyrics to songs, attempts his hand at poetry, or sketches. It depends on his mood, but he marks his journal with goals and things he wants to achieve. It's so unlike him, but he's already seeing the benefits. And every day he writes the same thing on top of the day's page, mimicking what his father said to him over and over again: make good decisions.

When he spent New Year's Day in his cottage watching the Bowl games, he made meaningful New Year's resolutions this year, and finally, he's seeing that some change is starting to happen.

He's hungry for something new. And more than that, he's finally ready to see the world through an optimistic lens.

*

Over the last few weeks, Reid's approach to change is paying off. He's noticed that the smallest adjustments can have the biggest payoffs. It's all new to him, but he's finding that he's committed to giving himself the opportunity to make a transformation that's worthwhile.

Reid gets to the tavern early that night, and says hello to Dave, the guy who books him for the gigs. They share a bit of small talk, and Dave asks how ready the duo is for tonight.

"Pretty ready. My partner's good...really good. You'll like his stuff," Reid tells him. Dave nods and wishes him luck.

Dimitri rolls through the door ten minutes later, and needs help carrying his equipment inside. Reid gives him a hand, and Dimitri admits he's nervous.

"It's different than playing at the bookstore," Dimitri says. "There, I'm just background music. Here, it's more about performance."

"You'll be great. You know you're good, dude. You've got this. And remember, they're all drinking in here, and the music tends to just be background noise, even though there's a small stage area," Reid tells him, as if he's a pro and not nervous at all, when in fact, he's actually pretty nervous himself. And for good reason.

After setting up their area, testing the keyboard, amps, and their mics, they settle in and get ready to play. There's a good crowd, and Reid has reserved two tables nearest to them for their guests.

Just as Reid takes a sip of his soft drink, Eva walks through the door. She's smiling and waves to him, and he points to the table up front. She looks pretty. Well, Reid always thinks she looks pretty, even in the early mornings without makeup, looking naturally beautiful, walking Brownie. Soon after, Meg comes through the door, looking stylish. Along with Meg is an attractive blonde woman Reid's never seen before, and the two sit next to Eva. They begin talking and making their introductions, the women shaking hands and ordering their drinks.

A few minutes later, Dimitri's father walks through the door and gives his son a quick wave. He's happy to see his Dimitri's dad come to watch his son play music. Dimitri seems to really love his dad, and Reid is somewhat envious of their solid relationship. He wishes he and his father could come back together in that way—but he knows it will take some time.

As they strike their first chords and begin their first set, their new friends begin to take notice. They play well together, and Reid's voice starts off a little shaky from nerves, then begins to settle as they move into the second song. Reid catches Eva's eye a couple of times, and Meg gives a "thumbs up" sign and a little wink to them both after the first song. She seems pretty pleased with their song choices, and he can see her singing along and clapping.

Dimitri's playing is impeccable. He's right on point with the songs, and his background vocals are holding up well. The accountant turned musician-thing seems to be working for him, and Reid feels himself chuckle inside. And then, just as he's focused on hearing Dimitri's harmonies, he feels his heart jump. His mother, father, and Emme all walk through the door, a total surprise. Emme knew he was playing tonight. He had told her all about it over the phone, and she said she'd never heard him this excited about playing before. She must have put his parents up to it. He can't remember the last time his parents heard him play—actually heard him play. He's overwhelmed to see them there, and they wave to him as they look for seats.

Reid swallows hard during the instrumental interlude, and Emme smiles broadly at him. His family finds room at the table with Nicholas, and Reid, looks around at all these people he's either known all his life or just met in recent days and can't recall feeling this kind of kinship since...he's not sure he's felt it since his early college days.

Something is shifting for him. Maybe this time he'll get his act together.

Finally.

Dimitri

Saturday, February 9

After they finish playing their third set and the gig is over, Dimitri is on a high. He hears the applause, and feels as if their first run at being a duo was pretty successful. When he played his first notes earlier, his hands were shaking from the fear of it all—he's never truly put himself out there like this before. That, in itself, is an accomplishment.

"Wow, that was amazing," Meg says to him, as he comes off the stage and sits down with the group. Reid is saying hello to his parents, sister, and Dimitri's father, while Dimitri talks with the ladies for a few minutes. "Who knew you two could play like that? I'm so impressed!" Meg says.

"Thank you. I think we are surprised as well," he says.

"Dimitri, I'm sorry to be so rude. This is Lily. I don't think you two have met before," Meg says.

"No, I don't believe we have. Nice to meet you."

"You, too," Lily says. "I'm glad Meg asked me to come tonight. This was really fun. I enjoyed hearing you two play."

"Thank you," Dimitri says, not at all used to compliments.

"Meg said this is the first time you two have played together in public. Is that true?" Lily asks.

"It is," Dimitri says, taking a drink of water.

"Well, it seems like you've been playing together forever," Lily says.

"Did you get your first dollar?" Eva asks him.

"What first dollar?" he says back.

"Your first dollar for playing as a duo. It's a momentous occasion! I want to frame it, you know, for the bookcase?"

Dimitri laughs. "Gotcha," he says. "I'll make sure I get it to you for framing."

After talking with them for a few minutes, he turns around and sits at the table behind them where Baba is sitting. His father gives him a high-five, something Baba is fond of doing, and Dimitri appreciates his support. "You're out late on a Saturday night," Dimitri says to him.

"It was worth it," he says. "That was really fun to hear you two play."

"Well, I can't thank you enough for coming," Dimitri says.

"Are you kidding? It's my pleasure," his dad says. "I love hearing you play, son."

Meg walks over and says hello to Baba. "Did you enjoy that, Nicholas?"

"I really, really did, Meg," Baba says to her. "And we have you to thank for introducing them."

"Your son was on it tonight," Reid says to Baba.

"I'd say you were both on it. That was tremendous."

Reid looks at Dimitri and slaps him on the back. "That was fun, wasn't it?" he asks, laughing.

"It was," Dimitri says. Then, Reid introduces him to Emme and his parents. Emme shakes Dimitri's hand and apologizes for having to leave early, saying she has to take her parents home and then drive herself back to Towson.

"Are you sure you don't want to crash at Mom's or with me?" Reid asks her.

"Next time," she says, kissing Reid on the check and shaking Dimitri's hand. "The kids have early activities in the morning."

Dimitri says goodbye to Baba, and Reid and Dimitri are left with Meg, Eva, and Lily. They sit at the table and enjoy a lighthearted conversation. Dimitri learns that Lily owns a boutique up on State Circle and that she and Meg are recent acquaintances. He wonders briefly if Lily also got a letter. In fact, he wonders who at the table hasn't received a letter.

As they all chat at the table, Dimitri watches Reid and Eva. He wonders if there's something brewing between them; there's something about the way they look at each other—and don't look at each other. He hasn't known Reid for long, but he knows he's solid. Maybe there's some history of screw-ups in his past, as he's mentioned, but he seems to be a good guy. Who among us isn't a little broken? And the little he knows of Eva, she seems like a gem. She's been fun to work with, and he's excited to see what she does with his place.

But the one who intrigues him most at the table is Meg. He leans back in his chair and studies them all as they talk. It's Meg who has brought all of them together, whether they all realize it or not. There's something about her that is mysterious and alluring. And don't think he hasn't noticed how she looks in that red dress she's wearing, or the hazel color of her eyes.

She throws her head back in laughter, and he watches the joy on her face.

He wonders if his face looked anything remotely like that during his playing tonight—because he certainly felt that way, even if it didn't translate through his facial expressions.

For the next hour, they share stories, get to know one another better, and Dimitri is thankful for these new people that have been introduced into his life. It's refreshing.

*

When everyone leaves and it's just Dimitri and Reid loading up Dimitri's car with his equipment, Reid asks him if he had a good time.

"It was a great time," Dimitri says. "I'm glad Meg connected us."

"She seems to have connected all of us," Reid says, scratching his head. "Isn't that weird? I mean, all of us at that table were somehow brought together by Meg." Dimitri's glad to see Reid recognizes this as well and has come to the same conclusion.

"It's a little weird, but great at the same time," Dimitri says. "So, speaking of that, I know we haven't known each other that long, but I may have a business proposition for you."

"Really?"

"I'm trying to work some things out, but are you free on Monday?"

"What time?" Reid asks. "I'm finishing a job for a client."

"Around lunchtime? I want you to take a look at something with me."

"Sure. I can make time," Reid says, readjusting the guitar across his shoulder.

"Okay. I'll text you the address of where to meet me. Sound good?"

"Yup, sounds good. I'm intrigued."

"Yeah, and I may be off my rocker, but we'll see," Dimitri says. He stretches out his hand to shake Reid's. "And, hey man, thanks for tonight."

"You bet," Reid says.

Dimitri climbs into his car on more of a high than he ever got playing tables at the casino.

Meg
Sunday, February 10

Meg can't shake the dream she had last night. It was about Will, and in the dream, he was in trouble. Internalizing these types of dreams and taking them to heart as empaths often do, Meg worries that it is a forewarning of something. She summons the courage to pick up the phone and call him. It's been two years since they've spoken, and she wonders if he will even take her call. Calling her former fiancé? It feels completely inappropriate for her to check on an old flame—on someone she loved—especially because it ended in such disappointment and misery.

On the third ring, she hears a voice on the other end of the phone pick up.

"Hello?" he says, groggy, and asking as if in disbelief.

"Who is it?" she hears a familiar female voice say in the background. When he lies to her and says it's someone from work, he tells Meg to hang on. She hears him shuffle to another room for more privacy to have the conversation.

"Meg?" he says, after a few minutes of relocating to speak to her without ears listening. She can hear the birds chirping in the background, so she assumes he stepped outside to have his conversation.

"I'm still in your contact list, I suppose," she says.

"You are," Will says. "What's up? Why are you calling me?

Last I heard, you never wanted to speak to me again. Don't you hate me?"

"Hate's a pretty strong word. I don't hate anyone," she says calmly. "I had a very bad dream about you, and I wanted to make sure you're okay."

"Wow. It must have been a pretty bad one for you to actually pick up the phone and call me after almost two years. Was I dead in the dream?"

"Not yet."

That was an intentional—and somewhat malicious response. She knows she's got him a little freaked out now.

There's an awkward silence that fills the air. Will always knew she had an ability to receive strange premonitions or sense emotions from people. He'd watched her attend to the sensations she would glean from others, and she knew it spooked him sometimes. And when she finally decided to attend a seminar at a local university with Bev Bronstone, the empathy guru who wrote the seminal book about empaths, he knew she was serious. Attending that conference was freeing for Meg; she had finally found her people—people who understood what it is like to live with full-blown empathy every day of their lives. It's how she learned that it's okay to love deeply but with boundaries, that taking care of yourself is important in order to care for others, and that gut feelings are, indeed, very, very real. Plus, she could finally attach a name to something she'd experienced her whole life.

After the pause, Will speaks again: "Well, that's good, I suppose. I'm fine. How are you?"

"Fine."

"Well, you don't seem to have much more to say. You just wanted to make sure I was still here?" In the background, Meg hears a door shut, then the whir of a coffee machine. He always had coffee first thing in the morning.

"Pretty much, unless you have anything to say."

"Is this where you want me to apologize yet again?"

"Maybe," she says, taking the bait. Why not? "An abundance of apologies never hurt anyone."

"Okay, I'm sorry once again. I'm sorry I screwed up."

"More than a screw up, I'd say," she says. "Especially, since she is there, and you are still with her."

"What? Are you gazing into your crystal ball?" There it is. The witch dig. It doesn't take long for him to try to make her feel like an outcast due to her empathic nature. It's his go-to verbal ammunition.

She knows enough to take a deep breath, and she contemplates hanging up on him. Meg can hear her heart beating, and not in a good way. Anger still dwells within her.

After a minute, Will speaks again. "The truth is, there will never be enough apologies for you. You still want me to feel bad about it all? I'm trying to get the money together to pay you back."

"Take your time. It's not urgent," she says sarcastically. She dealt with him when it all went down, when he took the money she'd saved and used it for himself and his own projects—or whatever—without her knowledge, never to pay her back. And of course, there was the issue of Cecelia—her best friend—who went behind her back and slept with Will, and who is curled up next to him now. Meg thanks God she didn't marry Will as planned. She is grateful for unanswered prayers. He's Cecelia's problem now.

Meg regrets picking up the phone. She should have shaken off the dream; she shouldn't have called him. She should have marched on with her life as he had done all those months ago. How can some people move forward and never look back, especially when there was love at one time? It was unfathomable to her.

"Okay. I still feel bad, but we've all moved on, right?" His voice is cavalier. She's incensed.

She doesn't answer him, and yet she hangs on the line. He really can't help himself.

"Okay, Meg," he begins again. "After two years and a lot of unanswered phone calls and text messages, you finally decided to reach out to me because of a bad dream you had?" he asks.

"Yes," she says.

"Well, jeez, thanks. So very, very kind of you."

He strikes a nerve with her by saying that. She's always been kind. During their time together she was nothing but kind to him. Every single ounce of her being was committed to their relationship in which she gave, and he took. He took and took and then never paid back what he took. He stole from her. She breathes deeply, collects her thoughts, and responds accordingly.

"Well, it's better than anything you ever gave—or repaid. I'm truly sorry I called this morning. Better for us not to have contact again, unless of course, you'd like to mail me a check, in which case, mail it directly to Brodie's Books in Annapolis," she says, and she hangs up before he can say anything else.

Her reaction to him is not without its effect on her. Meg stands frozen, shaking, for minutes afterwards.

*

Later, on the walk to work, Meg chastises herself for dialing Will's number, for making the call, for having to subject herself once again to his infantile banter and smug voice. One thing they don't tell you about empaths is how much they feel—deeply feel—so much so, that while they have the capacity to forgive, they also have the means to cut people out of their lives if they dare cause too much angst. There is such a thing as a boundary. She is still learning how to set up effective ones.

Will caused her angst. No, wait, she thinks, let's rephrase that. Will causes her angst. Still.

She dislikes feeling this way, and when she opens the door to the bookstore, her body loosens a bit from the tense feeling the conversation with Will left in her body. There's a certain comfort that comes from stepping inside her bookstore and feeling at home. Clarke's standing near the door with a big smile on her face. Meg loves her work, the store, and she can't imagine it not always being here for her.

"Good morning, Meg!" Clarke says, excitedly.

"Good morning. You're awfully cheery this morning," Meg responds, getting herself settled behind the check-out counter.

"Three book clubs," Clarke says. "I've already sold over forty books in the last thirty-five minutes. Lots of books flying out the door. Your store is having a very good Sunday morning."

"At least that makes one of us," Meg says.

Clarke looks at her sideways, and Meg realizes that she's never really told her about Will. She always tries to be positive and bright. "Is something the matter?" Clarke asks her, looking concerned.

"Oh, you know, old baggage." Meg fiddles with the "reserved" copies on the shelf behind her, reorganizing them.

"What old baggage?" Clarke stops what she's doing and focuses on the conversation.

"Former fiancé baggage. You'd think after two years, I'd be done being angry about how I was treated, but every once in a while, it still gets to me," Meg says.

"I didn't know you had been engaged. Did you run into him or something?" Clarke asks, knowing nothing of Meg's past relationships. Strangely for Meg, it feels slightly therapeutic for her to open up a bit.

"I had the unfortunate pleasure of talking to him on the phone," Meg says. "Okay, enough about that. So, we've sold a lot of books this morning?"

Clarke smiles at her and takes her coat. "Yes, a very good morning. I'll take this to the coat rack and get you a nice, hot cup of coffee. Take a deep breath. It's going to all be okay."

"Sounds lovely," Meg says.

*

At two-thirty, Meg is creating a new window display to draw customers into the store. *Game of Thrones* is set to air its final season on television, and she's dedicating the front, paned window to the books by George R.R. Martin. She bought merchandise that she's displaying along with the novels, and although she doesn't typically like shows with extreme violence, *Game of Thrones* is the exception for her because of the characters. She's always been a fan of complicated and intricate characters that keep you guessing.

Which might explain her past affinity for Will.

Complicated, smart, sexy, and someone with an unusual amount of confidence, Meg had been drawn to him from the second they met at a mutual friend's cookout. There was something about Will that was so familiar, as if she had met him before—or in another lifetime—the sensation of comfort overpowering at times. They had fallen into step together so naturally, spending every waking moment in each other's company. She fell in love with him instantly, as quickly as someone falls for a favorite food or film. Meg couldn't get enough of him, could swallow every iota of his being whole, always wanting more of him. He had proposed on the streets of their favorite little small town after eating lunch in a restaurant at the top of the hill. Months later, when Will's demeanor began to change and she found out about Cecelia after following Will one night when he claimed to be working, the pain that shot through Meg's heart was something she'd never felt before. She had loved Will and trusted him; he had put all of her faith in him. As well, she had loved Brodie albeit in a completely different way, but the net result of losing both relationships was loss. Tremendous loss.

She never confronted Cecelia to her face, her supposed best friend. Meg simply ended her relationship with her full stop. Afterwards, Cecelia had tried to reach out to her, but Meg refused to have communication with her. It was easier for Meg to block both Will and Cecelia from her life. The excruciating pain of losing Brodie was hard enough during that time. The added cruel treatment by her fiancé and friend was insufferable.

Truth be told, Meg had never felt that low in all of her life.

That was the turning point.

That was when she decided to pick up and move and begin a new life thanks to Uncle Ben and Aunt Nancy. They always say you have angels watching over you, and she swears two of her angels are here on Earth. Brodie may have had a hand in it, too, if you believe in heavenly angels.

Admiring the handiwork of her window display, when she lifts her head, Meg sees Dimitri outside making faces at her through the glass. She laughs and waves. She looks at her watch in disbelief that it's already a little before three, and he's come to play the piano in the store from three o'clock until close.

"Hi, Meg," Dimitri says, coming through the door and approaching her. "It's looking good from the outside."

"Yay!" she says.

"I loved those books," Dimitri says, pointing to the window. "Such an escape from reality. Do you watch the show?"

"I do. Totally addicted, and it's not even typically what I like. It's a little raunchy and over the top at times."

"I hear you," he says. "I also wanted to thank you for coming last night."

"Of course! I can't get over how good you and Reid sounded together. You must be so happy," she says.

"It was fun. I did have a good time once I got past the nerves." Meg watches him fiddle with the keys in his hand.

"Nerves? What nerves? I couldn't tell you were nervous at all," she says. Her blood pressure returning to normal, Meg's thankful for the conversation. It's steering her away from obsessing about Will and Cecelia. She's got to put them out of her mind. Thinking of them always makes her feel off balance.

"Well, I was nervous," he says.

"Are you nervous playing here?" she asks, innocently, pointing to the surroundings of the bookstore.

"Only around you," he says, with a wink, and walks toward the back to take the stairs to the second floor.

Meg's eyes follow him as he climbs the stairs. She feels the pull again, and it's right then that Meg sees him. Truly sees him. She has guarded her heart for two years, and it's been exhausting. Maybe everyone is not like Will. Not everyone will hurt her the way Will did. Perhaps, she thinks, it's time to be vulnerable again if she's ever going to give another relationship a try. She has cut herself off from potential hurt and pain long enough, turned down dates and set-ups, and while she puts up a good front, living alone, managing this store alone, writing letters and helping people who need help, she recognizes at that very moment that she's tired of wallowing in the hurt and the fear of trying again. Writing the letters has been both a diversion and therapeutic, allowing the focus to be taken off herself in order to help others, but it may be time for her to fully heal, as well. Perhaps she should write herself a letter, she thinks, amused by the thought of it.

She has so much love to give. She wants love in her life. And children. Although it may sound cliche, Meg wants to raise a family and grow old with someone.

Who knows? Maybe someone like Dimitri is the right type of person to allow in, even if she proceeds slowly and cautiously, to see what might happen if she actually is brave enough to let someone else see her as she is—the broken bits, the hopeful wishes, and the need to feel love again.

Eva
Thursday, February 28

Eva waits outside her office on Church Circle for Dimitri to arrive. She has found a few things at a nearby furniture store she wants him to show him in order to put the finishing touches on redecorating his place. His house has been fully repainted, and Dimitri loves the new color schematics. Earthy tones mixed with greys and blues make the house feel a far cry from the pinkness of its previous existence. As well, he's updated the kitchen countertops and bought sleek, new appliances for the house. Reid even came over during the week and hauled unwanted items to Goodwill. Eva loves how it's all looking. Dimitri's bookshelves are coming together nicely. Furthermore, while the décor doesn't exactly scream "man cave," the tones are much more tranquil throughout. He seems quite pleased so far.

As they stroll through stores, Dimitri picks out a muted globe for his desk, book ends for his bookcase, and a standing lamp that will go next to his leather chair. Eva has taken so much time on those bookcases, framing and laminating items and collectibles to display along with his books. The two of them have spent a lot of time redecorating, but Eva hasn't minded at all. It's a great outlet for her creativity that doesn't require writing copy or setting up a promotional campaign for a client, something she can do with her eyes closed. She's having fun with all of it.

Shoving everything into the trunk of Dimitri's SUV, they drive back to his house and unload. They plug things in and place items on shelves. Eva also unpacks a box full of Dimitri's special mementos she had framed—a couple of vintage baseball cards, a piece of music that Dimitri wrote years ago, and of course, the dollar bill he made from playing in his first-ever duo.

Dimitri and Eva stand back, admiring the bookshelves, and Eva moves in closer to adjust a few things.

"Well, I'm happy with it. How are you feeling about it all?"

"It looks fantastic. It feels so much more homey, if that's a word," he says.

Eva chuckles. She knows exactly what he means. She had to make her own place feel that way, and she also hopes she made Reid's cottage feel that way. Looking around, she feels good about the work she has done here. It's almost ten o'clock by the time they finish, and she grabs her purse and begins to leave. Dimitri puts a check into her hand, but she refuses it. He insists and asks her to take it, thanking her for all her time and energy. She has no idea how much he's paid her, and she doesn't really care. She did it because she wanted to—and because Reid put her up to it.

"So, how do you feel about doing this all again?" Dimitri asks, standing with her at the doorway.

"What? What do you mean?"

"How do you feel about doing it all again, except, maybe this time, with a business?"

She crosses her arms as she stands in his new foyer. "I'm not sure I'm understanding you. Did you just buy a business?"

"I'm seriously considering it. I have one more walk-through next week. And I'm not really buying it. I'll be renting space and starting a new business—with your buddy."

"With Reid?" Eva is pleasantly surprised to hear this news.

"That's the plan."

"What do you two have up your sleeves?"

"We're thinking of opening a music store. A place where people can buy instruments and sheet music, and also take lessons. We're also hoping to have a stage area where musicians can showcase their talents for recitals and events."

"Like a Music and Arts Center?"

"Yes, but cozier. More like Music and Arts Center meets a rathskellar, or like a fireside chat, music in the park, or musical poetry slam. It's a new concept we're working on."

"Reid didn't say anything to me about it," Eva muses.

"I don't think he wants to tell anyone until it's a done deal. And it's still in the works. I've had some money tucked away for children—savings I started when I was in my early twenties. It's not a lot, but it's enough to get us started without having to mortgage the house, if you know what I mean."

Eva's eyes are bright. She is happy to see good things happen to good people. She adores both of them, Reid and Dimitri.

"Well, you can count on me to help with whatever you need. And you don't have to pay me. I'll do it just for the fun of it."

"Thank you. I want to make it work," Dimitri says. "For a long time now, I've been wanting to do my own thing, branch out, work for myself. Reid can't afford to put any money into it yet, but he's going to manage it. He's tired of construction and working outside when it's cold. He's a smart dude and has a lot of patience. He's been lost for a while and is finding his way. He's wanted to try something new, too, but he's been limited financially. And then, we met. So, he pushed me out of my comfort zone by playing with him in public, and that made me realize that perhaps there's a hole we can fill as partners. So, now I'm going to push him out of his comfort zone, and he'll give lessons and manage the store. I think this has a lot of potential, if we can pull it off."

"I would say so. The only other competition I know of is in the next town over," Eva says.

"Yes. So, we need to get creative to make this different from that one." Eva can see the wheels turning in his brain. She's never seen him this excited.

"Sounds amazing," she says.

"I can take you to see the space as soon as I sign the deal. It's got a cool vibe already, but you could make it shine."

"Aw, thanks, Dimitri. Thanks for the vote of confidence. I'm happy for you guys."

"One more question," Dimitri starts to say. "How are you on guidance with men's haircuts?"

*

At ten-thirty when Eva rolls in, she sees Reid's light is on in the cottage. In fact, all the lights are on in the place. She makes herself a cup of chamomile tea and hangs her coat in the closet. Done with February and the cold, springtime can't come soon enough. Brownie is wagging her tail, wanting to be let out, so Eva opens the back door and lets her run around and take care of her business.

Then, she unfolds the check she had jammed into her pocket from Dimitri. Her eyes widen as she looks at the amount of money he paid her. He must have a lot of stashed cash somewhere, because she didn't expect him to pay her this kind of money. She's thrilled, but she is also surprised. Maybe she could start a side hustle. Who knows?

"Eva, are you in there?" she hears Reid's voice call through the door. Brownie is with him, and she opens it, letting them both inside.

"How did it go with Dimitri's place?"

"Great," Eva says. "Come on in. I can't wait for you to see it the next time you go over. I think you will really like it."

"Well, I think it's looking really good so far. You've worked your magic on it," he says, closing the door behind him.

"And he paid me really well, too. I didn't expect him to pay me that much."

"That was nice of him," Reid says. "Hey, can I talk to you about something?"

"Yes, you can. But first, can I get you a cup of tea or coffee? I just made myself a cup. Or hot chocolate. I have that, too."

"Ah, sure," Reid says. "Hot chocolate works."

Eva fiddles around the kitchen and Reid takes a seat at her kitchen table. She wonders what he wants to talk about; maybe he wants to tell her about the Music and Arts Center idea to see what she thinks.

She places the cup of hot chocolate in front of him with a container of marshmallows, and he plops a few into his mug. She sits down at the table across from him, and gives him her utmost attention.

"Now I can focus. I'm all ears," she says, taking a sip of her tea.

"Well, I have this thing—" and he stalls.

He seems nervous about asking her whatever it is he has to ask her.

"Okay, so you have this thing—" she says, hoping to help him spit out whatever it is he wants to chat about.

"Yes. Okay, let me just get right to it. I have this thing I have to attend. My sister is planning a party for my parents' 50th wedding

anniversary in Bethany Beach at a beach house on the ocean with catering and dancing—kind of a fancy party. I was wondering if you'd
be my date for it. I know it's a little weird because you've only met my
parents and sister at the tavern that night, but—"

"I'd love to," she says, interrupting him. She figures she will
save him from himself and his babbling. "I'm happy to do it. They are
very sweet people, and I'd like to get to know your sister better, too,
so count me in. Fifty years. Wow. When is it?"

"It's in a month. Saturday, April 6. I thought I'd ask you now,
so you don't make other plans."

"Right, because my social calendar is chock full of engage-
ments." She winks. He smiles.

"It seems to be of late," Reid says. "You and Dimitri have
been spending a lot of time together."

"Right. He's my 'client' that you hooked me up with, remember?"

"I do," Reid says. "It seems to have worked out."

"It has. And don't forget all the outings to come see you—you
two—play," Eva says. She's only missed one performance so far, so she
believes that's a pretty good indication of how she supports her new
friends.

"I know. I'm thankful," Reid says. He begins to reach his
hand across the table to touch hers, and for the first time, their hands
touch. "I really am thankful," he says.

Eva gives his hand a squeeze, and then stands up, not wanting
it to get weird or awkward between them.

"Well, if you're so thankful, I know how you can repay me,"
she says, grinning.

"Sure. You name it."

"I can't seem to get my closet doors in my bedroom to align

anymore, and the one door won't stay shut. It's sort of driving me crazy."

"Happy to take a look at it," he says.

"So, maybe tomorrow?" she asks, feigning that she is tired, which she is, and she has an early meeting in the morning at the office.

"Sounds like a plan," Reid says, and takes her cue. "I'll see you tomorrow then."

Reid opens the back door, and steps outside. Before she forgets, Eva calls after him.

"And don't forget to tell me what the dress code is for this anniversary party," she shouts. "I may need to get something spiffy."

"Spiffy," Reid calls back, "is that word still used today?"

Eva laughs, and shuts the door behind her.

*

As Eva begins to turn off all the lights, she remembers that she forgot to check her mailbox. She's waiting for the invoice for one last thing she had made for Dimitri. She opens the front door and grabs the mail, taking it back inside and placing it on the foyer table, when she notices a handwritten letter. She would recognize that handwriting anywhere. She knows it so well, from cards, old poetry, and letters and notes written in years gone by.

She grabs the letter opener and slices open the envelope. She sinks into her white, fluffy chair, retrieves the paper from the envelope, her hand lightly trembling, unfolds it, and begins to read it.

Dear Eva,

I hope this letter finds you well, and finds you hating me less and less with each passing day. I wanted to set things right, or at least apologize to you for my awful behavior and deception. You didn't deserve it. In fact, you deserve so much better.

There's no easy way to tell someone that you've fallen out of love with them, that you no longer love them in a way that is healthy for either of you, or that points toward a happy future. And what can happen during those times of complete uncertainty is that you talk with someone else about it. That someone else ended up being the person I unintentionally ended up falling in love with— again. I'm so sorry I allowed this to happen without coming clean first. My lack of happiness led me to do stupid, hurtful things. Please accept my sincerest apologies.

The truth, Eva, is that we both deserve better. We deserve more happiness than going through the motions, which is how I felt most of the time. And you deserve someone who loves you with his whole body and soul. You've always deserved that. You are kind beyond measure and the most giving person I've ever met. Even while knowing all this about you, sometime over the last two years, I began to feel alone, even though we were together. I can't describe it, and I won't try. I did love you, but as time wore on, I realized we just were not as compatible as "forever." If I could put my finger on one particular thing, I would, but I can't.

I wanted to share all of this with you because it is owed to you. It's nothing you did or said that made me feel this way. It just evolved, or I changed, or we changed, I'm not sure. I behaved like a complete jerk, and I'm ashamed of it. I also figured the only way you would "hear" what I wanted to say was if I put it down on paper so you might read it and not hang up on me.

Please know how much I did care for you, how for eight of those ten years life was really, really good, and that I know you are going to find the right person who will make you happy for the rest of your life.

My deepest apologies for causing you pain,

Kyle

Eva walks slowly up the stairs, holding the letter in her hand. She kicks off her shoes and curls up on her bed with her clothes on. Brownie assumes her position on the corner of the bed, staring at her with sad eyes, lightly panting. Eva's tears begin to fall on the pillow, dampening the pillowcase. She feels gutted; an ache resides in her heart. When she begins to drift off to sleep, still clutching the letter in her hand, she acknowledges that she needs this type of closure after all this time, even though the words in the letter are devastating to read.

Lily
Saturday, March 2

Lily's been out three Saturday nights in a row listening to the music of Reid and Dimitri at the tavern. They still haven't named their duo, so that's the name they go by right now. She has been enjoying getting to know Meg and Eva, and tonight, she is joining them for dinner before heading to the tavern to hear the guys play again. Cora doesn't know what's gotten into her mother.

"Are you having a mid-life thing?" Cora asks Lily, as she sits on the edge of the bed watching her apply lipstick and examining the flattering black sweater dress that hugs her in all the right places.

"What do you mean, mid-life thing?"

"Well, you're going out to bars like someone in her twenties."

"What else would you have me doing? I had no social life, and now I'm starting to have one," Lily says. "Plus, I've made a few new friends. You should be happy for me."

"I am, it's just that I don't know any of these people. How do you know I approve?" Cora asks.

"Because you trust me, like I trust you. They seem to be really good people."

"So, why hang out in bars all the time?"

Lily realizes the ridiculous nature of this backward conversation, the kid scolding the parent for going out and trying to have a good time. It's funny, and she's amused.

"Because the two guys actually play music in the bars. We are there for the music and to talk, Cora, not to drink our butts off."

"Well, why don't you invite them over for dinner one night so I can meet these famous new friends of yours?"

"I'll think about it," Lily says, leaning over to kiss Cora on the cheek. Lily grabs her handbag and puts her lipstick inside. "It's a nice idea, actually," Lily says, calmly. "And where will you be tonight?"

"I'm going ice skating with a huge group, then going back to Sammie's house for a while," Cora says.

"Okay," Lily says, turning off the light in her room and getting ready to head out the door. "Not too late."

"Uh, yeah, Mom. Heed your own advice."

Lily laughs. She can see Cora enjoys the ribbing she is giving her mother. The two of them had gone to the French cinema in Baltimore, taking Brad up on his offer of tickets to enjoy a night in Paris, and the movie was adorable. It made Lily want to go to Paris even more. Lily had made reservations at a French bistro in midtown before the film. It was a nice mother-daughter night out, and she sent Brad a text thanking him for the gift.

As Lily opens the front door to walk to her car, she is startled, and grabs her chest. "Oh my goodness, Brad! You startled me!"

"I'm sorry, Lily. I didn't mean to. I was just driving by and thought I'd check on Cora."

"Oh, sure. Yeah. She's inside. Feel free."

"Where are you going?" he asks, boldly.

"To dinner, and then out to hear my friends play some music."

"Really?"

"Yes, really."

"Okay," he says.

"What surprises you most? That I am going to dinner or that I have some friends?" she says. She can feel herself becoming defensive, and there's really no need for it. He has been cordial and friendly these last few months. Even kind.

"Oh, neither," he says. "It's just—"

Lily cuts him off. "Never mind. I'm sorry I snapped at you. I shouldn't have done that. I'm in a rush, and I need to get going," she says. She can see Cora pull the living room curtains aside as she watches her parents from the window. Lily's not in the mood for a conversation with Brad, nor is she wanting an altercation. They've had too many in the past, and they seem to be sailing into much calmer waters as they deal with each other now.

"I've got to go. Go on in. Cora's inside," she says.

*

The tavern is lively. The guys are playing well tonight, in perfect sync with each other. Lily even notices that they are smiling more, maybe because they're starting to feel comfortable playing together. The bar crowd is enjoying the music, and Lily, Eva, and Meg bonded over dinner earlier, and continue to do so as they sit at a table and talk as the guys play. Lily thinks about what Cora had said, about having her new friends over for dinner, and she thinks it may be a good idea. She broaches the subject with the ladies, asking if they are up for it.

"Maybe we could have game night, or something like that, too. Who else loves board games?" Eva asks.

"I do," Lily says. "Do you, Meg?"

"Sure. I'm up for anything."

They make plans to host a dinner/game night at Lily's and

decide to pick a date after speaking with the guys, who seem to be booking up in town. Reid and Dimitri have also been commissioned for some private parties and a wedding, according to Reid.

As the duo begins to play a second set, Lily leaves the table to use the restroom. Making her way back to the table, she stops, and stares in disbelief. She has to pull it together, remain cool. It's not one of her strong suits.

She shimmies back into her seat at the table, and Lily sees Meg take an interest in what's unfolding nonverbally. In fact, Lily can see that Meg is, in fact, fully attune to Lily's change in demeanor and flushed face. Lily gets the sense that Meg knows that someone is making her feel uncomfortable. Finally, Eva catches on, leans close to Lily, and whispers, "Why is that handsome guy staring at you, Lily?"

"You think he's handsome?" Lily asks.

"Empirically, yes, but I'm not suggesting I'm attracted to him." Lily laughs nervously at Eva's remark. Then it clicks with Meg. "Is that your ex-husband?" Meg asks.

"It is," Lily says, under her breath. "My daughter must have told him I was coming here tonight."

"Oh, the plot thickens," Eva says, looking delighted at the story she will now attempt to piece together.

Meg fidgets a little, and crosses her legs. Lily watches her, and senses something strange. She can't put her finger on it, but something about the moment feels...destined?

Brad nods to her, and Lily finally lifts her hand and waves to him across the room. She pulls out the empty chair next to her, and motions for him to come and sit with them. What else could she do? It would be unkind not to suggest he come and sit with them. Eva and Meg exchange glances. A banal thought crosses Lily's mind: what is happening? She tries to plaster a smile on her face.

Simultaneously, another less banal thought creeps into her brain, the one she has all the time, every waking minute of the day, the one that beleaguers her morning, noon, and night: if only I didn't still love him so much.

Reid

Sunday, March 17
St. Patrick's Day

Reid wakes up late on Sunday morning. He's been incredibly busy over the week, and he's become involved in things he never dreamed he'd be involved in three months ago. Ever since meeting Dimitri, since receiving that letter, and since beginning to take some initiative in his life, he has started to see change. He thinks back to the night he walked into Meg's store back in December. Was he the same man now? He didn't exactly feel the same at all. A few months later and something has definitely–shifted.

His contracting partner had been disappointed to hear that Reid is going in a new direction professionally. Quite frankly, Reid almost couldn't believe he was about to attempt something new himself. He's been building and fixing things for so many years that it feels surreal to him. And he hasn't told his folks yet, either. His instinct is telling him that this is the right gamble to take, that this might actually work. He has convinced himself that working at a music store is a wise decision. Reid has put his faith in Dimitri's business acumen, and as an accountant, Dimitri has thrown together a business plan, which the bank has already approved. And, when Dimitri showed Reid the space in Annapolis not too far from downtown, Reid became instantly excited to be a part of the new venture.

For now, with Reid's lack of funds, Dimitri is making the financial investment in the store. It's Dimitri's idea, and he shared with Reid that he'd always wanted to be an entrepreneur, to try to run things himself. Reid will manage the store. The launch is still several weeks away, but there is plenty of work to do to get ready. They have to create the space and alter it to house soundproof rooms for lessons, the staging area, the counter space, and the instrument showcase. Dimitri and Reid will hire teachers, order the equipment and the instruments.

Additionally, Reid can contribute by helping with the contracting work with his former construction partner, who is giving them a deep discount. The Reid and Dimitri duo has been booking well several evenings a week all over Annapolis. Things are beginning to come together. And Eva is on board to help with the aesthetics inside the store.

Despite that everything is moving along at a good pace, Reid can't shake the nagging worry he feels for Eva. She hasn't been the same over the last couple of weeks. She has completely withdrawn, and has made excuses not to get together, or to even have a cup of coffee. Reid hopes she will still be his date for the upcoming anniversary party for his parents.

The old Reid may have let her continue to hide in her house. But the new Reid is thinking otherwise.

*

He raps on the door, and then rings the doorbell. Brownie comes trotting up to the front door wagging her tail, as Reid stands on the porch with a gift in his hand. He's perched at the door holding a basket that looks festive for quickly running into town and buying it from one of his favorite shops—there's Irish soda bread, Irish tea, jelly, cheese, shortbread, and mustard, and an Irish chocolate bar.

Eva opens the door in her robe and fuzzy slippers.

"What's this?" she asks, looking at Reid in bewilderment.

"St. Patrick's Day cheer. I felt you might need some."

Eva runs her fingers through her long hair, which is completely unkempt and wild. Reid's not sure he's seen her looking quite this frazzled—she's always so put together—and yet he finds her stunning, the glow of her skin highlighting her big, brown eyes.

"Oh, thank you," she says. "That's so sweet of you. Do you want to come in? As you can see, I'm not really myself. Or I am myself, and that other version of me is a fraud. I'm still trying to figure it out."

Reid is not sure what she means, but he's determined to get to the bottom of it.

"Well, do you want to tell me what's going on? We've missed seeing you. Lily and Meg miss seeing you. What's happened?"

"Let's just say I got a letter."

Reid remembers seeing her letter on Christmas morning, the one he didn't read. He knows she got a letter, too. He knows its job is to help people get through tough times. He never even thought that it might work for some and not for others.

They walk into the kitchen and sit at her white farm table. She places the gift basket on the table. Despite her current state, the house is still neat and tidy, and she puts a kettle on for tea.

"Do you want to talk about it?" he asks. He catches himself, and he feels rather pleased. In the past, he wouldn't have cared about such trivialities.

"Not really."

Eva sits across from him and looks him in the eyes. He stares back at her, trying earnestly to allow his eyes to show that he cares, that he wants to hear what is happening. She crosses her legs, lowers her eyes, and then begins to talk.

"Ok, I'll share. As I mentioned, I got a letter," she says, swallowing hard, then pausing.

"I know," he says. "I got one, too."

Eva pauses for a moment. "What?"

"I got one from the bookstore, too."

Eva looks at him in disbelief. "Oh. No, I'm not talking about that letter. And how did you know I got a letter from the bookstore?"

Reid feels stupid for a second. He shouldn't have opened his big mouth. Now he has to come clean.

"When you asked me to take care of Brownie on Christmas morning, I saw the letter hanging out of your book on this table. I didn't read it, though. I only saw it."

"And you got one, too?"

"Yes. The night of Midnight Madness."

"Same here," she says. "But again, that's not the letter I'm referring to."

The kettle whistles, and Eva gets up, pulling two large mugs from her cabinet. She steeps the Irish tea bags Reid gave her in the boiling water and places the white mugs on the table.

"Do you want to tell me about the letter—the one not from the bookstore?" Reid asks.

Eva looks at Reid and her eyes begin to fill with tears. He feels uncomfortable for making her upset or forcing her to think about the contents of a letter that has obviously caused her pain.

"Well, you and I are friends now, so I suppose I can tell you," she says.

Hearing her refer to them as "friends" makes him realize something he isn't ready to acknowledge—that she sees him in that way only. Reid decides to process this information later. It also solidifies that he clearly has more in mind with her than even he is willing to admit. He understands at that moment that he has feelings for her.

"Okay, so tell me."

"Two weeks ago, I got a letter from Kyle. I'll spare you all the gory details, but in essence his letter said that he owed me an explanation for the way he left me, that out of the ten years we were together, eight of them were great, and that it's incredibly difficult to tell someone you cared for that you are no longer in love with them. And apparently, he said hadn't been in love with me for two years. Two years! Imagine how hurtful it is to hear that!"

Eva's voice is cracking, and Reid can see the pain in her eyes. At that moment, he wants to hug her. He feels angry at her ex for continuing to hurt her while attempting to relieve his own guilt, all while she is trying to move on from it.

"I'm so sorry," he hears himself saying to Eva. "I'm sorry you had to open a letter like that."

Eva looks at Reid, and the faintest half-smile forms on her lips. "Thank you. Thank you for saying that. And for the Irish basket. And for just being here on the property. If I haven't told you before, it's comforting having you here."

"I'm glad to be here," Reid says, meaning it.

"So, what did your bookstore letter say?" Eva asks, sniffling.

Reid begins to tell her the impact the letter has had on his life.

*

An hour later, Reid and Eva are looking at Eva's letter—the

bookstore letter. They are trying to figure out if it's actually Meg who writes the letters, or if it's someone else in the store. They also want to know how she decides who gets a letter and how many she actually sends inside books. The mystery of the letters is helping to change Eva's mood and is giving them something to focus on and talk about. She is curious, and she wants to figure things out. Of course, they could just ask Meg, but Eva thinks about it differently.

"It's our own little Annapolis mystery," Eva says. "We could be like Holmes and Watson."

Reid laughs. "But sometimes when you know the truth, you wish you didn't. All I can say is that our little letters, no matter who wrote them, came at the right time, at least for me. I probably wouldn't be living here right now if it weren't for the letter. And I wouldn't have met you. And I wouldn't have met Dimitri. Don't you think it's interesting how we have all connected with each other because of Meg's bookstore?" he asks.

"I guess there's truth in that," Eva says. "I just wish the words would help me the way they have helped you."

"Maybe you're not allowing your letter to help you," Reid says, again, feeling philosophical and not knowing where it's coming from. "I think you have to be open to it. I was long overdue for the kick in the pants. I wasn't headed in the right direction."

"There could be truth in that," Eva says, leaning against the island in the kitchen.

Reid feels daring, bold. They have bonded over the last hour. He feels the timing is right, even though earlier he may not have felt it was the right move.

He gets up out of the chair and walks over to her, looking down into her eyes that seem less hazy after their discussion.

"Do you know what I'd like to think? I'd like to think the

letters intentionally brought us together," Reid says softly, and then wraps his arms around her, and kisses her forehead. He wants her to know he cares, but he doesn't want her to think he is taking advantage of the situation.

She feels stiff, and he panics. He wonders if this gesture was not wise, if the move was too forward, if she is not ready for it. Then, seconds later, he feels her arms come from her sides, wrapping tightly around his waist, as she takes a deep breath and allows him to hold her for a few minutes in a warm embrace.

Dimitri

Saturday, March 23

Dimitri wraps up playing the last song of the day at Brodie's Books. The store is a little quieter than normal today, and he needs a quick bite to eat before he goes to the tavern to meet up with Reid. They're playing from nine until one in the morning, and Dimitri kind of wishes they weren't. They'd been busy all week looking over blueprints, placing instrument and sheet music orders, and interviewing potential music teachers for jobs. They committed to hiring four initial teachers, and they each would round out the staff for a total of six employees to launch. Dimitri is confident that number will be sufficient to get the business going.

Meg has already cleaned up the place and has dimmed the lights by the time he bounds down the staircase. He's got to muster up the energy to keep going until the early morning. Not that he's complaining; he's simply been moving at a record pace trying to keep everything in line, as they check items off their long list of tasks.

"Nicely done, once again," Meg says to him as he approaches the counter. "And your haircut! You look like a new man, Dimitri."

"I was hoping you might say that," he says, watching Meg blush a little. He certainly feels like a new man, and it's not just because he finally cut his hair, although his father will be quite pleased.

"You're playing tonight with Reid?" she asks.

"Yes. We're booked up almost every Saturday night through May. Reid's been diligent about keeping us busy."

"That's great, Dimitri. And please know, if life gets too hectic, you don't have to feel obligated here. We love having you, but I also know you've got bigger things on the horizon."

"Well, I don't know about that, but thanks for being understanding. So far, everything seems to be balancing okay. Are you heading home now? I could walk you down the street."

"Ok. I just need another minute to power everything down. Thanks. Would love to stroll with you for a bit."

Dimitri waits patiently, browsing some of the newer books Meg has placed on the "new arrivals" table. He loves that she owns this charming bookstore, and that she loves what she does. He's never asked about the letter he received, although he believes she wrote it and gave it to him for a reason. Dimitri needed that push. He'd lost a wife, a job, and a lot of himself over the last several years. And he hasn't been to the track or gambled anything away in quite some time. He threw away his last pack of cigarettes two weeks ago. Cold turkey. Full stop. He swears it was the letter. After receiving it, he knew something had to give. The truth was, he had lost faith in himself. He's done feeling sorry for himself.

And this woman's kind letter had made him stop and think.

"Here, let me get the door for you," Dimitri says, stepping ahead of Meg to hold the door open. March can be blustery in Maryland, and because Annapolis sits on the water, the wind can whip.

They walk down Main Street chatting. Meg is talking about how much Dimitri's playing is making her update her playlists at home. They stop in front of the tavern for a second where a new poster publicizing the music of Reid & Dimitri is placed on an easel on the sidewalk up against the building, so it doesn't blow away. They admire the poster, and Dimitri feels proud of it. Meg says that she's been missing out on a lot of good music, and that Dimitri is reminding her of songs she hasn't thought about in years, when Dimitri hears a voice call his name.

"Dimitri?"

Dimitri and Meg stop and turn to see the couple facing them. Standing in a white fur coat and a wide-brimmed hat is his ex with her new husband, arm in arm. The fur collar frames her face, and her bright red lipstick makes her look pale, while the husband sports a sleek, leather jacket with a cashmere scarf. In seconds, Dimitri can smell the expense of their outerwear along with the familiar scent of that horrible perfume she wears. It brings back bad memories.

"Hey," Dimitri says.

"Good to bump into you," his ex says. Only Dimitri can tell that her comment is dripping with sarcasm. "You look different," she says.

"Thanks, I guess."

Dimitri feels Meg move closer to him. He senses she understands who this is.

"So, you're playing music in bars now?" she asks, pointing to the sign, almost mockingly with an air of condescension.

"And bookstores," Meg chimes in innocently trying to help. Dimitri looks at her and smiles.

"And bookstores," he says, parroting Meg's words. He feels like an idiot.

"What happened to your job at the accounting firm that you have to play in bars now?" Dimitri can't stand her demeanor and that she's asking him a question just to belittle him in front of her husband and Meg. He absolutely refuses to introduce Meg to her, which would mean he'd have to call the vile woman by name.

"For the record, I don't have to do anything. I do it because I love it. I left accounting behind, thank God, because I could—because I never loved it. Opening my own new business soon. Anyway, would love to chat more, but we have dinner plans, and I have to get ready to play soon. So, hope you have a good night."

As if on cue, Meg slips her arm through Dimitri's, and they walk together into the tavern, heads held high, leaving his ex and her husband in the dust on the sidewalk.

*

"Yikes," Meg says, after they've been seated. They hadn't even discussed having dinner together, but Dimitri is thankful that Meg allowed him that small fib. "I'm sorry you had to endure that interaction."

"She's a horrible person, as you could probably see. I've dealt with her BS for years. Actually, it's great not to have to deal with it anymore. That poor guy. I know he has a ton of money and lives well, but really, when you have to live with someone like her, I feel a certain amount of empathy for anyone's future." Dimitri rubs his brow and picks up the menu.

Meg smiles. "The fact that you can have compassion for him shows you are a good person, Dimitri."

"I don't know about all that," Dimitri says, "but I've been there, and know how it goes. So, you'll join me for dinner?"

Meg nods. She is the perfect companion at this moment, and Dimitri is thankful that she was there for that confrontation. It was bound to happen. Annapolis is a small town, and you run into people all over the place, whether you want to or not.

They order a few things off the menu, and settle into their

table. "It's kind of lame that I'm taking you here for dinner. This tavern is my place of work, not exactly a special spot for a date night."

Meg's eyes widen. "Is this a date night?"

"I'd like to think it is," Dimitri says, leaning forward to look at her.

"Then, I supposed it's just perfect," she says, a sexy little smile moving across her face.

Meg
Sunday, March 24

Meg sips her coffee as she stands on her back porch looking at the light reflecting on the water. The sun is strong as it provides a little warmth to the otherwise fifty-degree weather. The blue skies are free of clouds, and she can feel spring trying to break through. In jeans and a light sweater, Meg is content to sit and take in the scenery before work. Dimitri was originally supposed to play at the store today, but something came up at their new music store, and he had to cancel. She fully expects that as soon as their store gets up and running, Dimitri may not have as much time to play at her bookstore.

When Meg had chatted with Dimitri between sets, she told him she would walk herself home, tired from the long day at the bookstore, and that she was looking forward to perhaps another "date night." Dimitri had actually kissed her on the lips—a quick, clumsy kiss but comfortable for two people still in the early phases of getting to know one another. It was momentarily awkward, as he leaned in, giving her very little time to process what was happening, and they locked lips for a quick second.

Thinking of it now, Meg smiles. He's a handsome and kind man. Maybe they'll have a chance to work on getting that kiss a little better next time. Her emotions swirling like a cyclone, she catches herself wishing and hoping there is a next time.

Before walking to work, Meg makes herself a cup of coffee and puts it in her travel tumbler, slips into her coat, and begins the walk to the bookstore. Striding over the Eastport Bridge, Meg notices how calm and clear the water looks. Experienced boaters are taking their boats out because the weather is cooperating. April is drawing near, and the weather continues to warm up a little each day. The morning sun is rising in the sky, and it reflects off the creek. Meg inhales deeply, filling her lungs with the crispness of the spring air, and picks up her pace as she descends the bridge into the city. She can't wait to take her own boat out, hoping Dimitri will be her first passenger this season.

When she arrives at the bookstore, she sees someone familiar standing outside the door with his back to her, seemingly waiting for her to open its doors. It's rare, but sometimes people do come to the store early to shop. When she looks more closely, she stops dead in her tracks and feels her hands begin to tremble, as something drops in the pit of her stomach.

When he turns to face her, he smiles, that cheeky grin, the one she had loved to see from morning to night, three-hundred and sixty-five days a year. The one she imagined seeing forever.

"What on earth are you doing here, Will?" she says to him, obviously stunned.

He's holding an envelope in his hands, and he waves it in the air. "I figured if you're gonna pay someone back, you might as well do it in person."

Putting the key in the door, she flicks on the lights, and everything inside illuminates. Will follows her through the door, and Meg watches his expression as he looks around and takes it in. Wide-eyed, he examines the place without saying a word.

"You've done well for yourself," he says. "I'm impressed."

"Thank you." No need for more than that, she thinks. Inside, she feels off kilter.

He walks toward Meg, reaches for her hand, and places the envelope in the palm of it. "If I could take it all back—every minute, every stupid move I made, every selfish bone and every disregard I had for you—I would. Hear me clearly, Meg. I am apologizing to you again for what I did to destroy our relationship and for the way I hurt you. I'm not proud of it, and I wish I could hit the 'rewind' button. All I can do now is say I'm sorry—truly, truly sorry—repay you, and hope that you'll forgive me."

His earnestness is apparent, and Meg swallows hard.

"I do forgive you," Meg says softly. For two years, she'd imagined hearing Will say these very words. Words that could have helped her understand. A cornucopia of feelings, memories, and emotions begin rising within her, things she's suppressed or had to get over. She feels off-balance, lightheaded. The man she loved with all of her heart, imagined having children and growing old with, is standing before her offering what seems to be a heartfelt and meaningful apology. In her daze, she imagines falling into his arms to hear him say it's going to be okay—all is forgiven—and that they can start over, but instead, she stands there stoically and nods.

"I'm glad," he finally says, after a moment of silence. "Thank you. I don't know if I could have lived with myself if you didn't forgive me." He seems contrite and mature, all his arrogance and pompousness subsiding. In this moment, he seems real, and he's here, and Meg wants to know more.

"Where is Cecelia?" Meg finally asks, figuring at this point, she might as well know the rest of the story about her former friend.

"We called it quits. Well, I called it quits. It wasn't right for either of us, though I knew better than she did."

Meg can't believe what she's hearing. She can't fathom that after everything he put her through, he's now standing before her admitting that the whole sordid triangle was detrimental to all of them. *Camelot*, she thinks. It's *Camelot* in real life, and all three of them have suffered.

Seconds pass, and the words of the moment float into the air, joining the other words housed in books, in memories, in histories, and in imaginations. Silence momentarily haunts Brodie's Books, and Meg and Will look at each other in a familiar way yet knowing that familiarity has slipped away. They are two changed and damaged people. The events of the past have affected them irrevocably.

Will takes a few steps toward her, and Meg blinks back tears she feels forming in her eyes. Mustn't cry, she thinks. Hold it together. This is the closure you need and have yearned for.

Will reaches for her and lifts her chin in a way that asks her to look at him. He holds her face, looking deeply into her eyes—the ones that once loved him back wholeheartedly and without question. He kisses her on the cheek softly. She allows this to happen without a fight, as if in a trance. When he pulls away, he simply says, "I'm sorry, Meg," and then she sees it. Perhaps there is a glint of remorse in his eyes. Perhaps he regrets the way he treated her.

No further words are spoken, and Will walks away from her toward the door. Meg stands frozen as she watches him go, the echo of silence in the bookstore replacing the chaos in her mind.

*

Hours later, Meg is still rattled. She tries to keep her emotions in check when she receives a phone call from Lily, who has decided to throw together that game night they had discussed. Reid and Dimitri do not have a scheduled gig, so Lily says it is the perfect time to host something at her house. Meg wants to say no to the offer, to go home and cry her eyes out and soak in her tub and listen to Adele, but she can hear the excitement in Lily's voice. It is not the right day to honor the boundaries she sets up as an empath. It is a time to interact with her new friends, and so she agrees to go.

"What can I bring?" Meg asks her.

"Just your beautiful self and a bottle of wine," Lily responds.

"I think I can handle the wine part," Meg says, her self-deprecating humor making Lily laugh.

"Oh Meg, you have no idea just how beautiful you are," she says. "Gotta run. Last minute cleaning. See you at seven-thirty."

Meg puts her cellphone in the back pocket of her jeans.

Two seconds later, her phone vibrates again. She answers.

"I assume you're going tonight?" Dimitri asks.

"Yes. Planning on it," she says.

"Great. I'd offer to pick you up, but I'll be coming from the store. I'll see you there?"

"Yes," she says. Meg is flattered that he is checking on her.

When the last customer leaves, she tidies up and powers down. She gave nine letters today to various customers she deemed needed a pick-me-up. The tenth letter is still sitting in her purse. She takes the check Will gave to her from her back pocket, opens the remaining envelope, and slides the check inside.

She figures she might need to re-read one of her own letters tonight. Or maybe she needs to receive some inspiration from someone else.

*

As she walks down Main Street and the sun lowers in the sky, she feels a chill run up her spine. She needs to go home and change and drive over to Lily's. The brisk walk is doing her good—the outside air feels therapeutic on her face.

Walking on the brick sidewalks, peering inside windows, her mind is racing from the events of earlier in the day. Will had driven all the way to see her, to pay her back the money she is owed, and to apologize once again. Will was right in this regard—he had apologized plenty, it's just that Meg had never really felt he meant any of it. Until today.

Sometimes on her walks, she stops and sits and listens to the water slap the docks. Sometimes she grabs an ice cream cone from the ice cream shop near the harbor and plants herself on a bench in the square. Sitting near the water, being on her boat, strolling the docks—these are ways her empath needs are satisfied—and she listens when the need to do so arises.

Suddenly, and without expectation, she sees Will again. He is sitting in the window of a restaurant alone. He doesn't see her, but she sees him. Her heart pounds, and for a moment she feels that pang she felt so long ago, that pang of wanting to be near him, talking things over for full healing, and departing as friends.

Meg passes by the window and stands alongside the restaurant so Will cannot see her. She can see his silhouette through the window.

Immediately, she begins to feel like a horrible person for not offering to keep him company. She wonders if he is staying in town. Wonders if he plans on staying for a while. Thoughts are flooding her brain. She is a good person...meant to do good for those she encounters...she believes in her heart that not helping and not caring for others is a sin of the greatest level. She pauses, takes a breath, and decides to walk into the restaurant to see if Will would like her to join him.

She has to eat. She could use a bite to eat before she heads to Lily's...

She places her hand on the door handle, and walks inside the restaurant. The hostess asks her if she needs a table. Meg says she doesn't, that she's meeting a friend. She steps inside the dining area and sees him across the room, near the window.

With a blonde.

They are holding hands across the table. He is smiling at her.

Without him seeing her, Meg quickly turns away and scurries out the door.

That was close, she thinks. Dangerously close.

Will has fooled her again. She has misjudged his character, wanting to believe he has changed, wanting to believe people can change for the better. While some people certainly can change, the truth, she has learned, is that Will plays women, and he probably always will. He lacks sincerity and true selflessness. He will always care about himself first. Everyone else is just a pawn in his game.

There on the sidewalk, she chastises herself for almost allowing her emotions to slip back to a place she promised never, ever to go again. She takes a deep breath and pulls herself together. She will no longer be involved in Will's twisted and toxic games.

She quietly thanks God that she didn't make a fool of herself, and she pledges never to allow any thought of Will to taint her brain.

It is over.

Nothing more will pass between them. Nothing ever, ever again.

Eva

Sunday, March 24

The light rapping on the back door at three-fifteen in the afternoon startles Eva. She's curled up on the sofa, deep into a new novel Meg recommended, when she hears the knocking. She knows it's Reid, as he's typically the only one who comes in through the back French doors.

"Coming," she shouts loudly enough so he can hear her. She's wearing leggings and a sweater, and her pink fuzzy slippers.

She opens the door, and Reid's got a smile on his face. He has shopping bags in both hands and has just come from the mall. Brownie is happy to see him.

"I could really use a second opinion on some of these things I bought. Care to lend an eye?"

Eva smiles at him. "I could lend both, if you like." Reid acknowledges her joke as he puts the bags on the sofa. "I would have been happy to have shopped with you," she says.

Reid stops and looks at her. "Honestly, I wasn't sure if you would go."

"Why not?"

"You've been in a funk, and I didn't want to push you to do anything."

"I appreciate that...but I think I'm getting over it, thanks mostly to your care and concern. And I re-read my bookstore letter, so there's always that."

"That's good. Glad to hear that. I read mine often, too. So, do you mind if I do a few try-ons? I need a couple of new outfits."

"For what?"

"Well, I'm going to be managing a music store, and I typically wear jeans with paint stains and holes in them, so I need a new wardrobe."

"You have a point there," Eva says.

Reid puts his bags down and glances at Eva's fuzzy puppy dog slippers. She sees him look at them.

"Are these causing you to second-guess asking for my opinion?" she says, waving her right slipper in the air.

"They do make a statement."

"As they should," she says, laughing.

"Can I change in your bathroom?" Reid asks.

"Use the office, it's got more room," she says, walking him over to the room, and she closes the door behind him.

He reappears a few minutes later in sleek trousers and a button down. She gives the thumbs up on that. Next, he changes into a pair of dark wash jeans and a pullover. Another thumbs up. She's noticing how good he looks in more fitted clothes, his physique perfectly suited to his clothing choices. She notices how fit he is, and how strong his arms are. His last outfit is a pair of dark slacks and a fitted shirt in a pale blue color. It's Eva's favorite.

"I knew you'd like this one. It reminds me of some of the pretty clothes you wear to work," Reid says, feeling triumphant. "I'm wearing this to the grand opening."

"It suits you."

"Oh, and speaking of suits, I have a dark grey suit that I'm wearing to the party for my parents, but I bought this new shirt and tie to go with it. What do you think?"

Eva examines the shirt and tie; they look great together, and she knows they will go well with the suit.

"Looks like you have a good eye, Reid Jones," she says. "All winners."

"And you're not just saying that, right? Remember, I haven't had any sort of day job that hasn't involved holding a hammer or a drill. I want to look respectable. I can't just wear jeans and a t-shirt like I do at the clubs. Dimitri's a sharp dresser. I have to try to keep up."

Eva laughs. "Yes, he is."

Reid doesn't know exactly how to interpret that comment, so he just keeps moving along to the next thing.

"I actually have something for you, too," he says.

"What do you mean?"

"I bought you a little something. You don't have to say you like it or keep it. I saved the receipt. But when I saw it, it just looked like you should be wearing it."

He jogs back into the office and grabs the bag that's intended for Eva. He hands it over, and she takes the bag by the handles, smiles, and thanks him.

"This is so generous and thoughtful," she says, surprised by the kind gesture.

"Well, open it first before you say anything," Reid says.

She reaches into the bag and sorts through the tissue paper; she pulls out a beautiful, turquoise chiffon dress. It's simple, with a ribbon sash. Very French inspired. Eva is stunned.

"How did you know my size? This is gorgeous!"

"Creepy as it may sound, when I fixed your closet doors, I

peeked at the size of your dresses. You're a small."

"I am a small. Although all this emotional eating might move me up to a medium."

"I don't think so," Reid says with a smile.

"Well, thank you, Reid. It's just so pretty. And I'm going to wear it to your parents' anniversary party."

There's an awkward pause, and Eva doesn't know whether to kiss him, hug him, or just leave it at "thank you."

Trying not to think too hard, her instincts guide her. She walks over to him and reaches up to kiss him on the cheek. "It is very sweet of you," she says.

Eva watches Reid's face blush, the two of them vulnerable in their own ways, and that tender moment makes her feel connected to him. She thinks for a moment and can't remember a time when Kyle ever bought her something to wear, especially not something as beautiful as this.

"Do you want to ride over to Lily's together?" she asks, interrupting the moment.

"That sounds great," he says, and she playfully punches him in the arm.

*

Eva examines her outfit in the mirror, and then opens the top drawer of her dresser and pulls out the letter. Knowing that Meg wrote the letter, and that Meg is now a friend of hers, gives it even more meaning now. Eva flattens the paper and reads it aloud.

When she is finished reading it, she places it on her nightstand. There's something in the words that she will never grow tired of reading.

Lily
Sunday, March 24

"Mom!" Cora calls, helping to set the table. "Do you want me to use the flowers as the centerpiece?"

"Yes," Lily shouts to her daughter from the top of the stairs. She's applying the last bit of her makeup as she slips into her tan pumps—a new pair that just came into the store. She's casual in her jeans and a light pink sweater. Over the years, Lily has become quite adept at multi-tasking, from helping her daughter with projects and getting her to events on time, to making dinner while paying the bills.

After she fixes her lipstick and combs her hair one last time, she descends her cottage's stairs to face her daughter, who is inspecting her outfit.

"That's some pink lipstick," Cora says.

"Too much?" Lily asks.

"Maybe, but what the heck, right Mom? You are the style queen in the middle of a mid-life crisis."

"Haha, very funny," Lily says, and makes a face at Cora. "Let me see what you've done to the table."

Cora is a visual person and enjoys working with her hands. She loves the arts and takes great pride in making things look pretty. Lily has been able to see the similarities between them over the years—their enjoyment of books, movies, arts and crafts, fashion and design—and she is happy that these similarities they share keep them together, never running out of things to discuss.

"Wait," Lily says, "why are there six place settings? We only need five—Meg, Eva, Dimitri, Reid, and me. Is that one for you?"

"Nope. Once I meet all your new friends, I'm going out. That place is for a surprise guest," she says, raising an eyebrow.

"You didn't! Cora Jane Webster!"

Cora smiles at her mother. "Don't be mad. I did. And I think you will be happy for my interference."

"Are you kidding?" Lily asks, incredulously. "Seriously, Cora. Are you kidding me?"

"I'm not, so it's a good thing you look so amazing and have a perfect meal ready to go."

"I cannot believe you did this!"

"Well, it seems you two have been spending more time together lately, and he did get us those tickets to our Paris night in Baltimore. I didn't want his feelings to be hurt that you planned a party without inviting him. And look at it this way—he's already met your friends!"

Lily can feel her face becoming flush. She knew she could have invited Brad if she had wanted to, but she wasn't sure she wanted her ex-husband here tonight. She's not prepared for that kind of mingling. After he left the tavern when he had tracked her down—AND spent time with her new friends—she could sense something was going on, and that maybe even he wanted to have a deeper conversation about things. Lily had put him off. She wasn't ready to forget the recent past that freely. Or was she? Loving someone deeply always makes staying angry at them impossible.

The fact that Cora has intervened on purpose and jumped in certainly indicates that she wishes her parents would reunite. It's written all over Cora's face, and it breaks Lily's heart to see her working to help fix what's broken. Lily and Brad have had cordial and surface conversations, but they have not discussed their relationship, its hurts, and its dissolution. Lily is afraid to talk about it, and she can tell Brad is tentative about it as well.

"Stop wearing that frown on your face, Mom. It's going to be fun. You always told me how compatible you and Dad were. Maybe you can just sort of...find that fun again. Plus, you won't have to have any serious conversations," Cora says. "All your friends will help with that. Added bonus!"

Her daughter knows her so well and can read her mind at times.

"I'm just very surprised that you would invite him without talking to me about it, that's all. It's my party." Lily is trying to remain calm.

"I know. I probably should have told you, but you might have whined about it like you're doing now. Besides, he told me how much he liked your new friends, and that he was happy you'd found nice people to hang around. I figured he's alone in that house, and he could probably use some new friends, too."

Lily folds her arms and looks at her daughter, the matchmaker.

"Just don't expect anything to come of this, Cora. Don't go thinking that we're going to run off into the sunset or anything. We're divorced, remember?"

Cora folds her arms, mimicking her mother. "Well, I'm not sure what your futures hold, but it would be nice if you could at least be friends."

Lily looks at her young daughter. At seventeen, she still wants her parents to work it out. The divorce was hard on her. She lives with

Lily and visits Brad every other weekend. And she's still living with the fact that her behavior on Brad's wedding day has altered his life. Is she hoping for a reunion so that she can dispense of her guilt and justify her actions? Lily has done her best to try to explain that she is not responsible for what happened, despite that Cora still believes it was all her doing.

The doorbell rings, and Lily must leave the analytical thinking for later. She's got guests to attend to at the moment. Slapping her face and telling herself to pull it together, she opens the front door with a smile.

*

Meg arrives first and gushes over Lily's charming house. After a quick tour, Meg stands in the kitchen talking to Cora about books and the bookstore, the two of them deep in conversation, when the doorbell rings. Lily opens the door.

Brad stands before her. They both look at each other for a moment, and Lily would give anything to be able to hear the thoughts that are running through his head.

"Hi, Brad," Lily says, as he returns the greeting with, "Hey, Lil," and hands her a bottle of wine. It's one of their favorites.

"Thanks," she says.

"Before I come in, I just want to make sure you're okay with me being here," he says.

"Sure. Cora invited you, so of course you are welcome."

"Yes, but you didn't invite me, and I want to make sure you're good with this."

"I'm good with this," Lily says, doing her best to believe the words she is saying.

"Are there other people here, too?" Brad asks.

"Yes. Just Meg, so far. The rest are on the way."

Brad looks puzzled. "Oh, okay."

"Wait—" Lily says, finally catching on to what Cora has done. "Did you think it was just us?"

"Well, us and Cora."

"She's sneaky, our girl," Lily says. "She's misled you. I'm sorry. I'm hosting a dinner party and game night with friends."

"In that case, I'll just drop off the wine for you all to enjoy."

"Nonsense," Lily says, suddenly feeling bad for him and the ruse their daughter created. "You're here now." She can see Reid and Eva getting out of their car. "You come on in. It'll be fun. I made some of your favorites."

"Are you sure?" Brad asks.

"Yes, I'm sure they're your favorites," Lily says with a wink, and then turns to say hello to Eva and Reid, who seem cheery as they arrive. Eva hands over a warm loaf of freshly baked bread from the local bakery, as Lily takes a whiff and leads them inside.

*

Lily pours the wine as her friends and Cora chat in the living room. She's happy that Cora is getting to meet them all in person, although she is annoyed by her antics and manipulation. Nonetheless, Lily watches Cora from the other side of the room and still feels proud of her—despite her intrusive attempt to get her father to the house tonight. Cora has grown into a beautiful, confident, and engaging young lady. How did this happen so fast? Lily catches Brad watching her, too, as Cora talks to Eva and Reid. As parents of this young woman, they nod to each other, clearly witnessing their daughter's growing maturity, and sense that even if they didn't have the capacity to last, they created a daughter who is representative of the best of them.

Lily takes a sip of her wine and wonders if there has been some sort of intervention that has taken place on behalf of all of them. She can't quite put her finger on it, but a sense of intrigue washes over her as she looks around the room and accepts her current station in life. At the moment, she feels unusually content.

*

Dimitri comes bounding in the door last, and Cora jumps up to greet him. After a few quick words of welcome, she escorts him to the dinner table, where everyone is waiting to sit. The appetizers are nearly gone, and all of Lily's new friends are having fun mingling.

"I'm sorry I'm so darn late. We had trouble with the final inspection."

Reid hears Dimitri say this, and he leans in for the discussion.

"What's going on with the inspection?"

"Oh, something with the electrical wiring and all the equipment that needs to be plugged in. Apparently, we need to add another fuse box. The electrician is going to come Monday morning and sort it out. Honestly, we just need to check this off and we'll be ready to go," Dimitri says.

"I'm so excited for you both," Meg says, smiling at them.

"We're pretty excited, too," Reid says.

"I signed up ten new students just today," Dimitri says.

"Are you kidding?" Reid asks, his face bright with enthusiasm.

"No. I'm not sure what's happening. Word is spreading."

Lily grabs the bottle of champagne, sensing it's a good moment to start the dinner party. Brad helps her pop the top. They pour the champagne into glasses and pass them around. Reid politely declines and grabs a water. Cora looks disheartened not to have a glass, so Lily pours one little mouthful.

"She can have my bit," Reid teases. Lily figures that if she's grown up enough to play matchmaker, she's grown up enough to have a sip of champagne.

"So, who wants to make a toast?" Lily asks.

They all look at each other and smile.

"I will," Cora says. The room becomes quiet for a second, and they all look at her, standing there in her Boho dress, her black military boots, and her two long, thin braids cascading down the sides of her soft curls. "I've actually never made a real toast before, so this will be fun."

"Well, then," Lily says, not at all sure where this is going but quite confident that she's raised someone squarely enough to pull it off, "let's hear it!"

Cora grabs the glass, in full command. "Here's a toast to all of you," Cora says. "My mother hasn't been this happy in a while, and it's wonderful to see that she's made some nice, new friends. I was never too fond of the old ones, but that's another story for another day. Anyway, I'm so glad I got to meet you all tonight." Then, turning to Lily, she says softly, "Can I tell them this was my idea?" and Lily laughs, and tells her that she can. "And this dinner party was my idea, because you know how parents always want to meet their kids' friends? I was feeling like it was time to meet my mom's friends that I kept hearing so much about, and now, here you are. So, 'Hello, new friends' and thank you for coming. Cheers and enjoy your food—you, too, Dad, because these are some of your favorites."

The friends all laugh, and Cora raises her glass. They all clink each other's glasses and take sips. Cora hugs her mom and dad, kisses them both on the cheek, grabs her purse and coat from the chair, and waves goodbye, slipping out the front door. "Gotta run to my own party. My friend Ginny's picking me up. Have fun, guys!"

So much polish, Lily thinks to herself, as she wonders for a second just who is raising whom.

*

After lots of laughter, food, wine, and a game of hilarious charades, the night winds down. It is a Sunday evening, after all, and by eleven o'clock, with a workday on the horizon, the party slowly comes to an end.

Meg grabs her coat and explains she has to open up her store early in the morning. Lily can relate, understanding this responsibility all too well. "We're working girls," Meg says. "We can't be partying until the wee hours."

"I can't stay up until the wee hours anymore either, ladies" Eva says. "I've been going all day, too, helping at the music store."

Reid has his eyes on Eva, rarely taking them off her. Lily notices that they've become closer, but she makes no mention of it when the two of them leave together after profusely thanking her for hosting such a great night.

When Dimitri sees Eva and Reid rise to leave and watches Meg begin to straighten up and collect her things, he stands as well, and thanks Lily for her hospitality. Brad shakes Dimitri's hand.

"Thanks, Lil," Brad says to her, as he stands at the door with Dimitri and Meg. "I'd better get going, too."

Lily is surprised that he's leaving along with the rest of them, but she maintains her smile, and thanks him for coming.

"It was such a fun night, Lily," Meg says. "Thanks for having us. I'll host the next one. Can't wait to do it again soon."

"Me, too," Lily says. The three of them walk out the door, and turn to wave goodnight to her, as she stands on the porch waving goodbye.

Lily turns and closes the door behind her and looks at the remaining mess she has to clean up. The ladies had helped her along the way, but there are still a few things that need attention. She walks over to the table that's adjacent to the front window and blows out the candle that still flickers. She can hear voices out on the front lawn, so she dims the front light to be inconspicuous as she peers from behind the curtains. She sees Dimitri drive away, yet Brad and Meg remain chatting on the sidewalk, the two of them engaged in an intimate conversation near Meg's car.

Lily can feel her heart sink a bit.

Meg is single. Brad is single. And perhaps Dimitri is just a friend to Meg. Lily jumps to the conclusion that maybe she has it all wrong.

All this time, Lily has been clinging to hope, a hope that maybe she didn't even want to `recognize. She cannot believe she has let herself be so vulnerable. After countless therapy sessions, she has not taken the advice of her counselor to "grow past things," as she had told her to do months ago. The mere fact that she is a hopeless romantic has once again made her look like a fool. She picks up what remains of her wine, takes a swig, and sits very still.

The impulse to look out the window again is strong—to see if they're still there—but she's frozen in place, her mind calculating scenarios she'd never even imagined until just now. When psychologists counsel you to "move on from divorce" when you were the one who was hurt, they forget to hand you a manual offering specific instructions as to just how one goes about doing it. It's easier said than done. No matter how hard she has tried, no matter how much she has attempted to move on, it's been impossible for her.

Imagining Brad with his young fiancée—a woman she did not know personally and had no interest in learning more about—was easier to do than having to imagine him with her new, sweet friend, Meg. But Lily can certainly understand why men find Meg so attractive; her kindness supersedes her natural beauty. Tears begin to form in her eyes, and Lily feels herself begin to—

Just then, Lily is startled by the knocking she hears coming from the front door. It begins as a soft rapping, and is followed by the sound of Brad's voice.

"Lil, can I come in?" he says through the door. Lily swallows hard and fights back the tears, straightening her clothes as she hesitantly gets up out of the chair, fearing what might come next, and opens the front door.

Brad is standing there in front of her holding the book about Paris she had given to him for Christmas. Lily looks at it closely, and then back at Brad. He is grinning from ear to ear.

"If you have a few minutes, there's something I want to show you," he says to her, "and there's something I need to say to you."

They walk back into the living room, and Brad motions for her to sit down next to him on the sofa, as he pulls out an envelope from inside the book, shows it to Lily. Then, he begins to tell her the story of a letter found inside a book that has changed everything.

Reid
Saturday, April 6

No matter how many times he attempts to tie his tie, it's still askew. Reid finally takes it off and decides to open the top button of his pressed, white shirt to see what his suit looks like without the tie. More and more men are going tieless, and Reid chooses to go with this new look—very Ryan Gosling, although, admittedly, he wishes he looked a little bit more like him. He can feel little butterflies in his stomach—a symptom of the anxiety he is feeling for both the anniversary party and for the grand opening of their music store, which is happening next weekend. He also considers today a first date with Eva. There is a lot going on, and he is feeling a little overwhelmed.

As he closes the cottage door behind him and locks it, he makes his way across the yard to Eva's back door; he can see her through the windows in the dress—the turquoise one he bought for her. She looks stunning. Reid can hear her crossing the hardwood floors in her heels from outside the house.

"Well, hello, handsome!" she says, opening the door wide. "Are you ready for the big event?"

"I think so," he says. "Ditched the tie. Do you think that's okay?"

"It looks perfect—very GQ," she says. "I'm ready. Just fed Brownie, and I'm all set to try to be the perfect date."

"Is that so?"

"Yes. I've been mentally practicing all week. It's time to step out of the on-deck circle and come up to bat. It's been a while, and I'm kind of out of practice."

Reid chuckles and looks at her, smiling at her baseball analogy. He feels lucky to know her, and feeling lucky is a recent emotion for him.

"Let me assure you—if you're out of practice, then I've been sitting on the bench for years."

She looks at him sideways.

"Well, mister, let's get you off the bench, then."

"Not just yet," he says. "You haven't heard me say that you look gorgeous—really beautiful, Eva. I like the hair up like that. It shows off your smile."

Eva blushes and thanks him, and Reid can't imagine where he got the courage to say something like that, but it's heartfelt, and he means it.

"A girl doesn't get a compliment like that very often," she says, imitating Mae West. "I'll take it."

Brownie is panting in front of them looking from one human to the other, and then curls up on her dog bed, putting her head near her front paws.

"We'll see you later, Brownie-girl," Eva says, and there's something in the way she says the pronoun "we" that makes Reid feel instantly at home with his date.

*

Two hours later, Reid and Eva arrive in Bethany Beach, Delaware. Eva is stunned by the beauty of the beach home owned by

Emme's best friends. It's a gorgeous place to celebrate the occasion. Reid explains that he and his family have vacationed in Bethany Beach for years, and it's where is father proposed to his mother.

As they tour the property and reach the top level, Eva and Reid look across to the Atlantic Ocean. Reid's father and mother are mingling with all their friends and family. Caterers pass around appetizers to the guests. When Eva and Reid get a moment to chat with his parents, they share how happy they are to see them, especially Reid, and comment on how great he looks. They greet Eva with hugs, as they are reintroduced to her.

Many of the eighty guests in attendance haven't seen Reid in years. He's kept himself away from everyone, embarrassed by his own setbacks and life choices, but today, he's feeling a lot better. He likes the suit. He's happy to be rebuilding the relationship with his parents. Emme has taken to Eva as well, and Reid watches them chat as if they are old friends. At one point, as Reid and his father are standing on the deck, Emme turns to him, and without anyone seeing gives him a thumbs up and a wink, indicating that she likes Eva very much. Emme's always been supportive in everything Reid does, and was his sounding board when life became difficult. Even when Emme didn't agree with his decisions, she loved him unconditionally. He realizes now he didn't appreciate her enough.

Later, as the DJ begins to play a lot of old standards and people take to the designated dance floor in the living room, Emme loops her arm through Reid's as Eva talks with Reid's mom near the dessert table.

"I like her a lot," Emme says, as they dance together. "You've picked a good one there, Reid."

"Don't put the cart before the horse," he says. "We're still just friends."

"Best way to begin a relationship, don't you think?" she says, looking him squarely in the eyes.

Reid nods. He also slips a check into her hand to pay his portion for the celebration. Emme winks back and thanks him.

"So, how's the 'I quit drinking' thing going?" she asks.

"Well, let's see. I haven't touched a drink since I told you I'd quit. I even went to a dinner party recently where there was plenty of alcohol, and I drank none of it. I'm actually pretty proud of myself. I feel better, too. I started running again."

"Are you kidding?"

"Nope. Running. I'm up to six miles every other day."

"Wow. I'm proud of you, too, little brother. You really seem to be turning your life around."

"Well, Em, I think we both know it's about time. Better late than never, I suppose."

*

Reid's mom and dad profusely thank Reid and Eva for coming to the party, enveloping them in massive hugs. Friends make speeches and toasts, and Emme's playlist is put to use for dancing. The cake, from a local bakery, looks like a wedding cake. Reid enjoys catching up with people he hasn't seen in a while. It is nice, Reid thinks, to spend the day with family and extended family and friends. He is enjoying himself.

Eva waves to him from across the room, the corners of her mouth turning up.

Reid waves back.

He's lost in the moment for a second, watching her as she interacts with his family, feeling proud to have Eva on his arm for the day. He knows he has grown accustomed to seeing that smile almost every day, and truth be told—even though the idea scares him a little— he has quickly realized more and more often that he might like to see that smile for the rest of his life.

*

By the time they return from the party, the sun is setting and the full moon is visible low in the sky as they drive over the Chesa- peake Bay Bridge, heading back to Annapolis. Reid is well aware that while they have been schmoozing all day long, there has been little physical contact between them, except for when they were dancing.

When he thinks back on his relationship with Lexi, it's easy to blame the other person for the demise. Was it ever good, he wonders, or was it an illusion? Time and distance force a person to see things more clearly, and he's willing to admit he was not a good boyfriend. He was a mess. He never did the things she wanted to do. He wanted her to hang out with his friends, his drinking buddies, and he rarely spent time with her friends and family. He was selfish, and he took ad- vantage of her kindness. He drank way too much. In hindsight, Lexi had every right to end their relationship. She wasn't getting what she needed, and he was too stupid to listen and alter his behavior, change his ways, or be responsible in any manner.

Listening to Eva share her experiences with Kyle heightened Reid's own revelations about his relationship with Lexi. It was yet another case of one person's selfishness camouflaged as something meaningful...as a sense of connection, and yet, it had disintegrated into...nothingness. Reid vows not to make the same mistakes he made with Lexi when faced with a new relationship. He keeps a record of reminders in his journal and has become a fan of inspirational quotes to help his mindset.

And the person he hopes to have that new relationship with is riding beside him in the car, chatting about how beautiful the party was, how nice his parents are, and how he's lucky to have such a kind, supportive sister.

She turns to look at him as they pull up in front of the house.

"Why don't we both get into some comfortable clothes, and then we can meet back up and eat these cannolis your mother sent home with me. I'm pretty sure the Orioles are on tonight. Care to watch with me?" she asks him, as they close the car doors.

Reid agrees, and fifteen minutes later, they are sitting in their sweats on the carpet, leaning up against the couch, eating cannolis, and watching the game. It's the fifth inning, and the Orioles are up by three. Brownie curls up next to him and puts her head on his lap. Reid rubs the dog behind her ears, her favorite spot. Reid sees Eva watching him pet Brownie out of the corner of his eye.

"Are you a little jealous of your dog's affection for me?" He loves Eva's eyes. They are big and brown and expressive.

"Maybe," she says.

Eva stares intently into Reid's eyes, and he can't stop looking at her. He swallows hard. Forgetting about Brownie for a second, Reid takes Eva's face in his hands and kisses her. She kisses him back, the cannolis roll off the plate, and Brownie trots over to the other side of the room, allowing the humans to have their privacy for whatever might come next.

Dimitri

Saturday, April 20

Dimitri arrives early to the music store, and despite being as early as he is, Reid has beaten him there. It's Grand Opening Day, and Eva has planned a ribbon cutting ceremony for ten o'clock. She also hired some face painters, ordered a balloon arch, and secured a couple of local celebrities to come and help kick off the store's opening. After creating the store's social media platforms and promoting their news for the last couple of months, the store is gaining followers and fans, thanks to all of Eva's experience with promotion. Publishing quick teaser videos and interviews with Reid and Dimitri, in addition to showcasing the behind-the-scenes look at the store's progress, along with clips of their performances, the social media strategy has worked. Dimitri promised to pay her for her time, despite her refusal to take any money for the work. "This is what we do for friends," she had told him.

"You should think about creating your own agency," Dimitri had told her. "Do you know how many people could use your services? You'd have so many clients who are entrepreneurs, but don't have the manpower to operate our events and social media."

"It's funny you should say that," she had said. "I've been doing public relations for years, and I have to admit, I have thought about going out on my own. Maybe someday."

Dimitri approaches Reid, who is working on the computer system. "Hey, partner," Reid says. "How are you feeling?"

"Good...nervous...excited. How about you?"

"Same."

They begin setting up the store for the day's events. Reid and Dimitri had both stayed late last night and didn't leave the store until one in the morning. The private studio rooms—all eight of them—had received the final touches last night. Instruments had been moved into the soundproof rooms, and Eva had Baba help for a couple of hours with her close friend, Ellen, to decorate the inside, making it look tasteful and festive. Ellen even brought her kids to help. Then, Reid and Dimitri powered up their computer system to ensure it was without glitches. They also stocked the final shipment of sheet music and paraphernalia that arrived late in the afternoon. The week prior, they had mailed out postcards to those on their mailing list from the website Eva had helped them create. Things seemed to be moving smoothly, and they knew they could not have gotten as far as they did so quickly without her help—and without guidance from Meg and Lily, who both had their share of entrepreneurial stories to tell about owning retail stores. Dimitri was thankful for all of their input.

Before long, musicians are lined up to play around the clock for the grand opening, and the first few arrive at nine and set up outside the store. For an April day, they realize they are blessed with warm temperatures, hovering around seventy-two degrees with low clouds, as they get ready to cut the ribbon. Eva helps with the celebrities and gets them settled. She also has the giant ribbon and introduces the guys to a couple of local reporters who will interview them before the ceremonies begin.

"Do you think we'll get a good crowd today?" Dimitri asks

Reid, as they stand outside, listening to their first act begin to play, the two of them feeling anxious about the launch.

"I think that if Eva is any good at her job, and I believe she is excellent at it, we will have a very solid day today," he says with a wink.

"We can't blame it on Eva if it's not good," Dimitri says back.

"That's negative thinking," Reid says, "and the two of us have had enough negative thinking to last a lifetime. It's time we change our mindset. And I was teasing. I would never blame Eva for anything. She's been a trooper. I have total confidence in her efforts to help us, and I know you do, too."

"Did I hear my name? Don't talk about me unless you're saying something flattering," Eva says, coming up behind them. She studies them for a second, and points to them both. "You're both nervous. I can see it in the way you two are standing with your arms folded and the expression on your faces. Now loosen up, uncross your arms, smile, and chat with your customers. They are starting to arrive. You must network and practice your public relations skills."

"Yes, ma'am," they both say.

"Ha ha." She looks at Dimitri, then at Reid. "It's going to be a great day. You're going to have a very good launch. Now schmooze and mingle! Remember, people will want to be a part of your brand because they know and like both of you."

Eva leaves them to it, and she begins to chat with people, check the store's decorations, organize the celebrity table, and chat with the local media. Her public relations hat is on, and Dimitri marvels as he watches her work from a distance. He wonders where all her confidence comes from and wishes he had more of it himself. It's been interesting to observe the way she works, and he's learned a lot from her about marketing and promotion. As well, Dimitri has noticed that Reid's become even more enchanted with her over these last few weeks, though he has downplayed their relationship.

When it's time for the ribbon cutting, a sizable crowd has assembled, and the local paper's photographer moves into place. Eva, acting as the emcee, gives a short overview of the store, its little history, and introduces Reid and Dimitri. Then, as Dimitri says a few words of welcome, he feels his heart pounding. He's genuinely nervous, and thanks everyone for coming. They cut the ribbon and officially launch the store: D&R's Music House. A few camera flashes go off, and Dimitri shakes hands with Reid, and they pose for a photo for the newspaper.

Dimitri watches Eva photograph the event with her own phone, no doubt for social media posts. He also takes note that she's taking a lot of photos of Reid. Dimitri smiles, as he is quite aware of the affection between them. And then he turns his head and notices Meg, Lily, Cora, Brad, Reid's family, and his own father, who are all standing slightly off to the side, but all together, chatting and taking pictures of the event. The fact that Meg and Lily have been able to leave their own businesses to come down to show support is endearing.

Dimitri swallows hard, wanting to capture the moment.

Baba walks up to him, a proud grin on his face. "Good thing you finally cut that hair—you didn't break the newspaper's camera," he teases.

Dimitri hugs his father. "Thanks for being here," he tells him.

"Your mother would be so proud. You may have hit some bumpy patches, but look how far you've come? I wish she could see how you've followed your dream. That was all she ever wanted for you. What we both wanted for you." Dimitri notices his father's eyes filling with tears.

"Aw, Baba," he says. "I couldn't have done any of this without you."

Meg
Saturday, April 27

On the night of the fire, Meg had crawled comfortably into her bed, and she recounted the delightful evening she spent with Dimitri and his father. Dimitri had asked her to join them for dinner, and she couldn't say no, despite working all day and having a slight headache. She'd taken Tylenol early in the morning to knock out the pain and had hydrated herself all day. She is prone to headaches because she doesn't drink enough water at work when she gets busy, and she sometimes doesn't care for herself as well as she should. She recognizes this as one of her bad habits that she needs to break.

Dimitri had picked up Chinese food, and they'd met at his dad's place. His father's cute home was neat as a pin, and they'd sat and talked at the dinner table for hours, listening to his father tell stories of his early years, raising his kids, the sacrifices he made along the way, and then the conversation turned to books. His father had admitted to hating to read when he was younger, but as he'd aged and began to find books that engaged him, his appetite for good stories grew.

"I can't tell you how happy it makes me to hear you say these words out loud," Meg had said. "When I opened the bookstore originally, it was to encourage people like you to open a book now and then...and maybe in the process, get them to love reading."

"I do love reading now," his father had said. "It took me a while, but I found my way."

"I know! I can tell you mean it," she had said, laughing.

"What do you like best about owning the bookstore?" his father had asked genuinely.

"Everything. The stories. The people. Helping them find a book that will be relatable or life-changing for them or just make them fall in love with a genre. I truly believe books have the power to change people. But ultimately, it's about connecting people together who share a love of reading and storytelling for me."

"And why do you write the letters?" Dimitri had asked. It came out of the blue.

Meg froze for a second. She knew Dimitri was referring to the letter she had put in his book when he was despondent and came into the store that December night. She also knew that at some point she might be asked about the letters by any of her new friends; she just didn't expect to be asked now, in front of his father.

"Well..." she had started to say.

"What letters?" Dimitri's father had interrupted, completely confused.

"The letters in the books," Dimitri had said. "I got one. It helped me get out of a dark place."

"I'm glad."

"What dark place? Someone please tell me about the letters in the books!"

And so Meg did.

She told them both the story of Brodie, how he loved when Meg would read to him. She spoke of his situation, of her commitment to him, of his funeral and death and the cemetery where he's buried. She shared the story of her aunt and uncle's generosity, and of the letter she received herself, from her friend John, and how it changed her life.

She told them about her prior career and how she knew she wanted to connect with people and become a part of a community, and that the idea of the bookstore and moving to Annapolis grew from fulfilling that need. Then, she got to the part of her story where she explained the letters as her own way to try to help encourage people, to let them know they're not alone, as she, herself, had felt alone many, many nights. She bared it all—even about Will—and told them that she is a full-blown empath and explained to them in detail what it means to be an empath. Sometimes, she had said, it made her feel particularly alone.

"Wow. It all makes sense because you are such a caring person, Meg," Dimitri had said when she had finished telling her stories. "I can see that, and we're still getting to know one another."

"Thank you, as are you," Meg had replied.

Dimitri's father had appeared engrossed by this story. "I'm enjoying getting to know you, too. How many letters have you placed inside books that people have received since you've been at the bookstore?" he had asked.

"Well, let's see...a lot. Ten a day since I've opened the store."

"Do you have any idea how many people you've helped?"

"Here and there, I do. Some people write back to me. But on the whole, the answer's no," she had replied.

"But that doesn't mean you haven't helped them. You very well may have," his father had said, matter-of-factly.

"I'd like to think so."

When they had finished marveling at the story, they played a couple of card games, and then Meg had excused herself because she was so tired and her head was still throbbing.

She had hugged them both goodbye, and Dimitri had kissed her softly on the lips. When she had said her final "goodnight," she left for home, ready to turn in for the night.

*

At three-fifteen in the morning, Meg shoots straight up out of sleep, sensing that something's wrong. She quickly turns on the light and takes a deep breath. Was it a dream? A nightmare? She feels hot under her covers and needs water.

She makes her way to the bathroom to splash cold water on her face, when she hears the phone ring. She runs to the nightstand to pick it up.

"Hello?"

"Is this Meg?"

"Yes." She can hear commotion on the other end of the line, the sound of a truck humming.

"Meg, I'm sorry to wake you, but there's a fire." It's Crystal, the woman who owns the children's clothing boutique across from Brodie's Books.

"What?" she asks, feeling a bit lightheaded.

"Your store is on fire, and the fire department is doing its best to put it out."

"Oh my God," she says, undressing and throwing herself into her jeans. "I'll be right down. Is it gone? Is the store gone?"

"It's—oh, honey, I'm so sorry to tell you this—it's in flames."

"Yes, but is it gone?" she asks, desperately.

"I can't tell," Crystal says.

She should have paid closer attention to the feelings she'd experienced all day. She'd felt a sense of gloom, or doom, or foreboding that she couldn't quite put her finger on. Yes, all day, she'd felt as if something had been off. The headache that rattled her was stronger than normal. She had felt off-kilter having to answer the questions Dimitri and his father asked about the letters. She's never had to tell her story like that before. And of course, Will's visit hasn't been easy to shake.

She is panicked. Her bookstore is burning. Everything she's worked for is burning. It's burning. She jumps into the car and drives over the Eastport Bridge and into the center of the city near the circle, where she can see the lights of the fire trucks flashing and lighting up Main Street, but the police have closed off the street. Her heart feels as if it might beat right out of her chest. She parks the car in an empty spot near the tavern and begins to run at a pace she didn't think was possible up the hill, her feet taking her near the flames so she can see for herself what is happening.

Brodie's Books is burning.

She stands and watches in horror as flames can be seen in the windows. Her livelihood. Her investment. Everything she has worked so hard for and that her aunt and uncle have worked hard for is burning inside her charming bookstore. The stories being torched must be wailing in pain as their histories are turning to ashes. She thinks of the piano on the second floor, the coffee bar, the unread letters in the box, the countless new books she placed on the shelves earlier today along with the old books, and the computer system that houses all of her financial transactions and records. Nothing will be left. It will all be gone. She is thankful no one was inside.

The firefighters are doing their best to manage the fire. They desperately try to put it out, to salvage what they can.

Crystal, the woman who had called her and lives above her

boutique across from Brodie's Books, sees her and embraces her in a hug.

"Where did it start?" Meg asks Crystal.

"They're not sure. It just spread so quickly through these historic buildings," Crystal tells her.

Meg stares at the flames, wishing she could scream or cry, while feeling helpless, scared, and the most alone she has ever felt in her life. She feels unstable, weak, and shaky.

Her heart is being ripped apart as she watches her beloved store bearing Brodie's namesake melt into the blaze as the smoke fills the dark skies, the flashing lights of the fire truck blinding her. Brodie's Books has brought her so much joy and new friendships. It hurts to stand there helplessly.

Meg scans the scene, as if this horror is happening to someone other than herself. She sees a male figure in the shadows across the street momentarily watching the blaze. The smoke is billowing so intensely that she bats her eyes trying to make him out, but she can't. The smoke hurts her eyes. When she looks again, the figure vanishes down the street toward the harbor, fading into the dark.

Something in her is triggered; she cringes and gasps for air. Crystal sees the distress on Meg's face and wraps her arms around her as they both slump onto the pavement, the dark plumes of smoke tainting the night air. Meg will never forget the haunting sound of the crackling fire or the noise of the hose drowning her beloved bookstore. These sounds and images will forever echo in Meg's memory.

Eva
Sunday, April 28

Eva first learns of the fire at Brodie's Books when she logs into her social media accounts in the morning, checking the news stories of the day. It's a habit she's grown accustomed to in her role as a public relations professional. There isn't a day that goes by that she doesn't comb through the local and national papers and assess the day's news. It's her responsibility to know what's going on in her city, as well as with her clients and their businesses. She sees the headline in the Annapolis newspaper:

Four-alarm fire damages two historic properties on Main Street in Annapolis

As she reads on, the article confirms that one of the stores affected is Brodie's Books. She continues reading the story, feeling a pit grow in her stomach.

"The fire department is investigating where the fire originated, but flames spread and burned for nearly forty-five minutes before firefighters were able to get the blaze under control."

Eva throws on her robe, Brownie following closely at her feet, and descends the stairs two at a time. It's seven in the morning, and she's darting across the back lawn, barefoot, to Reid's cottage. She bangs on the door. Within minutes, he appears, a little frazzled, in his boxers and a t-shirt and runs his fingers through his hair.

"What's going on?" he asks.

"There's been a fire," Eva blurts out.

"Where? What?"

"Meg's bookstore is gone," she says.

*

Within the hour, Eva has Lily on the phone. Reid calls Dimitri. They are due to open their own store at ten, as is Lily.

"Oh my gosh, Eva," Lily says, when she hears the devastating news. "My heart is breaking for her. Have you tried to reach her?"

"I've called at least fifty times, but her phone goes to voicemail and says the mailbox is full. We need to find her."

"I agree," Lily says. "I'll have Cora open the store today. I'll come pick you up, and we'll drive over to Meg's condo. She must be devastated. I can only imagine how I would feel if this had been my store. It's so shocking. My store's only a handful of stores away from hers. This could have happened to any of us retailers downtown."

Eva can hear the concern in Lily's voice, both about the fire itself and the worry for Meg.

"I'll see you in a few," Eva says, and ends the call.

Eva eavesdrops on Reid's conversation with Dimitri. She listens to what Reid's saying, as the two of them sit at her kitchen table nursing their coffees.

"...Sometime early in the morning...when did she leave your place?...we've been trying to reach her; she's not answering her cellphone...it's just going to voicemail." Reid runs his hand through his hair again. Eva notices this is something he does when he's nervous or uncomfortable—or afraid. She's still getting to know him, and they've certainly grown much closer over the last several weeks.

When Reid ends the call with Dimitri, he looks at Eva. "Where could she be? She must be crushed. I can't even imagine. That bookstore was her life and it was magical."

"It was," Eva says, feeling tears well up in her eyes. "We may never have met had it not been for that bookstore and those letters and the way Meg looks after people."

"I think we're all thankful for how she has brought us together," he says. "Now, what can we do to help this situation?"

"I'll let you know if we locate her," Eva tells him. Minutes later, Lily pulls up in front of Eva's home. She hugs Reid goodbye and tells him to call her if he hears anything–anything at all.

*

Lily and Eva pound on Meg's door, calling her name. There is no answer. Eva can feel her heart racing, and the look on Lily's face makes her even more concerned about the situation and their mutual friend. The three of them have formed a bond over the last few months, and they've begun to confide in each other. Eva feels proud to call Meg her friend, and she wants to try to help in any way she can.

When there is absolutely no sign of her at the condo, they walk the grounds, looking at every bench, nook, and dock along the walking paths. They check her boat and see it is still in its place at the dock. Realizing she is not home, they decide to drive up Main Street to check out the devastation.

They park near Lily's store, finding a spot around the corner for the car, and walk through the alley near Brodie's Books. Eva puts her arm around Lily's shoulder as they stop and look in disbelief at what remains. It's a mess. The fire decimated the store, and the smell of burning embers hangs in the air. Debris is portioned off on the sidewalk by lines of yellow tape and cones set up by the fire and police departments. There is a crew on site attempting to sweep up and clean the remains on the sidewalk. The windows are gone, and when they step across the street to view the store in its entirety, they can see the devastation through what's left of the windows.

"It's worse than I imagined," Lily says.

*

Not knowing what to do or how to help, the two canvas Meg's condo complex one more time. They ring her doorbell, they call her cellphone, and they wait outside on the bench near the entrance to the complex. They are at a complete loss of what to do or how to find her. They share how helpless they feel at the moment.

"I'm going to call Reid again. I wonder if they've heard from her," Eva says, grabbing her phone.

On the third ring, Reid answers.

"Hi," he says. "Still no news."

"And Dimitri hasn't heard from her?"

"No," Reid says, "and quite frankly, I think he's going out of his mind. The two of us can barely focus today. Can we meet you for dinner after work? We need to figure something out."

"Yes. Let's meet at my place. Lily and I will pick up pizza or something and we can put our heads together."

As the sun begins to go down, and still with no word from Meg, they meet at Eva's, worried sick about their friend. They try their best to eat, but it's difficult. Eva combs through her social media accounts looking for anything—any sign of Meg, or of any new updates from the local newspapers and television stations. There is nothing.

Lily's cellphone rings, and Eva, Dimitri, and Reid stare at her as she answers her phone.

"Hi," she says, as they listen to her, intentionally hanging on every word she says. "No, we have still not heard from her...no...no word. Are you heading home? Thanks for pitching in today, sweetheart. I really appreciate it."

"That was Cora?" Eva asks.

"Yes, she's just wondering what the latest is. She also said Brad stopped by to see her and was wondering if we'd heard anything."

"Call them back," Eva says, "and tell them to come over."

"What?"

"Yes, Lily," she says. "Tell them to come here."

They all look at each other, and Eva holds up a finger telling them to wait. Then, she excuses herself for a minute. When she returns, she is carrying a box of stationery.

"I have an idea," she says.

Lily

Tuesday, April 30

Lily had fallen asleep on the couch after she returned home from Eva's. Cora had gone to bed after working at the store all day and spending the evening at Eva's house. They had all continued to try to reach Meg, but to no avail. Their concern was growing exponentially.

When Lily's phone startles her out of her sleep at eight in the morning, she answers.

"Hello," she says, as she sits up.

"Something's happening on Main Street. We have to get there. And you also better read this morning's Gazette," Eva says.

"What?"

"I don't want to spoil it for you, but it seems your ex-husband kept a secret from all of us last night. Get your paper, read the editorial, and call me back," Eva says, barking orders and hanging up the phone.

Lily jumps off of the sofa, and jogs down the driveway to retrieve her copy of the newspaper. Anxiously flipping through the pages as she re-enters the house, she turns to the editorial page and sits on the sofa, leaning over the paper and reading the words aloud.

Dear Editor,

Two nights ago, Annapolis lost one of its newest gems and brightest spots on Main Street, a beloved store called Brodie's Books, to a horrific fire that ravaged the place. The owner's name is not Brodie; in fact, her name is Meg Ellis, and she's one of the kindest, gentlest, most giving people Annapolis has been fortunate enough to have as a shop-owner in its historic district. Those who have shopped at this adorable bookstore know it as a welcoming place—a place to find books, talk about books, shop for gifts, connect with book lovers—and yet the shop embodied so much more than all of that. It was a place of community, of goodwill, and where you could sit with a cup of coffee or delicious hot chocolate and listen to live music that made the store even more enchanting. The upstairs windows were often left open so the sounds of musicians playing the piano could entice folks to come inside to socialize, or simply to find a few moments of solace and escape from the fast-paced world in which we live.

That was the spirit of Brodie's Books, and if you've frequented the bookstore, you know what I am describing and that there is even more to this story.

You see, Meg has been writing letters to her customers for nearly two years. Each day, she writes letters signed by "Brodie" and slips the letters into book purchases for people she believes need a sort of "pick me up," whereby she shares a positive message or story to help people know they are valued and appreciated and that they are not alone. Each day for the last two years, she has written ten messages a day to people she wishes to help through the words she writes in her letters. If you multiply just how many letters she has penned, you'll calculate, as I have, that Meg has written over 7,000 letters to members of our community, just to let them know someone cares and that there is always support for them as they face challenges.

In the back of Brodie's Books, there was a mailbox where some recipients of the letters corresponded with Meg, and she always wrote back. And while this little endeavor of hers was kept somewhat quiet and written under the pen name of "Brodie," those who have benefitted from corresponding with "Brodie" understand that Meg is the author of the letters. Brodie, was in fact, a younger cousin she cared for during many summers spent in Maryland (with her aunt and uncle), and who passed away a few years ago from cerebral palsy. The bookstore is named for her beloved cousin who loved books, and who loved to listen to stories, especially when Meg would read them aloud to him.

Meg's story and that of her bookstore is worth sharing, because it's our turn now to give back to Meg. It's our turn to help her find the strength to rebuild her bookstore and restore her livelihood. It's time for us to reach into our pockets and find it within ourselves to give back, be generous, and help her, after she has helped so many of us. I, for one, am a beneficiary of one such letter, and not only did it make me realize what a mistake I had made in ending my marriage to my high school sweetheart—the love of my life—but Meg's words also gave me the courage to try to fix what's been broken and apologize. (L—you know I love you and our daughter, and I always have, as I recently told you. Meg's letter helped prompt me to ask for forgiveness.) The truth is, Meg's letter helped change my life.

Finally, to all of you who have received a letter yourself…didn't it make you feel hopeful? Restore your faith in people? Restore faith in yourself?

If you value our retailers in the historic district and what they bring to our city, I'm imploring you to find it in your hearts to help us give Meg a sense of hopefulness and get her back in business in time for the holidays—the true season of giving. We're Annapolis, our spirit is strong, and we have the power to make a difference and help those who need us.

Sincerely,

Meg's Friend,

Brad

Lily sits in awe as she reads the letter to the editor, written by her ex-husband, a man she loves even more right at this very moment.

She calls Cora's name as she climbs the stairs to get dressed, not caring if she wakes her, because she wants to share what Brad has written. As well, after talking to Eva, she knows there's something they need to do—all of them—together, as a family.

*

Hours later, after visiting the hardware store and purchasing a couple of large pieces of plywood and a can of red paint, Cora, Brad, and Lily paint the wood. They write a heading at the top of the board stating: LOVE LETTERS TO MEG. They cart the plywood to Meg's store—to Brodie's Books—where they post the first love letters to Meg and the store, the ones they all wrote last night sitting around Eva's kitchen table. Eva arrives with her camera and takes a hundred photographs. Later that night, she launches the social media fundraiser campaign and letter writing campaign to hopefully bring Meg back to Annapolis, back to her home, and back to the people who love her and miss having her in their lives. She tags her Instagram account in the site she has created, hoping Meg will see how much the community appreciates her presence in the city. And Eva sets up a fund online for people to make monetary donations.

The next morning, Lily dresses and takes the short walk down the hill to what remains of Brodie's Books and sees the plywood wall they had erected and propped up under the melted awning.

In awe, Lily sees the boards are covered in letters to Meg, and people are leaving books with inscriptions to Meg on the sidewalk as a tribute to the bookstore and what it meant—and still means—to them. Lily feels her eyes become misty, and hopes Meg will somehow feel the community's love for her. If only Meg could see the outpouring of love right now.

Reid

After he leaves the music store that night, Reid decides to drive up Main Street to see for himself what he has seen on Eva's social media accounts—the outpouring of love for Meg's bookstore. Eva has done a phenomenal job of becoming the storyteller for Brodie's Books. They all imagine Meg must have insurance on her business, but drumming up even more awareness of the store's current plight is what Eva does best.

Finding a space out front, Reid parks his truck and walks up to see the wall of letters for himself. The Annapolis newspaper has been covering the story, and the Baltimore news outlets have covered it as well. He wonders where Meg is at the moment, and if she even knows about the community's love for her store—and for her.

Dimitri had told Reid about Brodie. Dimitri also had told Reid what Meg had shared with Dimitri and his father the night of the fire—the story of why she writes the letters and why the store's called Brodie's Books.

"She named the bookstore after her cousin, who died of cerebral palsy—she took care of him every summer. This is a girl with a heart of gold," Dimitri had told him as they closed up the store earlier.

"And you love her heart of gold," Reid said, for the first time acknowledging that he knows Dimitri is beginning to have feelings for her.

"I think I might," Dimitri said, and then turned away. Reid has sensed a bond forming between the two of them, and perhaps it is even more advanced than he initially had suspected. "I just can't understand why she wouldn't reach out to any of us. Why wouldn't she reach out to you?" Reid asked. Dimitri could only shake his head.

Reid thinks about this conversation as he examines all of the letters. He guesses that Meg has gone home to Virginia or gone to stay with Brodie's parents, but ultimately, he doesn't know. None of them truly understands how devastated she must be feeling, and he wishes she would reach out to one of them. Perhaps Meg doesn't even know how much they all care for her and are thankful for her.

One thing Reid realizes is this: his life has changed from knowing them all.

And in particular, Eva.

This thought in particular gives him courage—the courage to finally tell Eva exactly how he feels about her.

*

Reid knocks on Eva's door, and she answers it.

"Hello, you," she says, with a smile. "Come in."

"Hi," he says, as he enters. "I stopped by to see what's happening outside Meg's store for myself."

"Pretty amazing, isn't it? I can't believe how much traffic we're getting and how people have become a part of this story in two short days. The newspaper wants to cover it again tomorrow."

He nods, watching her talk. He loves her energy, and her belief in goodness. But for some reason, the words he wants to say to her aren't coming as easily as he had hoped.

"It is so great," he says. He feels himself chickening out. He had come over with such confidence and feels it waning.

Eva pauses, sensing something is going on, something besides their worry for Meg.

"Is something else wrong? I mean, besides the obvious?" she asks.

"Well, it seems I've lost my nerve for what I wanted to say when I came through the door."

"Nerve for what?"

"For what I want to say to you."

"Oh, God," she says, looking concerned. "You're not moving out, are you?"

He laughs. "Hardly."

"Then what is it, Reid? You know you can tell me anything."

"And it won't scare you?" he says, moving a little closer.

"I don't think so," she says. "I hope not, anyway."

"Ok, here goes. I've been thinking about this for a while—probably since the first time we met, Eva, and certainly now, after all the time we've spent together. I have to get it off my chest. I think I'm falling in love with you. No, that didn't come out right. I know I love you. I love you. And what you're doing for Meg is—"

Eva walks toward him and puts her forefinger to his lips, as if to tell him to stop speaking.

"Thank you for saying it first. I think I've been wanting to say it, too. I love you back, Reid Jones," she says, seeing the relief on his face.

Reid is proud that he has taken his time with this relationship, and he didn't want to blow it. She had to be ready, and he had to grow the hell up.

He leans in to kiss her in the foyer, as Brownie wags her tail and pants at their feet, probably wondering what in the heck has taken the humans so long to say the words out loud to each other.

Dimitri

Dimitri locks the door to the music store at eight o'clock after he closes out the register for the night. He and Reid have organized several fundraiser concerts in conjunction with the tavern that they'll be performing this upcoming weekend and the following. They're also contributing a portion of their sales to a recovery fund for the bookstore, explaining to customers that Meg was the inspiration for their own store and is a good friend. Customers have been more than happy to help in any way they can.

Despite all of these actions, Dimitri is still feeling helpless, and is desperate to hear from Meg. She's been on his mind day and night, and he wonders why she hasn't reached out. It's been almost seventy-two hours since the fire. Until he hears from her, he has decided to put all his energy into something he can do for her.

Baba has called six times a day wondering if Dimitri's heard anything from Meg. He's as devastated as Dimitri is by the loss of Brodie's Books.

"I can't believe it happened the same night we all spent together. It's such a tragedy," he said to Dimitri. "I loved that store—and my heart breaks for her."

He knows how much his father adores her—and how much fun they all had together. Dimitri remembers the look in Meg's eyes as she would laugh at his father's jokes or play games in such a good-natured way as to make Baba happy. Then, she went to sleep and learned that her business was gone. Destroyed.

As he gets into his car, his phone rings, and he answers it.

"Hey," he says.

"I'm glad I left a little before you so that I can tell you that you've got to drive by the bookstore. You won't believe what it looks like right now. There are tributes to the store everywhere. Take a ride by it on your way to Eva's house," Reid says.

"Eva's house?" Dimitri asks.

"Yes—I told you. You are coming over to Eva's house, remember? There's more work to do."

"Okay," Dimitri says.

"Lily and Brad are on their way, too. Eva's making dinner."

"Okay, I'll see you in a few."

As he drives up Main Street, he can see the bookstore on the right. He pulls over right in front of it, and he can't believe his eyes at what's evolved over the last forty-eight hours. It's a veritable love letter to the store for all to see—letters plastered onto the red plywood, books left as tributes, and even some flowers with well wishes. His heart begins to sink. Dimitri's mind drifts back to that first day he walked into the store and Meg encouraged him to play the piano. He's loved every minute of playing music in her store and becoming part of the community. It was Meg who had inspired him to use his talent, to step out of his comfort zone, and she had introduced him to Reid.

The snowball effect of knowing her, of being a part of the little community she has created, gives him a sense of purpose, of belonging that he never felt when he was married to his ex, or even during the years before that. The letter in his book, Meg, and the belief that it was time to turn over a new leaf—they all gave him the courage to leave a career he hated and try his hand at something new. Additionally, over the last many months, he has become much closer to a father he greatly respects. He has worked to build a more meaningful relationship with Baba than ever before.

All of this came as a result of knowing Meg.

He chuckles at the thought of her *Game of Thrones* display. So many memories in such a short time. He admires the pride she took in the ownership of the place, and seeing her own passion gave him the courage to start his own business. Dimitri wishes he had told her all of these things, but he never did. Maybe she knows how much she has affected his life, but he wishes now that he had said the words.

Because words matter. Words truly matter.

Every word in every book, every word in each of her letters, every written and spoken word matters in relationships and in love, in forgiveness and in letting go, and in building and forging new bonds with people. Words mattered in the songs he and Reid had started writing together. Meg's beautiful, inspiring words had helped people, and the city of Annapolis is confirming that loudly and clearly through their supportive actions.

Dimitri wishes he could tell Meg all about it. He wishes he could see her and explain what is happening because she is beloved by everyone.

He stares at all the letters customers have left for the store and rubs his forehead, feeling entirely helpless, when his phone rings again. It's a number he doesn't recognize.

"Hello," he says, climbing back into his car. "This is Dimitri."

"Hi," he hears her say, "It's Meg."

"Oh my gosh—where are you? We've been worried sick about you!"

"Look across the street," she says.

He sees her leaning her back against the brick storefront across the street, and she gives him a little wave.

Dimitri feels a lump in his throat and motions for her to cross over and get into the car. She puts her phone in her pocket, opens the passenger door, and climbs inside.

"I lost my phone," she says, closing the door behind her. "This phone is my mother's. My new one arrives tomorrow. The night of the fire, I dropped mine somewhere along Main Street. After I searched for it and couldn't find it, I went back to my condo, packed a bag at five in the morning, and drove home to be with my parents to tell them what had happened. Then, I had to call my aunt and uncle—Brodie's parents—and tell them that I lost it all, all that they had given me to start the store with Brodie's nest egg. I've been dealing with lawyers and the insurance company. I needed to get away for a couple of days and clear my head. And then I saw what Eva's doing on social media, read Brad's letter to the editor, saw the post about the concert you and Reid are planning, and I dropped everything to come back to see this lovely wall of letters—what you are all doing for me. I should have called sooner. I was just so devastated. Anyway, I'm glad I'm here. I wanted to see for myself the messages that people were leaving. I have no words, except to say that 'My cup runneth over.'"

"That's okay. You've had all the words for a long time. Now it's time for us to find the right words for you."

Meg looks at Dimitri in the eyes as her own fill with tears—and in her eyes Dimitri sees something meaningful there: a relationship that they are building together, cautiously, but day by day.

"You are not alone in this, Meg. You understand this, right? You know I'm here for you."

Meg nods.

"There are some other people who want to see you and give you a hug. Is that okay?"

Meg begins to sob. Dimitri lets her cry, comforting her as the tears run down Meg's face. Dimitri hands her a tissue from his glove box as she dabs her eyes and takes a moment to pull herself together.

"You're going to be okay. It's all going to be okay," he says, and he reaches for her hand to hold it. She reciprocates by holding his hand tightly, and then places her other hand on top of his. She leans her body into his and places her head on his shoulder. After a few minutes of sitting in silence, Dimitri kisses her on the forehead and points the car in the direction of Eva's house.

Dimitri can't wait to see the expressions on all of their faces when they see the guest he's bringing to dinner.

*

"Knock, knock," Dimitri calls, as he raps on the door and opens it.

When Meg walks through the door behind him, Eva, Reid, Lily and Brad freeze for a moment before rushing over to her and enveloping her in hugs.

"Where have you been?" Lily asks. "We've been so worried."

Dimitri feels protective of her, and he stands close beside her as she explains.

"I lost my phone the night of the fire, and I went to visit my parents. I've been dealing with the insurance company and lawyers. I know I should have called you all, but I had to mull over my next steps with my parents and aunt and uncle. I was pretty distraught and was just trying to find my way. My mom let me have her old phone, and I was able to see what was happening on social media, so I came back today. I can't even begin to tell you how much I appreciate all of you and what you've done for me."

"Well, we are so relieved to see you, and we want you to have this because we appreciate you and what you've done for all of us," Eva says, handing over a wrapped book for Meg to open.

Meg looks at each of them and leans into Dimitri as she tears the wrapping paper and takes note of the title and the anniversary edition: *The Giving Tree* by Shel Silverstein. It's one of her favorites. Everyone watches her reaction in anticipation.

"Thank you so much, all of you," she says, getting choked up by their thoughtfulness.

"No," Eva says. "You have to open the book and read the inscription."

When Meg opens the cover of the book she looks up and smiles. The inscription reads: *To Meg, who gives so much. From your friends, who want to give back. With Love.*

It's then that Meg sees five handwritten letters addressed to her neatly tucked inside the pages of the book.

Meg

Sunday, August 5

As the sun begins to lighten her room, and she can hear the clanging of the masts of sailboats out her window, Meg places her two feet firmly on the floor and begins her morning stretches. Feeling the warmth of the day shining through the cracked windows, she allows the sunshine to warm her face. She takes deep breaths in and out, meditating on the last few months.

Meg opens *The Giving Tree* and takes out the letters. She gets comfortable and reads them. It's been four months since the fire, and strangely, she has realized that losing Brodie's Books in a fire was just a small part of her story, but it wasn't her whole story, just as Will was a part of her story. Meg realizes that all her little stories make up who she is—make up who we all are. There is so much more to come, and Meg grasps what is needed to face adversity: it's the desire to be resilient.

But resiliency by itself does not make a person, for if one lacks a wonderful support system, resiliency can become lost. Undoubtedly, the cast of local customers and friends she has relied upon these last few months has helped her find the strength to carry on. Meg could have crawled away from it all, found another job, moved back to Virginia, and wallowed in the disappointment. Instead, she lifted her head, realized her own vulnerability, appreciated her friends, and accepted the generosity of others.

Meg's empathic nature has helped her navigate the challenges of watching her beloved bookstore vanish in the middle of the night. She may never be quite sure if the figure she saw fade into the darkness that night was who her gut told her it may be; after all, she had seen Will in town. They had been face-to-face. Nevertheless, the coincidence of the fire happening so soon after their interaction made her question all of it. A hunch is a hunch, and yet, Meg has to come to terms with the fact that she will most likely never know if her intuition is correct.

The fire department did determine it was arson, and that perhaps it was her store that was targeted, but no evidence implicated anyone.

She takes a deep breath and exhales the negative energy out of her body. It doesn't matter anymore. Her responsibility is to rebuild. To move forward. To do it out of love, not bitterness.

And the beauty is that she isn't afraid to do it. Not after what her friends have done for her. Not after what her customers and supporters have done for her. She's a member of the community, and she vows that she will not quit—that she will continue to give back for as long as they'll have her.

Reid's former contracting partner is overseeing the construction and rebuild of the bookstore, and Reid even helps out in the evenings a few times a week to fast-track the reconstruction. Eva is helping Meg redesign the interior, and Eva continues to manage Meg's social media accounts. Meg hired Cora part-time before she goes to college to create artwork and crafts to give the store some personality. Clarke, Briana, and Jordan are putting their heads together for new programming, a more contemporary coffee bar and music ideas, along with innovative programs for kids. Lily, a fellow shop-owner herself, is Meg's trusted confidant about all things retail, and they have a standing lunch every Friday to strategize.

After she eats her breakfast and slips into a short sundress and her sneakers for the day, Meg prepares a little picnic lunch and drinks and heads toward her boat. The weather outside is perfect—not a cloud in the sky—and the water is calm. It's a day to be on the water in your sunglasses, feeling the wind in your hair. She penciled in this day off and is glad it's here. It's a day to just be, and to let go of responsibility for a while.

She walks down the pier and hops on the boat. She turns on the blower and tucks the canvas covers under the seats in storage. The Orioles play later today, and she knows they will listen to the game on the radio in the afternoon as they enjoy the sunshine, but for now, she turns the station to play today's contemporary hits when she hears him call her name.

"Meg!" he says, bounding toward her with a smile. He's got a bag of fresh croissants in one hand from the bakery in town, and a handful of daisies in the other. Meg notes how handsome he looks in his shorts, white shirt, and ballcap. She loves his handsome face, his dark, short hair, and his beautiful eyes. She loves his kindness and the way they are when they are together. She adores his father, too.

"Hello, Dimitri," she says, a big, broad smile taking over her face.

He boards the boat and gives her one of the sweet kisses they seem to have finally mastered over the last few months. They have both made a pact to let go of the past, and they are only looking to the future as they chart new waters.

Together.

Epilogue

Thursday, December 8
Midnight Madness

One year later, four individuals are intent on getting to an event on time.

The city is fully decorated in its Christmas greens; its white lights, its red bows, and its Christmas tree by the dock illuminate the area near the harbor. Carolers stroll Main Street singing Christmas favorites, merchants offer shoppers complimentary champagne and hot chocolate, and the restaurants and bars are packed with families and friends who enjoy spending the evening together in the name of goodwill and love.

Filled with gratitude, this holiday season is a much different experience for Eva, Lily, Reid, and Dimitri. Instead of drowning their sorrows over various drinks as they did last December, feeling depressed and isolated, a year later they have found a sense of connection, purpose, and friendship, all thanks to a woman named Meg who owns a bookstore.

And instead of a tavern, tonight's gathering will be held inside a charming, reconstructed bookstore located in Annapolis on Main Street in the historic district at the top of the hill near Church Circle. Over the last six months, the store has been lovingly reconstructed on its former site, rebuilt, and brought back to life. The insurance payout for the bookstore, coupled with the outpouring of donations and money collected from fundraisers and good-natured people, helped create a new version of Brodie's Books—an even brighter, lighter version of what had been there before.

The bookstore is inviting: its creamy walls, ambient lighting, and cozy decorations welcome back shoppers who had fallen in love with the former place, and it has brought new customers into the fold, as they watched the rebirth of the store happen in real time on social media and through the local news. Inside the bookstore, white lights are draped among books of every genre and style—a true mix of the contemporary and the classics. New displays have been erected to entice readers, both young and old, and active book clubs are creating a sense of community spirit.

The second floor, which has been partitioned off for the night, has been decorated in style, too. A decorated Christmas tree illuminates the corner of the room, and greens and lights hang from the black and white awnings and the coffee bar, recreated with a Parisian feel. An 8-foot-tall replica of the Eiffel Tower sparkles on the opposite side of the room.

Sitting caddy-corner on the second floor is an upright, white piano. The previous piano had been destroyed by the fire in April, and the new white one—its replacement—is a gift from the owners of the successful new music store down the road. Behind the piano, on the adjacent wall that is painted a warm pink, the numerous handwritten letters that had been received over the last several months are craftily displayed, using a decoupage technique that mimics wallpaper. Cora had designed it herself for the store. The handwritten letters are addressed to either "Meg" or "Brodie," but both are completely appropriate and sentimental.

Meg's bookstore will close at nine tonight, and she begins to ring up the last few customers. She wears her reindeer antlers and a big smile, as she profusely thanks each of her customers for the support they have given her over the last many months. After the final few shoppers leave, Clarke, Briana, and Jordan spend the next couple of hours getting everything into place upstairs—the food, the drinks, and the centerpieces on the ten tables upstairs.

When Meg and her employees hear the banging on the doors, they know the gang has arrived.

Dimitri enters first and kisses Meg on the lips. He looks elegant in his suit, his dark skin glowing. Reid and Eva follow closely behind. Eva's red satin dress hugs her curves in all the right places, and Reid looks sharp in his dark suit with a rose the same color as her dress on his lapel. He carries his guitar. Baba shows up next in his best suit, and various other friends, including Eva's friends Ellen and Emily, and Lily's friend Charmaine begin to enter the store, along with other family and friends. Meg has ditched the reindeer antlers and slipped into a knee-length silver dress and heels. She directs the nearly forty guests to the rows of chairs that have been staged upstairs.

This is what they wanted. This is what they requested.

Dimitri and Reid begin to play music—instrumental songs—while the catering from the tavern is put in place. Meg beams as she looks around the room at all these people—people she has come to love and can't imagine not having in her life. Over the last year, she is amazed at how her life has changed for the better.

Brad enters next, in his suit and tie, and moves near the window that overlooks Main Street. When Reid and Dimitri play *La Vie En Rose*, everyone stands to greet Lily and Cora, who are standing at the top of the stairs about to walk toward them, shining as brightly as the lights of Paris. Lily's gorgeous cream-colored satin dress accentuates her lovely skin, her radiant, glowing face, and her blush lips that cannot stop smiling. Cora's dusty gold dress from the boutique complements her mother's, and their happiness takes Brad's breath away.

Brad steps forward and takes Lily's arm, and in the other arm, he takes Cora's. The three of them stand together.

"I love you both," Brad says to them.

The minister smiles and greets everyone in the room. The second floor of Brodie's Books is alight with friendship, resilience and forgiveness. Everything feels new; everything feels right.

Those who have gathered watch as two people recommit to each other during an intimate and unforgettable night of magic, rooted in empathy, understanding, and love.

THE END

A note from the author

Dear Reader,

I hope you enjoyed this story. Whenever I sit down to write the next book, I always strive to tell character-driven stories that attempt to entertain and lift up readers. This story of an empath—of a person who can sense and feel things within her very deeply—had been on my mind for a while. I've watched a lot of Brené Brown TedTalks and read her books about empathy, vulnerability, and shame, and her research on the subject stuck with me. I began to research empaths, what it means to be one, and how their intuition and energy make them a compassionate force in our world. Empaths are intuitive, and it has nothing to do with voo-doo or being a fortune teller. So much about empaths intrigued me, and as I kept digging in, the research required me to take a self assessment. In that process, I discovered that I am one.

You may be an empath, too.

Thank you for reading *The Letters in the Books*.

Stephanie

P.S. *If you enjoyed reading this book, please consider posting a review online or sharing it on social media. As indie authors, we rely upon our readers to help promote our work. From an author's standpoint, writing is our passion; the tricky part is marketing. Therefore, any help you can provide by recommending the book, sharing it on your favorite social media platform, or posting a review helps us continue to pursue our love of storytelling.*

Big THANK YOU to...

Leni Parrillo, Anthony Verni, and Elizabeth Johnson for always agreeing to be the first set eyes of my books. To Jenny Bumgarner and Doug Parrillo who always offer advice when I need it. To my kids, Ellie and Matt, and my in-laws, Jo and Mark Verni, for their support. And especially to my husband, who happily goes along with all of this craziness.

To my mother, Leni, for allowing me to brainstorm with her and figure out characters and plot, and for being my super-proofreader. You are the best.

To my writing group and fellow scribes—Thank you for your support and inspiration: Colleen Young, Megan Musgrove, Dana Armstrong, Jere Anthony, and Sayword Eller. You all make me want to carry on, no matter what. This is a crazy business, and we need each other. So very thankful.

To my ARC readers—for reading and helping to launch the book.

To my Facebook friends who are always willing to offer input into cover designs and other random things I ask of them.

To my fellow Instagram writers: You all inspire me every day. So grateful for our "writing community."

To Melody Wukitch and her adorable bookstore, Park Books, for her support and for running a wonderful independent bookstore in our own backyard.

To Henry Wadsworth Longfellow, for writing beautiful poetry that can be remembered and quoted.

Book Club
Questions

1. Did you know what an empath was before reading this book? How would you define one in your own words?

2. Meg's character is the one who brings the other four main characters together. Which of the four—Eva, Lily, Reid, and Dimitri—did you identify with most? Why?

3. What do you think happened to Reid that isn't shared on the pages of the book? Do you think people get in ruts, flounder in shame, and can't get out of their own way sometimes?

4. Eva is devastated by the betrayal and desertion of Kyle, seeks a therapist, and tries to move on. What do you believe helped her move on permanently?

5. Cora plays an important role in the relationship between her mother and father. Discuss how a 17-year-old can sometimes see things that adults can't.

6. Meg's letter from John E. Anderson sets into motion her daily task of meditation and writing letters to people. Do you think she would have become the person she is had she not received the letter from Mr. Anderson?

7. What did Dimitri learn about himself after he lost his job, received a letter, and met Meg? What is Baba's role in Dimitri's story?

8. Lily's character covers a range of emotions throughout the novel. Explain Lily's scope and how she manages to always know who she is.

9. It's a fact that empaths can become attached to the wrong people because they believe they can help them change. Will, while not a major character in the story, plays a huge part in the last several chapters of the book. What does Meg's empathic nature illustrate when it comes to her ex-fiance?

10. Brodie's Books is named for Meg's cousin Brodie. Why was her relationship with her cousin such a huge part of who she becomes as an adult?

11. Empaths know that happiness has to come from within and that it's important to accept yourself on a lifelong journey of understanding who you are and what you can be. Discuss this concept as it relates to each of the characters.

12. Eva, Reid, and Dimitri are affected by Meg's letters, but not Lily, who did not receive a letter. What might have happened if she had received the letter instead of Brad? Did Lily need to receive a letter?

About the Author
Stephanie Verni

STEPHANIE VERNI enjoys writing realistic, hopeful fiction that tugs at the heartstrings and covers themes such as rebounding, forgiveness, loss, recovery, friendship, and love.

The author of *Beneath the Mimosa Tree, Baseball Girl, Inn Significant, Little Milestones, The Postcard, Anna in Tuscany, and From Humbug to Humble: The Transformation of Ebenezer Scrooge,* she is also the co-author of the textbook, *Event Planning: Communicating Theory and Practice.* Currently Adjunct Professor at Stevenson University Online, she instructs undergraduate and graduate communication courses.

Stephanie resides in Severna Park, Maryland, and enjoys spending time with her family, especially on the beautiful Severn River and in her hometown city of Annapolis. In addition to writing fiction, she dabbles in local travel writing, photography, and is an avid blogger at stephanieverni.com.

Books by Stephanie Verni

BENEATH THE MIMOSA TREE

Annabelle Marco and Michael Contelli are both only children of Italian-Americans. Next door neighbors since they were both five years old, they both receive their parents' constant attention and are regularly subjected to their meddlesome behavior. In high school and then in college, as their relationship moves from friendship to love, Annabelle finds herself battling her parents, his parents, and even Michael. She feels smothered by them all and seeks independence through an unplanned and unexpected decision that she comes to regret and that ultimately alters the course of her life, Michael's life, and the lives of both of their parents.

BASEBALL GIRL

Francesca Milli's father passes away when she's a freshman in college and nineteen years old; she is devastated and copes with his death by securing a job working for the Bay City Blackbirds, a big-league team, as she attempts to carry on their traditions and mutual love for the game of baseball. The residual effect of loving and losing her dad has made her cautious, until two men enter her life: a ballplayer and a sports writer. With the encouragement of her mother and two friends, she begins to work through her grief. A dedicated employee, she successfully navigates her career, and becomes a director in the front office. However, Francesca realizes that she can't partition herself off from the world, and in time, understands that sometimes loving someone does involve taking a risk.

INN SIGNIFICANT

Two years after receiving the horrifying news of her husband Gil's death, Milly Foster continues to struggle to find her way out of a state of depression. As a last-ditch effort and means of intervention, Milly's parents convince her to run their successful Inn during their absence as they help a friend establish a new bed and breakfast in Ireland. Milly reluctantly agrees; when she arrives at the picturesque, wa-

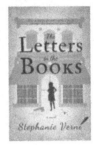

terfront Inn Significant, her colleague, John, discovers a journal written by her late grandmother that contains a secret her grandmother kept from the family. Reading her grandmother's words, and being able to identify with her Nana's own feelings of loss, sparks the beginning of Milly's climb out of the darkness and back to the land of the living.

LITTLE MILESTONES

The follow up novel to Inn Significant, recently divorced Olivia Bruno decides to leave her job in New York City as an event planner to live with her grandmother, Nan, in St. Michaels on Maryland's Eastern Shore, where she spent a lot of time as a child. Securing a job in town at a local bookstore, Olivia begins to pick up the pieces of her life by connecting with her grandmother's friends and other townspeople she meets along the way, including Milly Foster, who lives in nearby Oxford and runs an inn called Inn Significant, and Miles Channing, a local writer. Nan has lived in the town all of her life and has some stories of her own. Together, Nan and Olivia navigate their lives and appreciate the power of family, friendships, forgiveness, and listening to your heart. As well, Nan and Olivia find out that perhaps life is made up of little milestones.

FROM HUMBUG TO HUMBLE: THE TRANSFOR-MATION OF EBENEZER SCROOGE

How, exactly, did Ebenezer Scrooge stay true to his word and change in order to become a better person? What good deeds did he actually do to leave behind his life as an old miser and curmudgeon? What became of Tiny Tim? In this follow-up novella based on the great Charles Dickens' A Christmas Carol, long-time Dickens fan and writer Stephanie Verni imagines Scrooge's path to redemption that includes philanthropy, family, friendships, and love. Dickens fans will be treated to insights as to how Scrooge changed his ways in this heartwarming tale full of Christmas spirit as we revisit old Scrooge, Bob Cratchit, Scrooge's nephew, Fred, Isabelle, Tiny Tim, and more in this charming Christmas tale.

THE POSTCARD AND OTHER SHORT STORIES & POETRY

In this collection, which includes 22 short stories, you will read about tales of love, heartbreak, middle-aged meltdowns, gossips and unkind women, abusive relationships, a last-ditch message in a bottle, witches and brooms, baseball, and living with a grandmother, among others. Written over a span of twenty years, The Postcard and Other Short Stories & Poetry will warm your heart and leave you feeling as if you've made a few new friends among the pages.

ANNA IN TUSCANY

Travel writer Arianna (Anna) Ricci relocates from the United States to Italy for a year on assignment to cover the regions of Italy. She is also on a quest to write a story of love about La Festa Degli Innamorati—otherwise known as Valentine's Day—for her magazine's website. Living in her cousin's apartment in Siena in Tuscany, Anna meets her neighbor, Matteo, an older gentleman who lost his wife several years prior, and they form a friendship and begin to play cards every Wednesday evening, along with Matteo's son, Nicolo. Before long, Anna, who has suffered through two previous heartbreaks, uncovers a love story that spans decades, and learns a few things about love as she finds her own way in Italy.

***

To stay in touch with Stephanie and hear about her work, visit her website at stephanieverni.com, or email her at stephanie.verni@gmail.com to sign up for the mailing list.